AT THE GATES
OF DARKNESS

ALSO BY RAYMOND E. FEIST

AT THE GATES OF DARKNESS

BOOK TWO OF THE DEMONWAR SAGA

Raymond E. Feist

An Imprint of HarperCollinsPublishers

AT THE GATES OF DARKNESS. Copyright © 2010 by Raymond E. Feist. All rights reserved. Printed in the United States of America. No part of this book may be used or reproduced in any manner whatsoever without written permission except in the case of brief quotations embodied in critical articles and reviews. For information address HarperCollins Publishers, 10 East 53rd Street, New York, NY 10022.

Eos is a federally registered trademark of HarperCollins Publishers.

Designed by Joy O'Meara
Map designed by Ralph M. Askren, D.V.M.

ISBN 978-0-06-146837-7

For the ladies who make me look so good:

(in alphabetical order)

Jennifer Brehl, Emma Coode, Jane Johnson,
and Katherine Nintzel; rarely does an author
get one good editor, let alone four

CONTENTS

ACKNOWLEDGMENTS

As always, I am indebted to those who created Midkemia and allowed me to use it. Without their creativity the world of Midkemia would be far less vivid. So, Steve A, Jon, Anita, Conan, Steve B, Bob, Rich, April, Ethan, and everyone else who contributed, my continued thanks.

Thanks to John Bunting and Ralph Askren for giving readers so much more access than I could possibly provide myself.

Thanks to two people who always give support and friendship, Richard Spahl and Ray McKnown. And thanks to Kim McKnown for battling through and keeping me smiling every time I see her.

I also, once again, thank Jonathan Matson not only for far more than wise counsel and his business acumen, but for an abiding friendship that I cherish.

Thanks to my mother, still, for being there.

Lastly, and most deeply, to my children for their love and beauty; they still drive me crazy while keeping me sane and I am loving the adults they're turning into before my eyes.

AT THE GATES
OF DARKNESS

CHAPTER 1

SACRIFICE

Howls filled the night.

The blasted hills smoked and the stench of char filled the air. Hundreds of robed figures slowly wended their way through rocks to the huge clearing below what remained of a fortress's gate tower. A man of power stood atop the pile of stones, looking down at his followers.

On the opposite side of the clearing, another man hung back in the shadows, using his considerable skills to remain unseen, and wishing fervently he was just about anywhere else in the world but here. He took a slow, even breath, as much to calm himself as to catch his breath.

James Dasher Jamison struggled to keep his wits

about him. In the courts of the three largest nations in the region, he was a minor noble of the Kingdom of the Isles, a man who had inherited rank solely due to his lineage, being the grandson of the Duke of Rillanon; to most others, he was Jim Dasher, a businessman with some ties to crime in the city of Krondor; to a few, he was the Upright Man, leader of the Thieves Guild, the Mockers. And known to even fewer, he was the head of the Kingdom of the Isles intelligence apparatus, reporting directly to his grandfather.

In his slightly more than forty years, Jim had seen a great many strange and terrifying things—it came with his various positions. At times he felt he had become as heartless a bastard as those he had put down in the name of the Crown, or the Conclave of Shadows, with whom he often worked, but even a lifetime of blood and intrigue had not adequately prepared Jim for what he saw before him.

Already the dead numbered in the dozens, if not hundreds, as a massive fire burned around a circle of stakes, to each of which had been tied four human sacrifices. What had churned Jim's stomach as much as anything had been that the murdered seemed willing, even eager, to embrace their flaming death.

Around the edges of the clearing more sacrifices dangled at the ends of ropes, as only moments before Jim had witnessed them place nooses around their own necks then jump off small ladders, hanging themselves. Many broke their necks with an audible crack, but a few died by slow strangulation, kicking for what seemed far too long a time. Jim had witnessed more than his share of public hangings in Krondor but this was something far more horrific than a criminal meeting his just desserts. This was a willing self-sacrifice to as evil a creature as man could imagine.

The screams were lessening as the sacrifices finally, mercifully began to lose consciousness and die. Another score were impaled on wooden stakes, blood and feces filling the air with the unforgettable stench of death. Some quivered and twitched as their own weight drove the stakes deeper into their bodies, until finally succumbing to their wounds. Others gave out a death spasm then hung on the stakes, motionless.

Jim saw nothing here that could be called anything but insane. He turned his attention to the man standing atop the tumbled-down masonry of an ancient wall, holding his hands up in a welcoming gesture. His expression and bearing made Jim wish to turn tail and run as fast as he could, as far as he could. He had never seen this man before, but his description fit with what he had learned from Pug of Sorcerer's Isle and a Demon Master named Amirantha. The man on the stones above was named Belasco, and if what he had been told about him was true, Jim knew him to be one of the most dangerous men alive today, and certainly one of the maddest.

With a sweep of his hand, the magic user conjured an image, a shimmering likeness that hung in the air above his head, and which had the robed mob at his feet cry out in supplication and awe.

The image was of Dahun, and from what Jim had been able to learn over the last six months, the appearance of his likeness, as if he stood here in the flesh, meant his servants were closer to opening a portal for him. Dahun was twenty feet tall and roughly man-shaped, but with what could only be called a scaled black lizard's tail descending from his spine to drag on the ground behind him. His chest was massive and his stomach rippled with muscles under skin that started black at his feet, blended to red at his stomach, and turned crimson at his chest. His face was human, save for a massive, jutting lower jaw and large bat-like ears. His eyes were solid black orbs. Long tendrils of hair braided with human skulls hung to his shoulders. His brow was adorned with a massive golden circlet, set with a dark stone pulsing with purple light. The fingers of his left hand ended in black talons and flexed slowly, restlessly, as if in anticipation of rending apart his enemies. In his right hand he held a flaming sword. His hips were girded with a metal-studded kilt of scintillating red material, and two large leather bands crossed his chest with a massive golden emblem at the center, a flaming fist.

Jim spent a moment fixing the design in his memory. Then he glanced around and saw the slack-jawed, empty-eyed expression on those around him. It was clear they had eaten or drunk something in preparation for this ritual, so he attempted to mimic their shambling walk.

Feeling almost sick to his stomach from fear, Jim steeled himself and moved slowly to join those approaching the monster. Like the others he wore a heavy black robe and had pulled the cowl forward to conceal his features. The original owner of the robe was somewhere at the bottom of a deep ravine less than a quarter mile away, no longer needing the garment.

He scuffled his feet a little, moving slower than those around him, to keep to the rear of the crowd. He wanted everyone possible in front of him—he didn't dare be noticed and he wanted the opportunity to slip away should the need arise. He kept his hands up inside the sleeves of his robe—one hand held a dagger treated with a fast-acting poison that would render anyone cut unable to move within a minute, and the other a device constructed for him by a master artificer in Krondor, a ball that when shattered would emit a brilliant white light for ten seconds, more than enough time for Jim to slip away. It would leave those blinded unable to see into the shadows for at least another minute or two. Jim had a well-earned reputation for being able to slip away given the slightest opportunity, and with this crew he knew "slight" was the best he could hope for.

From the human onlookers, anyway. He couldn't be certain that everyone in attendance tonight was human.

Jim swallowed hard again and paused, forcing himself to confront the image of the monster above.

Belasco raised his hands again. Jim took only a moment to conclude the magic user was madder than a bug trapped in a bass drum. What was projected before the crowd was as horrifying a sight as Jim had ever witnessed, yet the magician was laughing like a delighted child. He was calling out to the faithful, but Jim wasn't quite close enough to hear the words, only the indistinct sound of his voice.

Jim inched forward and to the right as those in front of him slowly rose to their feet, for the group was coming together in the middle of what had once been a fortress. Perhaps five hundred of the faithful gathered. Jim glanced around, a sudden tightness in his neck causing him to worry about who might now be behind him. It was a sense he had inherited from his great-grandfather, something the family called his "bump of trouble." And right now it was starting to really itch.

As he suspected, figures moved along the rocks surrounding this flat area, what was once an ancient marshalling yard. The roaring fires made everything beyond inky dark, but Jim had mastered the trick of not looking at the flames if he could help it, keeping alert for flickering movement and reflecting highlights betraying those outside the light.

This ancient Keshian fortress once had a name, now lost in time. Walls and towers were mostly gone, so only one underground entrance a few hundred feet away led into tunnels and caverns, as well as the masonry upon which Belasco stood. Jim had no plan on entering that labyrinth. In Jim's great-grandfather's day it had been locally known as the Tomb of the Hopeless. Legend had it an entire garrison had been left to die. It once commanded the entrance to what was called the Valley of Lost Men. Jim reoriented himself, out of habit.

To his right was a gap in the rocks that would let him move swiftly to a trail north, an abandoned caravan route that ended in the Keshian port city of Durban. At the foot

RAYMOND E. FEIST

of these hills a half dozen of the deadliest thugs Jim could
find waited for his return. Five were cutthroats who occasionally worked for him in Durban; the sixth was Amed
Dabu Asam, his most trusted agent in the Jal-Pur desert region and the one he relied on to carry word back to Krondor should Jim not return by dawn.

To the left was an open expanse and then a sudden drop
down to a sheer cliff. Only the gods knew what waited
down in that desolate valley below, so Jim knew that should
he bolt he was certainly going to his right.

He glanced around, trying hard to look like just another devoted follower of the demon, mimicking the ritual
movements of the others. He hoped his constant glances up
toward the archers didn't call attention to himself. He knew
that very soon many things would happen, all of them bad.

Jim had been trying to find the nest of a group called
the Servants of Dahun, known to others as the Black Caps,
for over half a year. It had taken poring over reports from
his great-grandfather's days for Jim to decide to investigate
this ancient fortress.

Once home to a cult of fanatic assassins, the Night-
hawks, the site had been considered abandoned for a century. Obviously someone decided that now that no one was
paying attention, it might be a good time to reoccupy these
ruins.

The ancient fortress was close enough to Krondor and
the Empire City of Durban to allow quick and easy access
for these murderous dogs and it was far enough away from
any place a sane man would wish to visit that the chances
for discovery were small. Jim had almost gotten himself
killed twice getting here and now was counting the seconds
of borrowed time he had remaining.

He considered the family tales of his ancestor facing
down a cult of assassins here with almost no help. Jim
would take a fortress full of assassins over a mob of reli-
gious fanatics any day. The assassins might kill you and

it would probably be swift, but these lunatics might slow roast him over a fire and eat him.

Finally, Jim could make out Belasco's voice. "We are here to give blood and life to our master!"

As one the assembled mob chanted, "Hail, Dahun!"

Jim took an instinctive step back, glancing first to the right, then to the left. As he suspected, the crouching figures on the rocks surrounding this area were archers. He began sidestepping toward the closest boulder, a suddenly very distant-seeming twenty feet to his right.

With two rapid steps, Jim found a deep shadow beneath an overhanging rock. He had to crouch, which made doffing his robe more difficult, but in seconds he was almost invisible within the tiny pool of darkness. He reached back and from behind his neck pulled up a concealing hood that left only his eyes exposed. The material he wore was dull black, as were the blackened metal fastenings. He gripped his dagger and waited.

Belasco shouted, "Rejoice! Know your sacrifice brings us closer to our master's appearance!"

At that, the archers crouching in the rocks rose up and began firing at the gathered worshippers. Most stood stunned as those next to them fell. The eeriest aspect to Jim was the silence. A muffled exhalation of breath, or a faint grunt of pain, but no one screamed or cried out. With the wind whipping up dust, Jim could only catch glimpses of faces and none showed any fear.

They stood like sheep at a shearing, waiting until a bow shaft found its mark.

Jim needed to see no more. He scooted along under the rock and slipped behind it, circling around until he was behind the archer perched on the rock above where he had hidden. There was a small gap of ten feet of open ground he needed to cross to reach the next hiding place and he didn't hesitate. All eyes were on those worshippers falling around Belasco's feet and Jim knew that in a moment they would be dead and someone would be checking to see if anyone survived. He was determined to be as far away as possible before that moment.

Jim reached the second shadow and glanced around. Seeing no one nearby, he sprinted across a dozen yards of open space. An opening between two large rocks marked the entrance to a game trail that led down a short incline to the old caravan route to Durban. The eerie sound of the desert wind deepened Jim's apprehension as he half ran, half stumbled down the trail.

His nearly out-of-control flight caused him to bowl over a black-clothed figure waiting at the bottom of the trail. The two men went down in a tangle of arms and legs and Jim almost plunged his knife into the figure before he recognized him. "Amed!"

"Peace, my friend," said the Keshian agent as he regained his feet.

"What are you doing here?"

"When you failed to return, I thought to follow you a bit, in case you needed aid."

Jim glanced upward and said, "What I need now is to get as far from here as quickly as possible. Horses?"

"Down the road a little," said the spy. "I thought it reckless for you to come on foot, so I brought along a spare."

Jim nodded, and followed his companion. He had insisted on approaching the ancient fortress on foot, as all the supplicants were walking and a rider would have stood out. He thought he saw movement above and behind and with a quick tug on Amed's shoulder, had him kneeling at his side. Pointing upward and behind, he nodded once.

The nod was returned, Amed signaled his route up, and Jim nodded. Practiced in stealthy ambush, both men knew almost instinctively what the other would do. Jim would head back the way he came while his companion would loop around, approaching anyone following from behind. Jim waited to see if anyone came down the trail, and after enough time to ensure Amed was in place he started back up.

Reaching the top of the trail, he found Amed kneeling, inspecting trail signs in the moonlight. "I can't be sure," said the Keshian spy, "but I think whoever followed turned back when you headed down to the caravan road. Do we follow?"

"No," said Jim. "I need to report back as soon as possible."

"Magic?"

Jim smiled. "I wish. Those devices are only loaned out when necessary, and lately some of the older ones have stopped working. Pug is trying to find ways to restore them, but it looks as if a lot of Tsurani art is being lost."

Amed shrugged. "I know little of the Tsurani. Few ever venture this far south. And I have no desire to visit LaMut."

"It is less than a captivating city," said Jim. "Let's be on our way."

As the two made their way to where the horses waited, a man hidden deep in shadows watched them depart. He waited until they were gone down the old caravan route, then turned to trot silently back into the night. He reached the clearing now strewn with bodies to find Belasco waiting for him.

The mercenary said, "Master, it is as you have said."

The magician smiled and there was nothing akin to humor in his expression. "Good. Let Jim Dasher return to Krondor with his tale of bloodshed and dark magic."

"Master," said the killer. "I do not understand."

"I wouldn't expect you to," said Belasco as he sat atop the rock on which he had been standing. He looked at the carnage on all sides. "Sometimes you have to put on a demonstration to show your opponents what you're capable of accomplishing."

"Again, I do not understand. You instruct?"

"Ambition?" said Belasco, regarding the mercenary with a narrow gaze. "I'm not sure I like that."

"I do as you bid," said the man, lowering his head.

"Where are you from? You speak oddly."

The mercenary smiled broadly, revealing teeth filed to points. "I am of the Shaskahan, master."

Brightening up at that, he said, "Ah! The island cannibals! Lovely.

"Yes, I will instruct. Sometimes you wish your opponent to think they are ahead. Other times not. This time, I want them to concentrate on bloody murder and dark magic, as if I were another mad necromancer like my brother."

"This is to serve Dahun, master?"

"Of course," answered Belasco as if annoyed by the question. "Just not in the way you think." He stood up. "Get the horses," he shouted. "We ride south!"

The mercenaries all moved with precision. Of all the hired murderers he had at his disposal, this group was the most unswerving in their obedience and loyalty. The fanatics had their uses but were too willing to die for their "god," and Belasco needed those who were willing to kill and reluctant to die.

"Eventually," said Belasco to no one in particular, "Jim Dasher and his masters will decide the time has come to investigate the Valley of Lost Men. We shall have to prepare another distraction for them when they do!"

With that he leaped down from the rock and hurried to where a mercenary held his horse. Mounting up, he looked around to see that all was as he wished it. The fires would burn for hours, and the embers would remain hot for a day or more. The smoke and stench of death would drape this plateau for a week, but eventually the hot blowing sand and the scavengers would reduce everything to burned char and dry bones, and even the charred wood and dry bones would eventually be carried away by the unforgiving winds.

He signaled and led his men down the steep trail into the Valley of Lost Men.

Sandreena, Knight-Adamant of the Order of the Shield of the Weak, waited at the docks. Her orders had been simple: meet with a Kingdom noble. She had no idea who it would be, but she had been told he would recognize her. She didn't know if he had met her before or had simply been provided a description; there weren't many members of the order who were tall blond women.

A pair of men covered in road dust approached down the docks. Their faces were obscured by the trailing edges of their keffiyehs being pulled up and tucked in, forming a covering for their noses and mouths—not unusual for men riding in from the Jal-Pur. Despite the oppressive heat, Sandreena stood motionless in her armor, her shield slung across her back and her sword within easy reach.

The taller of the two men came to stand before her and handed her a bundle of parchment. "For Creegan" is all he said, and turned and walked toward the end of the dock where a Kingdom trading vessel waited.

She wondered who this mysterious nobleman might be, but as he was obviously disguised as a local trader, she knew there were things at play that did not warrant scrutiny. Father-Bishop Creegan was always forthcoming with what she needed to know personally to ensure the success of her missions. Apparently all she needed to know in this case was that those papers needed to reach Krondor.

She moved toward the stable yard where her horse waited. If the unknown nobleman needed her to ride to Krondor with his bundle, then his ship was bound for another destination. She put aside her musings and stopped at a local stall. She would need a week's provisions and several skins of water, for from Durban to the first oasis was three days' ride. And from there to the Kingdom town of Land's End another four days.

Not looking forward to the task before her, but resolute in her devotion to her duty, she paid for the dried meat, dried fruit, and roasted grain that would be her only sustenance for the next week. She also needed a week's worth of feed as there would be no fodder for her mount along the way.

Considering her assignment, she let curiosity about the unknown Kingdom noble fade away.

Jim stood on the deck of the *Royal Sparrow,* a message cutter that had been turned out to look like a small coastal trader, renamed *Bettina* for the duration. The crew were among the finest sailors and marines Jim could steal from Admiral Tolbert's fleet, each trained personally by Jim at one time or another. They were forty-five of the hardest, most dedicated and dangerous fighting men afloat on the Bitter Sea, and more than once Jim had been grateful for their skills and loyalty.

He had along the way considered his chance meeting with Sandreena. Dressed as a court noble, he was unrecognizable to her, but covered in dirt with three days' growth of beard, he ran the risk that she might remember him as the Mocker who had sold her into slavery years before. He was relieved he hadn't been forced to take valuable time out to avoid being killed as he explained to her his role in all the things in her life that she'd most like to forget. Instead he considered himself lucky to now be surrounded by those loyal to him and the Crown, who would ensure he reached his destination safely.

Like Amed, these were among those few men Jim would trust with his life, and they would follow him to the lower hells. And given what he had seen over the last month, that very likely was their final destination.

Overhead a nasty squall was finally leaving the small ship behind, as it moved eastward toward the distant city of Krondor. The storm seemed to come in waves, and they had endured four days in a row of bad weather. Jim ignored the drenching he had received on deck, waiting to get in close enough to the island to disembark.

In the distance, through the gloom, Jim made out the looming dark castle on the bluffs overlooking the lone approachable cove on Sorcerer's Isle. As it had since the first time he had seen it, the sight of the structure filled Jim with a vague foreboding. He knew from experience this was a very subtle magic employed by Pug, the Black Sorcerer, and that it would pass once he entered the premises. He did note that the magically induced evil blue light in the north-most tower was absent, now replaced by a relatively benign-looking yellow glow, as if a stout fire burned inside.

Jim waited until Captain Jenson, master of the ship, gave orders to reef sails and drop anchor before he indicated he was ready to go ashore. He was now dressed in a simple, utilitarian fashion: woolen tunic and trousers, broad belt with sword and knife, high boots, and a large flop hat—all well made despite the simple look. He entered the longboat as it was lowered over the side, and waited until the first breakers drove it into the shallows to jump out. He was already soaked to his smallclothes, so waiting for the men to pull the boat ashore seemed to serve little purpose.

He was impatient to talk to Pug and his advisors, especially the Demon Master, Amirantha, and, he hoped, unburden himself with his intelligence; he wanted this to be someone else's problem. He had Keshian spies to catch, competing criminal gangs to crush, and a court life that was going neglected far too long.

He waded ashore, ignoring the water up to his thighs, sloshing into his boots. He wanted to get this obligation of his discharged and be on his way.

The pathway up from the beach was short and came to a divide. To the left it meandered up and over a ridge, then down into a vale where the sprawling estate, Villa Beata, had rested. Gutted by fire in an attack a year previous, it now lay abandoned, a testament to the wicked effectiveness of Belasco and his minions. To the right lay the stone-strewn path leading to the black castle.

Now regretting his impulsive jump into the surf, he trudged up the path, water knotting his stockings in his boots. Even with the rain, they had managed to stay dry until he jumped into the water. Not only would he have serious polishing to do to save the fine leather boots from the predations of seawater, he would have a heroic set of blisters to show for his impatience as well.

Sighing in resignation, he wondered if one of the inhabitants of the black castle might have a balm for his feet when he reached the gate. He crossed over a rickety-looking drawbridge—really well maintained and sturdy, but allowed to look as if it had fallen into disuse.

The castle itself was a study in theatricality. Originally constructed by Macros, the first Black Sorcerer, it had been magically erected out of a blackish stone, shot through in places with steel grey. The looming gatehouse had the look of an open maw, as if any who entered would be devoured. The empty courtyard was weed-choked and dusty, and the twin doors to the castle were ajar.

Jim knew as well as those who lived here that the decision to relocate from the villa to this miserable haven was part of a ruse to let Belasco and his masters think the Black Sorcerer and the Conclave of Shadows had been humbled, driven into a fortress where they huddled in fear and waited for the mad magician's next assault.

The truth was much more complex than that, Jim had quickly come to realize. As he approached the entrance of the forlorn-looking castle, Jim reflected on his changing relationship with these people over the last year.

The relationship between the Conclave of Shadows and the Jamison family had been difficult for twenty years. Jim's great-grandfather, the nearly legendary Jimmy the Hand, later Lord James of Krondor, had married Pug's foster daughter Gamina. In a sense, they were distant family, but along the way a division had slowly developed.

Jim walked through the empty great room, crossing before the massive fireplace. In ages past, this type of castle would house as many as a hundred members of a noble family, and retainers and their families, and on especially cold nights they could gather in this one room. He paused for a moment and considered the painful attention to detail undertaken by Macros the Black in constructing this place. Anyone exploring this near ruin would assume it had been built ages before its erection. Jim, not for the first time, counted the Black Sorcerer who built this place slightly mad.

As he mounted the stairs leading up to the one tower he knew to be occupied, he wondered how his great-grandfather would have viewed the current situation. By all reports of his nature, he would have been annoyed and amused by it, Jim concluded.

Pug had shamed the Prince of Krondor at that time, later King Patrick, disavowing his loyalty to the Kingdom of the Isles and virtually daring the Kingdom to assert its claim to control over the island duchy of Stardock, in the Vale of Dreams.

Jim recalled there was some issue with those running Stardock on Pug's behalf at that time, as well. Whatever the causes, truly, Pug had withdrawn to this island with his family and retainers. He had also begun the Conclave of Shadows, the secret organization that had become a major part of Jim's life, despite his wishing to have nothing to do with it at the outset.

Reaching the top landing, Jim paused, considering what he would report to Pug. Not only was he bringing intelligence of the most dire sort to the magician's attention, he was about to make a choice.

The relationship between the Jamison family and the Conclave became strained when Jim's grandfather had been summoned to the King's court, eventually rising to the rank of Duke of Rillanon. Jim's great-uncle Dashel had retired from public service, beginning the family's merchant presence in Krondor.

At times during his grandfather's administration of the capital city—and by extension the Kingdom itself—conflicts of interest had arisen between the Conclave and the Kingdom. James of Rillanon, like his grandfather before him, had been steadfast in his loyalty to the Kingdom of the Isles.

Jim reflected it might have been simpler for Jimmy the Hand—in those days the aims of the magicians of Stardock and the Kingdom were more or less in harmony. He wondered if his great-grandfather would have looked at this situation the same way Jim did.

Jim's father, William Jamison, and his uncle Dasher had both died in border wars with Kesh when Jim was a boy, and his great-uncle Dashel had no surviving sons. By the time he was twenty years of age, James Dasher Jamison was the sole surviving heir to the family, and both his grandfather and great-uncle had marked him.

Jim pushed aside flooding memories of the ruse used by both his forebears to get him to take over control of all crime along the Kingdom's Bitter Sea coast, and taking charge of the Kingdom's intelligence services. That he had found a knack for both and had made the criminal activities serve the Kingdom's intelligence interest hadn't made wearing two caps at the same time any easier.

And now he was on the verge of donning a third cap, as a fully committed agent of the Conclave. Pushing open the door to the tower's common room, he wondered if he was making the right choice.

He was confronted with two young women, knitting, while a third was putting wood on a fire in a small fireplace in the opposite wall. A group of three men huddled near the fire speaking in low tones. One young magician recognized him and said, "Jim Dasher, welcome!"

Jim nodded a return greeting and said, "Jason." He glanced around. "Where is everyone?"

"Scattered," said Jason, running his hand through his long blond hair, pushing it back from his forehead. "Pug's sent many of the younger students home or to Stardock, while most of the rest of us have been moved to safe locations." He indicated the others in the room. "A few of us stay here to keep a lookout for any more trouble, and convey messages. What do you require?"

"I require to speak to Pug," said Jim, not masking his impatience. He held up a sphere of dull golden metal. "This doesn't work. I had to take a fast ship from Durban to get here."

The magician took the sphere and said, "The Tsurani transport spheres . . . we've not had any new ones in years." He looked at it and his tone was one of regret. "I fear most of the artificers who made them perished on Kelewan. The few who survived . . ." He shrugged.

Jim knew Jason meant those few were struggling with the rest of the Tsurani survivors on their new home world, or perhaps were living quietly in LaMut. And, without saying as much, implied that if the Conclave had access to newer devices, they would have them. "Most of those we have are decades old, my friend," Jason said softly.

Feeling a fool, Jim said, "Yes. You're right. Now, may I speak with Pug?"

"Pug's not here," said Jason.

"Where is he?"

As he glanced over at his companions, the young magician's tone was apologetic. "We don't know. We haven't seen him for nearly a month now."

Jim said, "Then I need to speak with Magnus."

"He's gone as well," said Jason. "Come, sit by the fire and rest. We have means of sending word, but it may take some time."

"By 'some time,' do you mean hours or days?" asked Jim,

pulling off his leather gauntlets and moving to a stool near the fire.

Jason only shrugged, and Jim felt his frustration return in full. He knew his crew would wait until he either sent word or returned, so he felt little need to move away from the warming fire. Thinking of nothing better to do, he sat back against the cold stones and wondered just where the two magicians might be.

CHAPTER 2

Foreboding

Lightning flashed across the sky.

Amirantha silently counted, and then came the distant boom of thunder. Looking at his old companion, Brandos, the Warlock of the Satumbria said, "The storm is moving away from us."

The fighter nodded, remaining silent as he sat on a low stool, attentively cleaning his armor. He hunched over near the fire burning in the ancient keep's fireplace, barely able to fend off the chill in this tiny room, perched near the top of the occupied tower.

Amirantha had been amused the first time he had come here, to visit the legendary castle of the Black Sorcerer. Now he found it old, drafty, almost stifling in its familiarity and a place locked in the grip of sorrow. After a year of living with these people, the usually solitary Demon Master felt a sense of understanding their pain and anger. Whatever had passed for normalcy before the attack on Villa Beata and the death of Miranda, her younger son Caleb, and his wife Marie, along with a score of students, that normalcy would never return.

Among the very few bright moments over that year was the return a month previous of Brandos, who had traveled down to their home near the city of Maharta in Novindus, with his wife Samantha. But even the unrelentingly cheerful woman had been unable to do more than momentarily lift the pall of gloom that constantly hung over this place.

Pug and his surviving son, Magnus, would come and go, and at times there were interesting discussions on matters common to their interest. Amirantha was forced to concede he had broadened his understanding of demons and the demon realm more in the last year than he had in the previous fifty years of solitary study. Often it was a case of having similar information, but interpreting its significance in a faulty way, and he had helped Pug identify misapprehensions in his knowledge.

But those times were growing more infrequent, and Pug and Magnus were absent for longer stretches, as they saw to the matters pressing upon their secret organization, the Conclave of Shadows. Amirantha and Brandos had not been invited formally into that organization, but there was a tacit understanding that they were now part of this effort, willing or not. Amirantha had no doubt they had the means to ensure he didn't leave with the vital knowledge he possessed, so he considered having a choice in the matter moot.

He stood and stretched, making a small motion with his head indicating Brandos should look out the small window. The old fighter put aside the leather jerkin he had been cleaning, stood, and walked over to his friend—a stepfather as much as anything else, despite the fact he now looked ten years the old magic-user's senior. "What?" he asked softly.

"Rain is going to play out soon," answered the Warlock as he looked out into the late afternoon murk.

"You look bored."

"Constantly," said the Warlock. "When I first came here, I will concede I did so with some anticipation, finding those I counted kindred souls, and thought for the first time in my life I might have colleagues with whom I could share my knowledge as well as learn from, and at first it was like that, but lately . . . ? Now, what do I find instead?"

"Children."

Amirantha smiled. The magicians remaining here with Pug and his son, Magnus, were hardly children, yet his foster son reminded Amirantha that he had a tendency to be dismissive of most everyone he met because of his long life and the perspective it offered. Yet Pug was even older, as were others who came and went from this island. Miranda, Pug's late wife, also had been older, and her sudden death had been a grim reminder to Amirantha that long life and experience are not defenses against mortality.

"Hardly," said Amirantha. "Still, for the most part they're in the formative stages of their education, training, and power. None of them have been practicing their arts for more than twenty years."

Brandos returned to his stool and took up the leather he had been cleaning. Applying a generous dollop of leather soap to his weapon's belt, he said, "Sort of makes you wonder where all the grown-ups went, doesn't it?"

Amirantha stared out the window. "Indeed." He craned his neck a bit and looked out and up. "I'm ready to go outside. Being cooped up here is hardly a treat."

Brandos sighed, looking at his unfinished cleaning. "Well, a short walk. I could use a leg stretcher." Looking at his friend, he added, "Samantha says I've been as irritated as a bear woken from hibernation lately, so maybe it'll do us both good."

"It's been four days of rain."

"It's an island in the middle of an ocean, Amirantha. It's late fall. There's going to be a lot of rain."

Muttering as he opened the door, Amirantha said, "Not an ocean. It's a sea."

Brandos shook his head but said nothing.

Amirantha descended the stairs to the common room below, and let out a long silent sigh. He knew his foster son understood his argumentative impulse was born of frustration. After the destruction of the villa used by Pug, his family, and students, there had been a flurry of activity. The dead were burned, the wounded tended, and there had been conferences among Pug and his most trusted advisors. Those conferences and discussions had animated the Warlock in a way he had rarely known, and had never shared with another; he had discovered he was happy.

Continuing down the stairs, Amirantha realized that part of his annoyance was the stark contrast between that early energizing period of reorganization here on the island and what he endured now. One night two months ago, everything changed. Pug and Magnus vanished, as had more than thirty of the most powerful of his magician colleagues. Abruptly what had been a somewhat crowded keep was occupied by less than a dozen souls.

The month when Brandos had traveled south to fetch Samantha had been the loneliest time in Amirantha's life, and he was vexed at discovering that fact. He had a strong opinion on matters of his own conduct and appearances, and missing his foster son did not mesh well with them. More than once he had cursed himself for letting another person grow close to him, especially one he was destined to outlive by a very long time—assuming they both survived the coming struggle.

Reaching the floor of the tower, they entered the common room and saw an unexpected presence.

"Jim Dasher!" said Amirantha in greeting.

Jim rose from his stool before the warming fire and said, "You still here, Amirantha?" He extended his hand and they shook.

He then exchanged greetings with Brandos, as Amirantha said, "My lingering here was at Pug's request. He can be persuasive."

"Ah," said Jim, nodding. "He wouldn't let you leave."

Brandos snorted, and Amirantha said, "He was insistent, and truth to tell I found many things here to be interesting."

Glancing around the stark hall, Jim said, "Really?"

Amirantha smiled. "Well, not so much lately, but the first nine months were fascinating."

He motioned for Jim to move toward the large doors. "My quarters are adequate but hardly commodious, so I thought to step outside for a breath of air now that the rain has nearly stopped."

Jim nodded and fell into step behind him. "I just came in from the . . ." Jim began, then he stopped himself. "Actually, I'm supposed to report directly to Pug on this matter." He looked hard at Amirantha, then said, "Still, there is much about what I've seen that concerns you."

"Really?" said the Warlock, then he fell silent, content to let the mysterious noble-turned-spy-turned-thief speak when he was ready.

As they reached the entrance to the yard, they paused on the verge of the doorway, feeling the occasional raindrop blown in by the freshening wind. Jim motioned for the Warlock to continue and they left the relative warmth of the keep entrance for the soggy ground of the ancient marshaling yard. As Amirantha had judged, the rain had fallen off to almost nothing and the wind was freshening a little; it already felt drier.

"So, you were about to say?"

Jim appeared annoyed. "I can never tell who knows what around here."

Amirantha laughed. "I can tell you this much, my friend: no one left here is without some power and ability, despite appearances to the contrary. Pug ensured all the students were safely away within a day of . . ."

"The attack," finished Jim.

"I was going to say the death of his wife and son." Amirantha sighed. "Never having children, I can only imagine a bit of what he's going through. I certainly had nothing to fairly compare what he was like before that, scant hours really, but . . ." He shrugged.

"There's been a change," said Jim. He looked to the west where somewhere behind the clouds the sun was lowering toward the horizon. "He knew I was about some business of consequence, yet there's apparently no means for contact; that is unlike him. It's as if he's . . ." Jim shrugged.

"Distracted?" offered Amirantha.

"More," said Jim. "Distant in a way that troubles me."

"I don't understand."

Jim smiled slightly. "I don't expect you to. I hardly know the man well, despite our somewhat tenuous kinship."

"Kinship?"

Jim said, "My great-grandmother was his foster daughter."

Amirantha's eyebrows went up slightly as his expression indicated surprise. "Tenuous by blood, yes, but otherwise?"

"We are not close. It is a long story, a family matter, and really not pertinent to the discussion at hand."

Amirantha shrugged, to convey that if Jim didn't think it important enough to speak of, that was enough. "Perhaps, but apparently we have ample time. Enlighten me."

Jim stared off into the darkening afternoon gloom and said, "While Pug and I may not be close, I do know a great deal about him, for his role in Kingdom politics has been significant, since long before I was born."

"Obviously," agreed Amirantha. "Given the rank and

status of those who have been to visit since I was first made aware of the Conclave's existence."

"So in my . . . other duties, to the Crown, I've been required to read a great deal of history, much of it penned by my own forebears.

"Pug is, if anything, a man of strong convictions and he pays attention to details. He is not the sort to let important things slip by. Yet lately . . ." Jim took a deep breath. ". . . this is unlike him."

"By this, I expect you mean *this*," Amirantha said, indicating the cold, nearly empty castle with a wave of his hand.

"I would have expected the man I knew, the one I studied, to have begun reconstruction on the villa at once, almost defiantly, as if telling his enemies that they would not prevail."

Amirantha nodded, pursing his lips as if thinking, and remained quiet for a moment, then asked, "How much time do you think his enemies spend studying him?"

Jim inclined his head slightly as if conceding the point.

"Would it not seem, given what has happened here, that Pug also realizes he's under a great deal of scrutiny? By all reports, in one form or another, these enemies of his have been coming at him for years."

"If you assume that there is one intelligence behind a series of assaults on this world going back more than a century and a half, yes. But that is an assumption."

"A better one to make," observed the Warlock, "than thinking this land is merely beset by a string of coincidental afflictions.

"I may not be the master of magic on Pug's scale, but I know enough about the other realms to know this is not a series of odd happenings." He paused, and Brandos recognized his expression. Amirantha was frustrated. "Over the last year I've heard enough references to things such as the Pantathian Serpent Priests—with whom I am familiar—and the Riftwar, and the Great Uprising, and all the rest of it to believe there is one intelligence behind all of this, one agency that has targeted this world, perhaps this nation, even perhaps this island, for reasons known only to them, but irrespective of those reasons, the consequences for this entire world are dire."

"I agree," said Jim, "but tell me your reasons."

"The Pantathians exist in the distant mountains to the west of my home, yet stories of them travel; they are a strange race, and they have been thought to be obliterated numerous times, yet they linger.

"They serve an ancient hate, a woman symbol they call 'mother of us all' and kill without remorse any who will not serve her.

"The Emerald Queen, whose army savaged my homeland before traveling halfway around the world to come to the Kingdom, was a demon in disguise." Suddenly Amirantha became animated. "Do you have any notion of how remarkable that is?"

Jim shook his head.

"I will bore you with a long lecture—"

"And he will," interjected Brandos.

"—some other time, but suffice it to say that demon possession on that level, of an already powerful magic user . . . it's unknown to those of my calling."

Jim said, "I still don't see the connection."

Amirantha seemed to fight for words. "I can't explain . . . I mean, it's as if I'm on the edge of understanding something, but I'm not quite there yet. Just, it's more than a feeling, Jim." He looked at Brandos and said, "Am I one to leap to conclusions?"

Brandos shrugged, then realized it wasn't time for a jape; it had been a serious question. "No, you occasionally become convinced of your own brilliance, but you are hardly rash." He paused, then added to Jim, "He's gotten us almost killed several times through miscalculation, but that's the point; he was wrong, not unconsidered. If he says he's on the edge of understanding something larger than is apparent, I'd believe him."

"Well, then," said Jim Dasher. "Is there any way I can help?"

"Only if you can supply more information than I've been privy to lately."

Jim was silent a long moment, staring out into the fading light.

Brandos cleared his throat and said, "I'm going to be inside; I should ask Samantha to hustle up something for you to eat. I imagine you're hungry."

Jim smiled. "Thank you, Brandos. That would be fine." After the old fighter had left, Jim said, "He should be a diplomat."

Amirantha laughed. "Hardly, but he can be discreet at times."

Jim paused, then said, "Very well. I expect that Pug will ask you in to listen to my report anyway, as you are the expert in demons."

Amirantha nodded. "That elf, Gulamendis, is the only being I've met who knows as much or more."

Jim looked uncomfortable. "Those Star Elves make my skin itch. But they're a matter for another time." Jim told the Warlock what he had witnessed in the distant Jal-Pur desert, and when he was finished he asked, "What do you think?"

Amirantha said, "I think we need to find a way to fetch Pug back here as soon as possible."

"Why?"

Turning toward the keep, Amirantha said, "Come with me."

He didn't wait to see if Jim followed, but hurried inside the keep. He glanced around the common room and asked the four younger magicians there, "Where is Jason?"

One of them pointed toward a door that led to a small

room Pug had occasionally used as a private office. Amirantha went to the door and knocked once, then opened it. Jason sat behind the tiny desk that Pug had installed in this former storage room and was squinting at a paper under the dim glow of a single candle. The tiny window above hardly admitted any light on the brightest of days, and on a day such as this, it might as well be midnight. "Yes?" he asked, apparently untroubled by the sudden entrance.

"Pug," said Amirantha. "You need to summon him at once."

Jason sat back. "And how am I supposed to do that, given I have no idea where he is?"

Amirantha glanced sidelong at Jim, then said, "I count Pug many things, but fool is not one of them. Even if you don't know where he is, I'm certain he's left you means to contact or summon him, should the need arise. The need has arisen."

"Really?" asked the younger magician. He looked at Jim for corroboration.

"I think so, as well," said Jim.

"Very well," said Jason, rising from behind the small desk. "Come with me." He picked up the candleholder.

He led them out of the room, across the floor of the keep's great hall. Brandos stood near his wife beside the large hearth where a pot of stew was simmering. The old fighter shot a questioning look at Amirantha, but with an inclination of his head the Warlock indicated to stay where he was.

Jason led them up a flight of stairs to the upper floor of the main building, and down a long hall that traversed the building, to the tower opposite the one in which Amirantha resided. The single candle Jason held was the only light on that floor. To the best of the Warlock's knowledge, that tower was empty, save for an enchantment on the top floor that caused an ominous blue light to glow whenever a ship approached sight of the castle.

They walked up a circular staircase, to the second to the last floor, and Jason opened a door. The room was bare, save for a construct of wood, two curving poles that sat atop a base of what looked like metal. Amirantha glanced at Jason and said, "Tsurani?"

The young magician said, "Design. Pug built it."

"What is it?" asked Jim.

"A rift gate," said Amirantha. "What our friends the Star Elves call a portal."

Jason went to a small shelf near a shuttered window and pulled down a small cloth bag. He handed the candle to Jim, then knelt and carefully opened the bag. Reaching inside he pulled out an odd-looking device, a square box with odd designs and some strange levers and wheels on it.

"This was created by some artificer up in LaMut, of Tsurani heritage, but not a Tsurani. It's a little ungainly compared to the old Tsurani devices." He shrugged as if what he was saying was merely trivia.

He put it on the base between the two poles, tripped one of the levers, and stood back. "I have no knowledge or ability when it comes to rift magic," said the magician. "It is difficult and outside my interests. Only Magnus and a few others know much about it, and no one knows what Pug knows. Against the need of summoning him, he had this constructed."

Suddenly a whooshing sound filled the room, and a crack of energy, followed by a shimmering between the poles. Then a grey void, with scintillating colors faintly running over the surface, like oil refracting light on water, could be seen.

"Pug will get the alert in a moment. He should appear as soon as he is able."

"Do you know where he went?" asked Jim.

Jason said, "We only know what he tells us."

Long moments dragged by, then suddenly a figure stepped through the rift. A short man with a closely trimmed beard, Pug still wore the ancient fashion of the Tsurani Great One, a simple black robe and cross-gartered sandals. "What is it?" he asked as soon as he was through.

Jason inclined his head toward Jim and Amirantha, and it was the Warlock who spoke. "We're being played for fools, Pug."

Pug's brow wrinkled as he asked, "What do you mean?"

"I'll explain," said Amirantha, "after Jim tells you what he saw a few days ago in the Jal-Pur, but it would help if we had another with us."

"Who?"

"We need an expert on death."

Pug looked slightly amused. "I know just the fellow." He turned and held up his hand, and the Warlock could feel shifting magic in the room, though Jim only perceived it as his "bump of trouble" starting to act up. After a moment, Pug said, "You two, follow me." To Jason he said, "Put away the toy when we're through." He stepped into the rift and Jim turned and said, "Send word to Captain Jenson to weigh anchor and make for Krondor. I'll find him there." He turned and followed Pug.

Just before he entered, Amirantha turned to Jason and said, "You also might tell Samantha that Jim and I will be missing supper tonight." He then followed the other two into the rift.

CHAPTER 3

SERGEANT-ADAMANT

Creegan motioned with his hand.

Sandreena entered his quarters still covered in dust from the road and feeling hunger pangs. She had paused long enough once she had given her horse over to the stable boy to drink deeply from the well behind the temple, but she hadn't eaten anything but a handful of dried fruit and some nuts since leaving Land's End. Her order was mendicant and there was no shrine or temple in Land's End, so she was still surviving on what she had purchased in Durban with the last of her coin.

The moment she handed her documents to the Father-Bishop she knew something was wrong, something that had nothing to do with the message she had just delivered. He waved her to sit in a chair across from his desk and said, "The Grand Master has passed."

She took a deep breath, closed her eyes, and made a short prayer to the Goddess to care for the old man on his way to Lims-Kragma's domain. He had been a good man, almost saintly, and Sandreena had no doubt he would be rewarded with a place higher on the Wheel of Life.

The Father-Bishop remained silent while she prayed, and then when she opened her eyes, she discovered him staring intently at her. "Father-Bishop?"

Creegan smiled and it was not a friendly or warm expression, but rather that of a man finding humor in a very dark place. "The end of life is not necessarily a cause for sorrow, daughter," he said, using the form of address usually reserved for minor members of the Order—it clearly communicated the difference in their ranks. She was uncertain why, but knew he did nothing without a reason. "The Grand Master served the Goddess well, for many years, and earned his final rest.

"But the timing of it is . . . inconvenient." He stood and said, "I must leave at once for Rillanon, for the convocation is only a week after the funeral, and the selection of the new Grand Master is now more critical than is usual."

She knew he was referring to the matter of the demon host, the "Legion" as it was called, that was out there somewhere, threatening to bring its ravages to this world. Few within the temple, and even fewer outside, even knew the threat existed. Sandreena did only because of circumstances, and the trust in which Father-Bishop Creegan held her. And fewer still knew of the relationship between the Father-Bishop and the Conclave of Shadows led by the magician Pug.

She merely nodded her head and said, "I understand."

"I know you do, Sandreena." He rose from the desk, came and sat on the corner before her, looking down at her. "I have never told you, but there is a beauty to you that few notice."

She was a little startled by the statement. There had always been an underlying tension between them, as she found him a very attractive and powerful man, but his reputation as something of a womanizer and their respective ranks had always kept any inappropriate behavior in check.

He held up his hand before she could speak. "I don't mean your physical beauty—as impressive as that is when you choose to let others glimpse it—but rather a beauty of strength and purpose, what you've overcome and managed to achieve despite a desperately difficult beginning. It is . . . admirable." He stood up and moved to the window and looked out, saying, "We may get more rain."

The rain along the coast had made her trip even more difficult, so she hoped he was wrong.

"I am leaving you in charge of the Order while I'm away."

Her eyes widened. "Me?"

"I'll send back Father-Bishop Bellamy, to assume my duties, but in the interim, you will take my place here."

"Take your place?"

Creegan shrugged as if it were of no importance, but said, "I will be the new Grand Master." The way he said it, she realized it was a fait accompli. He glanced over and smiled. "This was decided long ago. So, I will dispatch Bellamy as soon as the convocation is over, and you will then return to your duties, to do whatever he asks, for he will be speaking for me. Until then, you must take charge here."

"Why me?" she asked softly.

"You are the only one I trust, Sandreena." He came back and sat behind the desk. "Only a few know of what is really going on out there—I'll leave you a list and you will not trust anyone not on it—and you've also earned it. Your almost getting yourself killed isn't what I'm talking about, but rather you keeping your wits about you and your keen understanding of the political reality you found yourself in without warning.

"Few members of the Order would have coped so well with demons and secret alliances."

"The Mother-Superior?" she asked.

Creegan smiled. "She'll object, of course, but as she has no standing within the Order, I'll smile, nod, and suggest she get packed if she's to leave with me on the ride to Salador."

Sandreena nodded. The Mother-Superior had ambitions of her own and would be actively seeking her own allies in her bid to attain the office of High Priestess of the Grand Temple once the convocation began. The current High Priestess was older than the Grand Master so Sandreena judged there would be another convocation in Rillanon in the next few years.

Creegan said, "I suspect she'll dismiss your promotion quickly and start the endless flattery I will be subjected to along the way."

Sandreena couldn't help but smile. The High Priestess might be pleased to see Creegan leaving Krondor—their relationship had always had a contentious element in it, but with his rising to the highest calling in the Order, that suddenly made him an even more important voice in the temple, and he would have a great deal to say about the succession when the current High Priestess stepped down.

"You'll only need make one quick courtesy call—which I suggest you do now, before I let her know of your promotion."

"Promotion?"

"Of course. I can't leave a Knight-Adamant in charge of the Order in the Western Realm. Effective immediately, you are now a Sergeant-Adamant of the Order, but will bear the office rank of *adiuvare*. It's an old title we rarely use, but it's still recognized. So your official title will be Adiuvare-Sergeant-Adamant. Once Bellamy comes here, you will become just another Sergeant."

She tried not to smile. "Just another Sergeant," he said. As a rule, Knight-Adamants had to serve for twenty years to obtain the rank of Sergeant and few lived long enough. She was certain she not only was the youngest Sergeant in the Order, but perhaps in the history of the Order.

"I will do my best not to disappoint you, Father-Bishop."

"If I thought there was even a remote possibility of that, I would have given someone else the job," said Creegan. "Now, go make your call on the High Priestess, get something to eat, and rest. I think you'll discover this post is nothing close to as easy as you think." He motioned with his hands at the pile of papers and said, "More men have been defeated by reports than all the steel of all the swords in history." Then with his right hand he made a dismissive gesture and she rose, bowed slightly, and left his quarters.

Under any normal circumstance, she would have been elated at the promotion, for it would have been a signal that the Goddess had found her service noteworthy. This circumstance felt like it was not a gift, or reward, but a heavier burden. Still, she chided herself, if the Goddess wished to place an even bigger burden on her, it would only mean greater service, and that the Goddess deemed her able to meet the demands of office.

Still, she thought as her stomach growled, she wished she could get something to eat before calling on the High Priestess.

Sandreena made her call on the High Priestess, who was as Creegan predicted: distracted by the need to leave the next day for the arduous ride to the port of Salador, where she and Creegan would take ship to Rillanon for the convocation to elect the new Grand Master of the Order of the Shield of the Weak. The High Priestess had no official duties regarding the Order, but as every prelate of rank would be in attendance while the Order conducted their ceremonies and went through the motions of putting Creegan in charge, everyone else would be playing temple politics.

Sandreena was glad that she remained behind, even if she had responsibility for the Order in Krondor, which meant supervising the Order in the entire Western Realm of the Kingdom of the Isles.

After she had finally eaten, Sandreena had returned to the common barracks of the Order and had given her dirty tabard and clothing to a servant to be cleaned. She preferred to care for her own arms and armor. She went to the communal bath, enjoying the fact of it being empty, and gave herself over to a completely thorough cleaning.

While she scrubbed her filthy hair, she considered her feelings about Creegan's departure; it was as good as ordained since she had first met him, yet there was always this feeling . . . She sighed.

Encountering Amirantha months before, after that nearly fatal attack on Sorcerer's Isle, had caused her to revisit feelings she would rather ignore. Creegan also had that effect on her. With Amirantha it was something she wished she had never done, but with Creegan she began to suspect it was going to be something she regretted not doing.

Her order was not celibate, though like most people given over to a calling, personal issues were always of lesser importance. Still, as a woman in her prime, she was feeling certain needs asserting themselves.

She had never considered family a blessing, given how she grew up, yet now she wondered about being a mother. She knew nothing about raising a child, because no one had raised her. Her mother was early on lost to drugs, drink, and men, and no father had been at hand. Being ill-used by men since she had begun to blossom had given her a very unforgiving perspective on them.

There were two she had come to care for: Brother Mathias, who had rescued her from her Keshian slave master; and Father-Bishop Creegan, who had been her mentor, though she was beginning to think he was more important to her than that.

There were two men she wished dead. A blackheart who was called Jimmyhand by some, Quick Jim by others, who had controlled the brothel where she had served as a high-priced whore when she was little more than a girl. He had been the one to sell her to the Keshian. And Amirantha. He had charmed her, lied to her, and used her, and had lived down to her general judgment on the worth of men.

A tiny pang told her she didn't truly wish Amirantha dead, but rather she wished he had been telling her the truth; even when she saw him last, her sudden lashing out and knocking him to the floor had been followed instantly by regret. She wished somehow she could tell him that he had hurt her, but that would make her look weak.

Picking up a bucket she poured water over herself, cleaning away the dirt and soap. She bent over at the waist and ran a comb though her hair, squeezing water from it. The water was hot, but the air was cold after the passing storms and she felt gooseflesh on her skin.

She decided to forgo the meditative steam and retired to the barracks. She donned a simple white shift and turned in early. She was a sound sleeper and should others of her order enter, she was sure they would not wake her. All she wanted for this night was a sound sleep with no dreams.

Morning brought the departure of the group traveling to Salador, led by the High Priestess and the Father-Bishop. As Creegan had predicted, the High Priestess was as deferential and warm—to the point of cloying—as it was possible to be to the soon-to-be-named Grand Master of the Order of the Shield of the Weak.

When she had awakened, Sandreena had discovered a new uniform had been laid out for her across the footlocker at the foot of her bed, and atop it sat a new tabard, this one emblazoned with a chevron and crown above her heart, signifying her new rank of Sergeant. She couldn't resist smiling as she beheld it. She was not a prideful woman by nature, but she did like how seeing this badge of honor made her feel.

She had dressed and postponed a morning meal to be in the marshaling yard when the Father-Bishop and the others left.

Father-Bishop Creegan smiled when he saw her approach and put his hand on her shoulder. "The fate of the Order in the west is in your hands now, Sandreena." He leaned in so no one else could overhear his words and he said, "There's something on my desk you need to read; it's the report you brought to me. Act on it at once. I don't know exactly what you need to do, but I'm sure it will be the correct choice. I'm not telling you what I would do; this must be your decision."

Almost impulsively, he kissed her good-bye, but rather than a mere touching of the lips, he lingered a scant instant longer, and just before it became something both of them needed to worry about, he pulled back. "May the Goddess go with you," he whispered.

She could only nod, words failing her. As he mounted his horse, she managed to return the benediction. "May the Goddess go with you, Father-Bishop."

The High Priestess was fussing about her mount, a mild palfrey but still spirited enough to make the older woman show concern as she sat uncomfortably on the small horse. It was obvious the High Priestess would have preferred a litter, but the need to be in Rillanon by the date of the convocation prevented that more sedate mode of transport. She would be very sore and unhappy by the time they reached Salador.

The party moved out and as soon as they cleared the gate, Sandreena hurried to Creegan's office. Atop his desk lay two pieces of paper and the bundle she had carried from Durban.

She looked at the first, which had her name on it. She opened it and read: "Sandreena, if the Goddess wills it, we will meet again. Know the Order's trust rests with you and I have faith you will discharge the duties I've given you as well as if I undertook them myself. I've left you a list of those whom you may rely upon"—she knew he meant those who would be trusted in dealing with the Conclave and the matter of the demons—"and a report you must attend to at once. May the Goddess go with you." It was signed only "Creegan."

She looked at the list and found it had only five names on it. Four were priests and one was the orderly assigned to this office, the only member of the Order of the Shield who apparently knew about the Conclave of Shadows.

She looked up to see the man named on the list, a Prior of the Order, Brother Willoby. He was a round-faced, stocky man with a constantly worried expression. He said, "Sister? May I be of service?"

She sat down in Creegan's chair and said, "I will let you know, brother."

"I will be outside if you need me," he answered. The clerical branch of the Order were administrators. Unlike the Knights, they worked within the temples, as lay priests, but they were not properly of the clerical calling. These were men and women who had the calling, but not the strength of arm to serve in the field. Like most of the Knights, Sandreena hardly gave the priors a moment's thought, but she suspected she might come to appreciate them when she looked at the rest of the documents beside the desk that would require her attention.

She took the list of names and folded it up. She would burn it later. She already had memorized the names.

Then she opened the report given her by the nameless Kingdom noble and read it. She put it down, picked it up, and read it a second time.

Standing up, she shouted, "Willoby!"

Within a moment, the cleric appeared, asking, "Yes, sister?"

"Three things. First, do I have a second-in-command?"

The question seemed to startle him for a moment, as she was the Father-Bishop's *adiuvare*. "Why, no," he said, "I mean, you are the second-in-command, but with the Father-Bishop gone, you are . . . I mean, no, there's no one designated as such."

"Very well," she replied. "You are my *adiuvare,* as of now."

He blinked, then said, "I guess that's all right."

"As I am currently the highest-ranking member of the order west of Malac's Cross, of course it's all right."

He seemed to take this in stride as she stood up and put the report under her tunic. "Next, have my horse made ready with a week's provisions."

"Your horse?" asked the clerk.

"Yes," said Sandreena. "I need to depart on a mission today."

"But who . . . ?" he began, then saw her looking at him. "Me?"

"You're in charge until I get back," she said.

He was almost speechless, but nodded and said, "I'll have your horse made ready, sister."

She waited until he was gone then indulged herself in a low growl of frustration. "You bastard," she said softly with Creegan in mind. "That kiss . . ." If she had mistaken it for some sort of signal of passion withheld over the years, reading the report and thinking of what Creegan had said rid her of that notion. It was a kiss of apology. Yes, she thought, he wouldn't tell me what he would do if he was staying, because she was now doing exactly what he would do, which was send her out on a mission that would most likely get her killed.

Swearing at the curse in her life that was men, she moved out of his office and headed to the armory to see if her new-found rank would get her better armor and weapons.

CHAPTER 4

DEATH MAGIC

Pug held up his hand.

The two black-armored guardsmen at the door to the ancient temple were startled to see the three men appear apparently out of a grey void that had not been there moments before. Pug said, "We're here to see the High Priest."

Amirantha looked up at the sky and saw a dark, starry night, clear and dry. "We're somewhere to the east, aren't we?"

Jim said, "Rillanon. This is the temple of Lims-Kragma."

Amirantha said, "That makes sense."

No one on the world of Midkemia would have more knowledge of all aspects of death than the

High Priest of the Goddess of Death. The two guards still appeared unsettled by the sudden arrival, but their duty was to defend the portal only if obvious attack was under way—most of the time they were merely there to see that those coming to offer prayers for the departed remained orderly. One finally indicated with a wave of his hand that they were free to enter.

They passed through a large antechamber, replete with frescoes of the Death Goddess showing her as a warm, welcoming figure who was the eventual judge of every mortal being. That led them into the vast hall that was the main cathedral of the Goddess. Along both side walls, tiered benches were erected for contemplation and prayer by the faithful, while along the back wall two rows of shelves held hundreds of votive candles, most of which were alight. A burning flame to light the way of a loved one into Lims-Kragma's halls.

Pug took a moment to regard the heroic statue, some twelve feet high, of the Goddess, holding out one hand in a welcoming gesture, and in the other holding a silver net. The implication was obvious: no one escaped the drawer of nets, but she welcomed all equally. Pug found the image somewhat ironic, as he had been very adept at avoiding her welcome in the past, though the bargain he made with her was taking its toll on his mind and heart.

Three priests were praying before the statue, while off to one side several petitioners to the Goddess's mercy for a recently departed loved one lit candles and offered prayers. One of the priests saw the three men approaching with purpose and rose to greet them.

"Pug," he said in a neutral tone, inclining his head in a less than warm welcome. "What brings you here?"

"I need to speak with High Priest Marluke," said Pug. "The matter is most urgent."

"It always is, isn't it?" said the priest dryly. "Yet I am

certain the Holy Father will consider it urgent, as well. Please, follow me."

He led them past the statue, to a small door between the base of the edifice and the first row of burning candles and opened it. He motioned for them to go through, then followed, closing the door behind.

Down a long hall he led them, into a large room without decoration. The only items in the room were four chairs and a simple wooden table. "I'll inform the High Priest you are here," he said.

At that moment, a door opposite the one through which they entered opened, and an elderly man in a simple black robe, different only from Pug's in that it had a cowl thrown back, entered the room. "He already knows," he said. "You may leave us," he instructed the priest. He was tall, though starting to stoop a little with age, slender to the point of gauntness, and his hair was light grey bordering on white. But his dark eyes were alert and keen and his smile engaging.

As the younger man departed, the old prelate held out his hand to Pug and they shook. "As if you could pop into my temple without me knowing it," he said dryly. Then he said, "Ah, Jim Dasher, or is it Baron James Dasher Jamison today?"

Jim shook his hand as well and said, "Today it's Jim."

"And who is this?" asked the old man, waving the three of them to sit.

"Amirantha, Warlock of the Satumbria," said Pug.

The High Priest's eyebrows rose. "A Warlock!" He sat as soon as the others had taken seats. "I've sent for wine and food, if you're hungry."

Jim nodded approval.

Looking at Amirantha, the High Priest said, "Leave off the serious discussion until my servant has come and left. Until then . . . I thought the Satumbria obliterated."

"All but me," said Amirantha without emotion. "We were always a small nation—just a loose confederation of villages, really, scattered around the northern grasslands of Novindus. The Emerald Queen's army ended our existence."

"Ah," said the High Priest as his servant entered. All four men remained silent as food and wine were served, then the servant withdrew.

The High Priest looked at Pug and said, "No matter how many years pass, you look no different." He turned to Amirantha and said, "When I first met our friend here, I was a young priest, just ordained, working in the temple at Krondor. This fellow had several encounters with the High Priestess serving there." He looked regretful. "A wonderful woman, really, if you got to know her. She was my mentor and it's because of her I now hold this impossible office that was thrust upon me."

He looked again at Amirantha. "I suspect years after I've gone to meet Our Lady, he will still look as he does."

Amirantha only nodded politely.

Then the old man's manner changed. "Now, enough of reminiscence. What brings you here at this late hour?"

Pug said, "I am not sure, myself. Amirantha, Jim?"

The Warlock said to Jim, "You begin."

Jim had just bitten off a large hunk of bread and cheese, and was forced to wash it down with red wine, and after almost choking a bit he said, "Very well." He related his entire experience out in the Jal-Pur desert, describing the scene of slaughter and self-sacrifice as best he could. Given his years of training in observing detail, the narrative lasted almost a half hour.

None of the others spoke until he was finished. Pug said, "That is horrible, indeed." He looked at Amirantha and said, "You demanded we have an expert in death. Here he sits. Now, what in all this troubles you, that we are not seeing?"

Amirantha had been preparing for this question since he had first heard Jim's account. "Nothing that Jim observed makes sense. I will explain, but first let me ask you this, Holy Father: how much demon lore do you understand?"

"Little, truth to tell," answered the old man. "Our concerns here are in preparing the faithful for their eventual journey to Our Lady. We are put upon this world to let a fragile humanity understand that this life is but part of a much more profound journey, and that by living a just and honorable existence, when they meet Our Mistress she will place them upon a proper path toward ultimate enlightenment. Beyond that, our knowledge is much like anyone else's, we gather information where we may, share what we know with others"—he indicated Pug with an inclination of his head—"and have in turn been given the benefit of their wisdom." He laughed. "Besides, I was told to work with Pug."

Amirantha looked surprised. "Told to? By whom?"

"By Our Lady herself," said the old priest. "It is rare to have a visitation by the Goddess, but it does occur. Usually it's a revelation for the faithful and is proclaimed throughout the land, but in this case I was told to help Pug in whatever way I could and to keep my mouth shut." He laughed. "I may be the only High Priest or Priestess in the history of the temple to have a personal revelation and be unable to boast of it."

Amirantha said, "Then to understand what I must tell you, I shall have to tell you a story I have already shared with Pug and Jim."

Amirantha detailed his childhood, describing his existence on the fringes of Satumbria society, his mother's role as "witch" and her being tolerated by the villagers because of her skill with potions, herbs, and unguents. "She was also very beautiful; as a result, she bore three children by three fathers, none of whom would claim us."

He went on to contrast his brothers and himself, explaining how the eldest, named Sidi, had murdered their mother for the sheer pleasure of it. Of his next eldest, Belasco, he painted a portrait of a man obsessed with surpassing his brothers in any endeavor, one given to rages at the thought of being bested, and someone who had, for reasons Amirantha only vaguely understood, been trying to kill his younger brother for nearly fifty years.

"I can't even begin to guess which slight, real or imagined, set Belasco off on his quest to see me dead, but it hardly matters." He paused to sip some wine as his throat was dry.

The High Priest observed, "An interesting family, certainly, but I'm failing to see how any of this has to do with what Jim reported to us."

"I'm getting there, Holy Father," said Amirantha. "I recount my history so you'll fully understand what I believe is behind that exercise in murder." He paused, gathering his thoughts. "My eldest brother Sidi—whom you may also know as Leso Varen—was insane by any measure. He was mad when he was a child and only got more so as he grew. By the time he killed our mother he was a remorseless monster with no sense of humanity. His obsession was death magic."

The old priest nodded. "I recognize the name Leso Varen, and know he was a necromancer of prodigious art and from all reports, a font of evil."

"Whatever you read would not do the man justice," said Amirantha as Pug nodded agreement. "If there ever existed a shred of humanity in his being, it was extinguished long before he became a player in this monstrous game we find ourselves in.

"But Belasco is of another stripe; he is a man consumed by envy and rage, and jealous of any feat or skill achieved by my brother or myself. But unlike either of us, he has his own skills and talents, though he often leaves them aside to emulate our achievements. His dabbling in necromancy or demon lore, that I can see. But anything as murderous as the scene Jim described is . . . it's not something he would normally be a party to. Neither is serving a demon, no matter how powerful."

"Why?" asked Pug.

Sipping his wine again, Amirantha said, "Because Belasco would choose death before he would willingly serve anyone or anything."

"There's more," asked the High Priest, though it wasn't a question.

"Belasco also would not be a user of this sort of death magic. Here's the conundrum: whatever else death magic is good for, it's almost of no use whatever to those of us who are trafficking with demons."

Pug looked suddenly very interested, as if he wished to say something or ask a question, but instead said, "Go on."

"Holy Father," asked Amirantha, "what use is death magic?"

Pug realized the question wasn't rhetorical, but rather Amirantha asking a question to clarify a point he was about to make.

"It's an abomination," said the prelate. "Death magic, necromancy, are misnomers, for really what it becomes is the foulest form of life magic. At the moment of death, that which we call life leaves the empty shell of our bodies—it is what some call the *anima,* others call soul—and that energy is the fundamental core of being. The body is transitory and will fail, but the life which leaves it is eternal"—he held up a finger for emphasis—"unless something prevents that energy from translating to Our Mistress's hall."

Amirantha appeared impatient. "I'm sorry to interrupt, but the heart of the question is, what can you do with that energy if you trap it, bind it, intercept it somehow?"

The High Priest sat silently for a moment, then said, "An excellent question; the answer is beyond my knowledge.

"What little we know of necromancy is due to our having spared no effort to stamp it out; it's an abomination against the nature of Our Mistress to prevent a soul from returning to her for judgment." He turned in his chair and shouted, "Gregori!"

A moment later his servant appeared, and he said, "Ask Sister Makela to join us, please."

The servant bowed, and the High Priest said, "The sister is our Archive Keeper. If she doesn't know of something, she knows where to look to find out about it."

"I have already visited the Ishapian Abbey at That Which Was Sarth."

The old prelate smiled and shook his head. "The Ishapians are a noble order, and we venerate them, but despite their authority and knowledge, they tend to vanity from time to time. Their library is prodigious but hardly exhaustive. There are things that have not found their way into their library."

"But have into yours?" observed Jim.

Smiling even more broadly, the High Priest said, "We all keep our prerogatives. What we find is ours unless we wish to share with others." Then his mood turned somber. "And much of the knowledge we do not share is of the sort about which you inquire; some things are best kept secret or at least closely guarded by those who understand them best." He turned to Amirantha. "While we are waiting, I believe you had other points to make?"

"You are perceptive, Holy Father. Beyond my ignorance of the nature and purpose of this death magic, or as you pointed out, the stolen life force, I have never in my study of the demon realm found any connection."

Pug said, "A thought I've been holding for a few moments is there is something from my past that should be mentioned." He looked at the three other men and said, "Back when the Emerald Queen's host sailed across the ocean from Novindus and invaded the Kingdom of the Isles, their leader, the Emerald Queen, had been replaced by a seeming of her, a false guise worn by a demon named Jakan."

Amirantha tilted his head slightly, as if pondering this.

"What is not known to any but a few of us who were there—" He hesitated a moment, remembering that among those who had been present at the events he was about to describe was his wife, Miranda, and he felt a pang. "I was about to say, this was not about simple conquest, but rather a massive assault to reach the city of Sethanon."

Jim's brow furrowed. "Why? Sethanon had been abandoned since the end of the Great Uprising. There was nothing there."

Pug said, "Even your Kingdom annals were not privy to what took place below the city after the sacking of Krondor and the final victory at the Battle of Nightmare Ridge."

Pug paused, gathering his thoughts. Then he said, "During the Chaos Wars, the Dragon Lords fashioned a mighty artifact that was called the Lifestone. I never had the opportunity to fully study it, as it was deemed so dangerous we left it—" He considered the wisdom of revealing the true whereabouts of the Oracle of Aal, and decided not to burden his companions at the table with that information. "It was hidden in a deep cavern below the city." He looked at the High Priest and said, "I believe the Lifestone was constructed from captured life elements, as you have described."

The High Priest snorted. "Ishapians! I knew they were keeping something from us. Long have we been curious about what happened at Sethanon at the end of the Great Uprising, and why King Lyam never attempted to rebuild that city. The official reasons were that it was no longer an important stop along a trade route, or that it was cursed . . ." He shook his head and sighed.

"The Ishapians knew only what we told them," confessed Pug. "All we knew was the Lifestone was a vessel of great power and the demon Jakan was determined to reach it."

"But why?" asked Amirantha. "What use would a demon have for that artifact, no matter how powerful it is?"

"If we can deduce that," said High Priest Marluke, "then we might understand why your mad brother is so interested in wholesale slaughter and death magic and what that has to do with this demon he serves."

Amirantha sat back and sighed. "Perhaps, but I don't think so."

"Why?" asked Pug.

"Let me ponder a while longer before I venture any more speculation," answered the Warlock.

"Can't we, I mean you, study this Lifestone now?" asked Jim.

Pug shook his head in the negative. "It was destroyed before the demon could reach it."

The expression on the High Priest's face revealed distress. "Destroyed?"

Pug raised his hand in a placating gesture. "Perhaps that's the wrong word. The elf queen's son, Calis, managed to unbind the confining magic, and the trapped life energy within was set free."

The High Priest appeared almost delighted at that news. "A blessing! Those souls were freed to resume their journey to Our Mistress!" He looked eagerly at Pug. "What was it like?"

"Difficult to describe, Holy Father. A crystal to all outward appearances, the Lifestone pulsed with green energies, but when it was . . . unraveled is the only word that fits, a flurry of tiny green flames . . . floated away, in all directions."

The High Priest sat back and said, "In the ages of our temple, no such manifestation of the actual act of translation has been documented. Occasionally we have reports from one of our priests, priestesses, or lay brother or sister, and a few have reported glimpsing a tiny green flash." He sighed in resignation. "There are so few overt signs of the reality of what we do. Those of us who have been blessed by a visitation from our Goddess . . ." He looked at his wine cup and took a sip. "It is difficult at times to convince the faithful. So few actually have experienced the divine."

Pug resisted the urge to remark on that, as he felt he had had more than his fill of experiencing the divine. Several encounters with both Lims-Kragma, and Banath—the God of Thieves, Liars, and a host of other malfeasances—made it clear the gods were as real as the chair upon which he sat, so faith was never an issue, but he certainly felt as if he was their creature at times, and that left a sour taste in his mouth if he dwelled upon it too long.

The door opened and an elderly woman in the garb of a priestess entered, followed by a younger woman in similar attire. "You called for me, Holy Father?"

"Sister Makela, we have need of your knowledge."

"I am at your disposal," she said as Jim rose to offer the older woman his chair. She smiled, nodded her thanks, and took the seat. She was as old as the High Priest, and frail in appearance. But she shared the same lively gaze as the Holy Father.

The High Priest outlined what had already been discussed, finishing with a question: "Have there been any exhaustive studies on the exact nature of necromancy, specifically what use the life force robbed from Our Mistress might have to the necromancer?"

Without a moment's hesitation, the old woman said, "Exhaustive, no. Several volumes of opinion exist, and I can have them brought up from the archives if you wish, Holy Father. The evidence suggests that the necromancer usually has one of two goals. First, to control the dead, harboring enough life energy to animate corpses to do his bidding."

"Why?" asked Jim.

"A dead servant can have several advantages," suggested the librarian. "It is impervious to death, obviously, and can only be stopped by the utter destruction of the body.

These so-called undead can be prodigious bodyguards or assassins. They can exist in places where the living cannot long survive, stay underwater for a few hours, or in a room cursed, protected by poisonous vapor, or some other passive defense harmful to the living. Moreover, they can kill with plague or infection as well as weapons.

"The difficulty is they decay, as do all the dead, though life magic can be employed to slow it for quite some time."

"What's the other reason to use life magic?" asked Pug.

She sighed, as if this was distasteful for her to discuss. "To extend their own life, after death, to continue their consciousness in their mortal shell, rather than journey on to Our Mistress to be judged."

"A litch," said Amirantha.

"Yes," agreed Makela. "It is the ultimate defiance of Our Mistress and the natural order of things. But the toll is great, for the mind of the magic user who extends his life this way is the first casualty of such evil; litches are universally mad, from all reports."

"Madness does not preclude cunning and purpose," observed Pug.

"True," said the High Priest.

Amirantha looked at the librarian and said, "Is there any mention in the annals of any ties between such magic and the summoning or controlling of demons?"

The woman regarded the Warlock in silence for a moment, then said, "Demons are creatures of the other realms, beings not answerable to the laws and natures of our own world; we have almost no dealings with such practices. This is more the province of other orders, those who serve Sung the Pure or Dala, Shield of the Weak.

"They may have heard of some such knowledge, but I have not." She looked at the High Priest. "Is there anything else, Holy Father?"

"I think not, Makela. I thank you for your knowledge."

She rose, bowed slightly before the High Priest then

moved toward the doorway where her aide waited. As she reached the door, she paused, turned, and said, "I have thought of one thing, though."

"What?" asked the High Priest.

"A passing reference, nothing more. In ancient times a war was fought with a cabal of necromancers, which was strange for that; they tend to be solitary types.

"But it was their name that I recall now as being the thing most odd. They were the Demon Brothers."

Amirantha said, "Is there more?"

"Only that they were called that." She tilted her head slightly as she thought. "It was something I found odd, really." She looked from face to face in the room as she said, "We always assumed it was simply a name, describing the cabal much as you might call them something evil. But the more I think on it, it may be more than this, for the accurate translation of that ancient name would be 'Brothers to Demons.' I hope this helps." She nodded, as her assistant opened the door, and they departed.

The High Priest said, "Perhaps this is of some use to you?"

Pug said, "A great deal, perhaps." He rose and Amirantha followed suit.

Gregori appeared and ushered them from the room and left them to their own devices in the large main hall of the temple. Jim asked, "What next?"

"Sarth," said Pug. "The Ishapians are accommodating but not particularly helpful in this, but now we have something specific to investigate."

"The Demon Brothers," said Amirantha. "A very odd name for necromancers." To Pug he said, "Do we need to advise those waiting for us at the island that we're not returning soon?"

Pug said, "I'll see to it after we reach Sarth."

"Good," said the Warlock. "Samantha grows very short with me when I fail to show up for meals on time."

For the first time in recent memory, Pug laughed. Everyone in the temple turned and several of those before the votive candles stared, while some glared, for laughter was almost unknown in this place.

Jim said, "Now would be a fair time to depart, I think."

"Stand close," said Pug and he held out his hands. Each man gripped Pug's forearm, one to a side, and suddenly they were in another place.

CHAPTER 5

LEGACY

Amirantha gawked.

Jim also was astonished by the scale of the room in which he found himself, but managed to retain a small shred of decorum. Pug motioned for them to follow and led them deep into the vault.

Vault was the only word to describe the room, for the ceiling rose up into a gloom that prevented the unaided eye from perceiving its height. Massive columns rose to support the unseen ceiling, and row upon row of shelves were lined up in orderly fashion. The aisles between them, with the intersecting spaces separating them, provided a chessboard of areas. At each intersection a slender stand was erected, a graceful ironwork that bent over in a swan-neck fashion ending in a hook, from which hung a small crystal bound by a metal chain. The crystal provided illumination, just enough to allow those in the room to see to the next lamp.

"Amazing," said Amirantha, as he regarded row upon row of books.

Jim echoed his tone when he said, "I've been in the Royal Archives in Rillanon, but this dwarfs them in scope. How many volumes, Pug?"

"I'm sure I have no idea," said the magician. They moved between row after row of shelves, some vanishing up into the gloom, with ladders set on rails along the wall. "Perhaps the librarian can tell you?"

"This is Sarth?" asked Amirantha.

"That Which Was Sarth," corrected Pug.

"I don't follow," said the Warlock.

Turning with a wry smile, Pug said, "Before the invasion of the Emerald Queen's army, the Ishapians abandoned their abbey near the town of Sarth."

"I still am not clear as to the odd name," said Amirantha, following Pug down a long narrow passage between vaults.

Pug stopped and said, "The Ishapians have a prophecy, or perhaps 'had' is a better word. It said that a great upheaval would come upon the land and after the destruction of the west, all that would remain would be 'That Which Was Sarth.'"

Amirantha looked at Jim, then Pug, and said, "Was Sarth destroyed during the Emerald Queen's invasion?"

"Essentially," said Pug, "though the old abbey itself was relatively intact. How would it have fared had the brothers still occupied it . . . ?" He shrugged.

"So, they made the prophecy come true," said Amirantha, as Pug resumed walking.

As the Warlock and Jim joined him, Pug said, "Perhaps. Or perhaps there's another destruction headed our way, and this place, 'That Which Was Sarth,' is what is destined to survive."

"Exactly where are we?" asked Amirantha. "I assume underground, as I have not noticed anything remotely like a window in the last two vaults."

"We are very deep underground," said Pug. "As to where, I promised the monks I would not reveal that location unless given leave. As I transported you here by magic outside your understanding, it's safe to assume you would have no way of finding your way back here should the urge visit you."

Amirantha chuckled. "Indeed."

They reached a large door and Pug pulled it open. Inside was a small room, with a table fully occupying half its area, over which stood a white-haired magician in black robes. "Father," said Magnus to Pug as he entered. Then he greeted Amirantha and Jim.

Next to him stood a monk in the simple light brown robes of the Ishapians. He was a nondescript man of middle years, with a round head topped by a thatch of brown hair cut with a tonsure. He inclined his head in greeting and said, "Pug. You bring guests?"

"Brother Victor, these are friends. This is James, Baron of the King's Court in Rillanon, and great-grandson of Lord James of Krondor, also known as Jimmy the Hand."

At that the monk smiled. "We have a story about your ancestor you may not know," said the monk.

"And this is Amirantha, a Warlock of a people from across the great ocean, the Satumbria. He is something of an expert on demons and I have need of his wisdom."

"Your vouching for them grants an indulgence," said the monk. "But the Father-Superior might not be so kindly disposed."

"Which is why I came straight here," said Pug with a nod.

The monk smiled. "So when I mention, in passing, your visit, I should do so, what? An hour or so after you depart?"

"That should be ample," said Pug. "We don't plan on staying long, unless there's a need."

"Well, then," said the monk with a wry expression, "what do you seek this time?"

Magnus turned to Amirantha and said, "We've been challenging Brother Victor's nearly inexhaustible knowledge on every subject imaginable."

The monk held up his hands, palms outward, and said, "Hardly that."

"He is the living repository of where everything in this vast library is placed," said Pug.

Amirantha said, "Prodigious is the only word that springs to mind. Don't you have some sort of written record?"

"Of course," said the monk, "and a dozen brothers labor ceaselessly to update it as new material is found and sent to us, but until they do, we make do with scraps of hastily cobbled together notes, and this." He tapped the side of his head with a forefinger.

"What do you know of the Demon Brothers?" asked Pug.

The monk went almost completely motionless for nearly a half minute, then he closed his eyes. "I believe there's a mention of them . . ." His eyes widened. "Wait! I'll be right back."

The four men remaining in the room exchanged strange glances, which became expressions of curiosity as time dragged on. "Right back" became a half hour when the monk finally returned, a dusty old leather-bound volume in hand.

"It should be in here," he said as if he had merely stepped out of the room, then reappeared.

"What is it?" asked Pug as the monk laid the book down on the table and gently opened it.

"It's a chronicle of one Varis Logondis, a Quegan trader who lived about four hundred years ago. He was a compulsive journal keeper who felt every detail in his life was worthy of mentioning.

"In fact, most of his life was remarkably un-noteworthy,

unless you are an aficionado of travelogues, long discourses on mercantile trends of the day, or the state of Varis's digestive health at any given moment in his life. But, in passing he remarks on many issues of the day, useful in providing corroboration or refutation of other histories and accounts of the time.

"But one remark in particular stuck with me over the years." He scanned the page. "Ah, there it is. Let me read— the dialect is somewhat antiquated and his spelling is atrocious. 'In the evening, we came upon a village, by name Hamtas on Jaguard, whereupon we were welcomed at an inn by name, the Restful Station. There did we encounter soldiers of the Empire, at their ease after a battle.

" 'I remark on this for two counts'—reasons is what he means, I am certain—'that first they were not of the militia, yet were Legionaries from Queg that had been haste posted to this region, and last that they had struggled mightily against the Demon Brothers and their living dead.' "

"Back then most of the Bitter Sea was still under control of the Empire of Great Kesh," Pug remarked.

"What's interesting about this passage, Pug, is that it supports two other sources we are aware of, one in our possession, another not." He looked at the magician and his two companions with a satisfied smile. "Varis wrote sixty-five volumes over his lifetime, so I had to skim a couple before I could find this passage." He pointed to the page and said, "The source we possess along with this is a fairly standard tally of captured goods returned to Queg by the expedition encountered by Varis. We know that Varis was surprised to find Imperial Legionaries in that town instead of local soldiers; it implies something significant was being undertaken. Legionaries were only stationed in three garrisons around the Bitter Sea at that time: Durban, Queg City, and Port Natal. They were not used unless there was an uprising or some other menace of equal weight.

"If we look at what that expedition brought back with

them, we encounter an unlikely list of things; along with an unusually short inventory of gold, silver, copper, and lead, livestock and slaves, we also see a very long list of idols, books, and scrolls."

Pug looked interested but uncertain of what was being said to him. "It sounds as if they raided a library."

The monk smiled. "There were no libraries, either Imperial or maintained by any order of temple known to us at that time, anywhere west of Malac's Cross or north of Queg, in the Empire! Oh, some rooms of books here and there, but nothing that would require a detailed cataloguing that the Empire was so famous for at that time." There was a merry glint in the man's eyes as his smile broadened.

"What is it?" Pug said, unable to resist returning the man's smile.

"It's your Demon Brothers!"

"According to this inventory of captured items, over a score of volumes came from the 'frateri demonicus,' which is very bad Quegan spelling for Demon Brothers, or more accurately, Brothers to Demons!"

"The necromancers?" asked Pug.

"Not a common name, by any measure," said Brother Victor. "And there's more."

"More?" asked Magnus a moment before Jim echoed the word.

"The title of a volume; the maker of this list was, by any measure, barely educated. Legionaries were not as a rule much better educated than the common Keshian Dog Soldiers of today. The officers read and write—a necessity for giving and receiving orders—but the common soldiers, no. Either this list was compiled by a relatively uneducated officer, or the task was given to one of the common rank who claimed to write. In any event the title given is *Libri Demonicus Amplus Tantus* or *Really Big Demon Book*."

Amirantha laughed. "I speak Quegan, and it's nothing I recognize."

"It's four hundred years old. I originally thought the scribe just didn't understand that 'Amplus' and 'Tantus' have similar meanings—ample and large—but it occurs to me now our less than scholarly scribe was trying to describe two aspects, that it's a physically large volume, and also that it's important. 'Tantus' can mean 'of such great size,' but 'amplus,' besides ample, can also be read to mean 'of great importance.' So, what you may wish to consult is a very large, very important book concerning demons, written by a four-hundred-year-dead necromancer."

"I don't suppose you have that volume here?" asked Amirantha.

"No," said Brother Victor with a regretful expression. "I wish we did. It sounds fascinating from what you have revealed."

"But you know where we might find it," suggested Magnus.

The monk nodded. "If it still exists."

"The Imperial library in Queg?" suggested Magnus.

Pug said, "If the book was among the property seized by Legionaries, and if they didn't loot the library when recalled to Kesh during the abandonment of the north . . ." He tapped his chin in thought. "Likely. Gold and other valuables they'd take south with them. Books and scrolls? Not as likely. Certainly it's the place we can start looking."

Brother Victor said, "I must leave as the evening prayer is about to begin. I assume you do not need me to show you out?" His merry expression revealed he already knew the answer.

"No," said Pug. "Thank you, my old friend."

"No, thank *you* for all you have given. Too few people know what they owe you, Pug. Until we meet again," he finished, then turned and left the four visitors alone in the library.

Magnus said, "We have a problem, Father."

"I know," said Pug. To Jim he said, "Queg is the one court where we have no friends."

Jim sighed, as he could anticipate what was coming next. "I thought you had agents, or at least 'friends,' everywhere."

Pug gave him a tight smile. "Queg is strategically unimportant. We manipulated some information their way during the invasion of the Emerald Queen. They believed they were attacking a foreign treasure fleet, while instead they ran into her armada, half the Imperial Keshian Fleet, and the Kingdom Navy. Not wishing to attack nations they were at peace with, they did their best to loot a few ships which instead of treasure held angry soldiers. It made them distrustful of information that doesn't come from reliable sources.

"To the point they resisted all attempts to infiltrate their intelligence."

Jim smiled ruefully. "I know. I have had the same problem."

"How about Kesh?" asked Magnus. "Have they anyone within the Quegan Court who might prove useful?"

Jim slowly shook his head. "No, they're just as annoyed by their former cousins as the Kingdom is. If Queg didn't have as formidable a navy as it has, they'd have been reabsorbed by the Empire a century ago or conquered by the Kingdom. There is not a lot on that island that is worth owning, but they are a serious annoyance, and while they may not be strategically important to you, Pug, controlling that island would prove a significant advantage to Kesh or the Kingdom."

"Which is why neither of you will let the other gain control," finished Magnus.

Amirantha said, "Back to the point, if you don't have anyone in that court, how do you propose to find out if this tome exists?" He smiled dryly. "Are you just going to show up one day and ask to browse the shelves?"

Pug got a distant look for a moment, then he slowly smiled. "That may just be the thing."

"What?" asked Jim. "I was certain you were going to ask me to swim ashore, sneak into the library, and steal the book."

"No," said Pug, looking amused at the suggestion. "You're going to use your rank to get the Prince of Krondor to send you, with three advisors"—he indicated the three of them—"on a scholarly project, to correct some distortions of the truth in our own history. This will play to the Quegan vanity as you will explain that their place of glory will be forever enshrined in the annals of the Kingdom, and you would like permission to let your three scholars spend a few leisurely days browsing the shelves of the Imperial Quegan Library."

Jim's face went through a spectrum of emotions, from surprise, to doubt, to agreement, and then to delight. "Play to their vanity!"

"Yes," said Pug. "Then when we find out if the book is there, you can sneak into the library and steal it."

Jim rolled his eyes. "Can't we just glance at it for a while?"

"No," said Amirantha. "We will need to study it, and that may take weeks. If it's some ancient variant of the Keshian language, we'll need to find a scholar who can help us understand it."

"And the Quegans would love to know why we're spending all our time studying one ancient, obscure text on demons when we're supposed to be looking at their own histories," finished Magnus.

Amirantha said, "It would be helpful if you could convince those Star Elves to let their Demon Master come back once we get the book." Shaking his head slightly as if he hated making the admission, he added, "There's a lot he knows that I don't. I taught him a few tricks when he was on the island, but I think if Gulamendis was with us, we'd work faster."

Pug looked at Magnus. "Have we heard anything from the Taredhel?"

Magnus shook his head in the negative. "Only through Tomas. He and his Queen still are in contact with the Lord Regent, but you know how elves are about taking their time."

"All too well," conceded Pug. "Well, first things first. Let's get the book." He looked at Jim. "Can you do it?"

"Of course I can. The Duke of Krondor is another eastern caretaker who doesn't really have any sense of what's going on in the Western Realm. He's content to hunt, drink, chase serving girls, and let me tell him all is well in the west. Then he reports back to the King that all is well in the west.

"I'll have my personal scribe draw up the messages to the Emperor of Queg and he'll just sign them when I put them in front of him. If you think it would help, I can put the royal seal on it and make it look as if the document comes from the King, himself."

"Forgery?" said Pug with newfound respect. "Is there no end to your larcenous skills?"

"Few," said Jim with no hint of modesty. "This will take a couple of weeks, and the sooner begun the sooner done."

Pug said, "Very well. Magnus, get us to the island, please, and then take Jim to Krondor."

As they assembled to transport to Sorcerer's Isle, Amirantha said, "I wonder how that demon-loving elf and his brother are doing."

CHAPTER 6

SURVIVORS

The demons attacked.

Gulamendis drew back his hand, his brow furrowed in concentration as he watched his brother from the corner of his eye. Laromendis had conjured a battle demon illusion that was all talons and teeth, muscles like iron drawn over by skin resembling the hardest dragon scale. Ignoring the relatively lesser threats of the two Taredhel magicians, the three demons threw themselves upon the most obvious threat. Demon logic was simple: dispose of the most dangerous foe, then turn attention to the lesser. Intelligence was not a prerequisite for harrying demons, those whose job was to seek out hidden prey and drive them to where the demon captains were waiting. All they saw was a rogue demon not of their cadre attacking them and they never for one moment considered the improbability of it all.

As long as the demons believe Laromendis's conjurations, they were subject to damage from it, and it lay about in frantic mayhem, slashing and biting, tearing and gouging. From bitter experience, Gulamendis knew the illusion would be good for only a moment or two longer, then the attacking demons would recognize it for what it was; Laromendis had never smelled a demon or experienced its magic aura, so those components were lacking in the conjuration, and as soon as the demons recognized the fraud, the two magicians would be assaulted.

Which is why Gulamendis had his wand at the ready. It was a treasure, gained by guile and subterfuge from the treasure trove brought from Andcardia to E'bar, the elven city constructed on the ancient planet the Star Elves called "Home," in their language.

The wand had been the only thing that had kept the two brothers alive for the last few days, which was beyond the expectation of the Lord Regent and other members of his Meet who obviously wished to see the two brothers soon dead. Only Tandarae, the new Loremaster of the Taredhel, was kindly disposed toward the Demon Master and Conjurer, but he wasn't in a strong enough bargaining position to keep the brothers from being dispatched to the Hub World.

The warning from the Loremaster had come in the dead of night, delivered to the brothers in their small apartment by one of Tandarae's trusted servants. It recounted a heated debate that had erupted in the Regent's Meet, and the few voices that had spoken on the brothers' behalf had quickly fallen silent. They were being sent to the Hub World, ostensibly to aid in the evacuation of the remaining defenders facing the Demon Legion, but it was a thinly disguised death sentence. The brothers' role in finding Home, aiding the Taredhel in contacting the Elf Queen and her consort, and any other service done to the People, was outweighed in their minds by the simple fact that these two magic users were legacies of the Circle of Light and not to be trusted. When the portals on Hub World were deactivated, anyone still there would be stranded, with no means to return to Home.

Now they fought for their survival moment by moment.

They were holed up in a relatively defensible position in the city, a cul-de-sac of apartments for laborers, long abandoned, but with only one approach. They had created a series of trip-wire alarms and alerts so they could rest. Their orders had been to remain until recalled, and both knew that the recall was unlikely to ever come, so they had hunkered down and only fought when demons somehow managed to catch sight or wind of them.

The three who battled the conjuration were minor demons, any one of whom the brothers could probably have bested in hand-to-hand fighting should the need arise, but three of them was more than enough to give pause to engaging them directly.

This was the third time they had used this ploy, the other two having taught them how to refine the illusion and ready themselves for the moment they would truly engage the demons in combat.

Gulamendis took his eyes from the struggle for a moment; his brother had to concentrate on the illusion, so it was up to the Demon Master to keep alert for unexpected intruders while they stood exposed in the open, atop the rise that led to the highest apartment on this small street.

Behind the struggle, Gulamendis saw something flickering in the distance, near the entrance to the portals. He hoped it was other elves answering a recall he and his brother somehow hadn't heard yet.

Hub World; here the portals—what the humans called

"rifts" between the worlds—were clustered. For reasons that in retrospect looked like the height of prudence now, an ancient Lord Regent had decreed that only one rift from each world would be allowed to come to this one place, this otherwise nondescript world that had been home to barely a thousand elves, just enough to ensure the portals were operating as they should.

The portal to Andcardia had been breeched long before, and shut down. There had been one maintained portal from Hub, to the world of Locre-Amar, and from there back to E'bar. Once that one was closed, there should be no access to Midkemia by the demons. At least none the Taredhel knew about. Unless the brothers could manage to keep the marauding demons who still roamed this world from reaching the last remaining rift, and themselves get to it first, they would be stranded here with however many demonic castaways still resided here.

And Gulamendis's knowledge of demons told him there were too many still nearby to give the brothers much hope of surviving.

Then the conjuration was broken, and Gulamendis extended the want. A sphere of silver light with pink and blue colors scintillating across the surface expanded around him, and as soon as it touched the demons they shuddered, went rigid, and fell to the ground at Laromendis's feet. They were in spasm, and neither brother knew they needed to act quickly.

At first they had simply used the wand, but a couple of quickly reviving demons had educated them to the need to weaken them in combat to extend the period they were stunned. Both brothers drew out large battle knives and began cutting throats as fast as possible. Gulamendis reminded himself that even though this death was nowhere nearly as dramatic or effective as his magical abilities to banish demons under the best of conditions, it would suffice. The demons' essences would return to their realm and reform, but by the time these three were reborn the issue of getting off this planet would long be decided. Not to mention, considered the Demon Master, that to the best of his knowledge, the portal to the demon realm had been sealed.

In a few moments it was over. The two tall elves stood covered in dark demon blood, the stench of carrion and sulfur making their eyes water. "That bought us a few minutes," said Laromendis.

His brother nodded. "I sense some to the south, but they're not coming closer. We should probably make our escape now."

"Which way?" asked Laromendis.

Both were tall, nearly seven feet in height, but proportioned like all lesser elves. Massive shoulders narrowed to trim waistlines above powerful hips and legs. Neither was by training or inclination a warrior, but both had been forced to learn the killing trade and had become adept at it. It helped that Gulamendis understood each demon's vulnerabilities and had communicated what he could to his brother.

"That way." Gulamendis pointed to the northeast. "There should be an alley and through it to the broad street; last portal should be there."

"I thought it was the other way," said Laromendis, pointing to the northwest.

His brother smiled. "So does everyone else."

"You have a plan?"

"Always," said Gulamendis, trotting in the indicated direction.

The small city that served as the home of those caring for the portals was a simple enough place to navigate under normal circumstances. A wholesale invasion by the Demon Legion was hardly normal.

They carefully made their way between buildings, stopping at every corner to peer around and be sure they were unobserved. There was a very small class of demons that could hide well, even to near invisibility, but Gulamendis's sensitivity to any demon's presence usually alerted them to their proximity.

They came to the last open ground before the entrance to the hub portal and Laromendis swore. "Fliers!"

Circling above like so many vultures were a half dozen flying demons. "Can you do anything?" said Gulamendis.

"I'm tired," replied his brother, "but I think I can manage a small diversion. Give me a moment to compose myself."

The Conjurer closed his eyes and called up the last reserve of his power and abruptly Gulamendis saw the illusion. It wasn't much as conjurations went, a slight scampering between two houses directly under one of the hovering demons, but it was enough to set the demon to shrieking and diving toward the imagined prey. The others were only a moment behind and they flew off up a side street. "Now!" said Laromendis.

The two elven magic users dashed for the entrance of the building Gulamendis had indicated and made it safely inside. They darted around the edge of the doorway and paused. In the gloom of the unlighted entry, they waited for their eyes to adjust and to see if any ground forces waited inside.

"Now," said Laromendis softly, "where are we?"

His brother squatted, back to the wall, and Laromendis followed suit. "While I don't make it a habit to eavesdrop, I did manage to be close enough to hear two Sentinels discussing the last recall. This is a building housing a single portal, one designed to be used by the last of us fleeing. Assuming we heard the recall." He pointed to a door. Every elf who had visited this world had come down "that way."

They were exhausted, tired to the core of their beings, but necessity made them rise and move to the door. Gulamendis closed his eyes a moment, then said, "No." His brother knew he meant no demon sign beyond the door.

Gulamendis opened the door and they moved slowly,

for whatever illumination normally employed was missing. In the distance they saw a faint light, which became a line along the floor as they reached a closed door. Again the Demon Master paused to see if he sensed any demons, but when he felt nothing, he gripped the latch and pushed aside the heavy wood.

The room was a mess. Bodies littered the floor and the single platform that supported the two magically imbued wooden arms between which the portal formed were so blood-spattered they looked as if they had been painted red. The stench was nearly overwhelming, despite the brothers having been subjected to demon carcasses for days.

The portal was inactive.

Gulamendis said, "Well, isn't this a surprise?"

His brother let out a long sigh of exasperation and said, "No, it's not. Those arrogant bastards in the Regent's Meet think they have everything under control and we're no longer useful. So, rather than trust us after all we've done . . ."

"Well, if I were inclined to give these poor souls the benefit of the doubt, perhaps they just didn't try hard enough to make sure we'd get the recall. From the looks of things here, it was a quick and dirty fight."

A sound behind caused them both to spin, daggers and swords at the ready, but instead of a demon, it was another elf, this one in the garb of a Sentinel. "I'm wounded," he gasped as he clutched his left side with his left arm, leaning against the edge of the doorway.

Laromendis motioned for his brother to care for the Sentinel, and said, "I'll see if he was followed." He hurried down the hallway.

"Let me see," said Gulamendis to the Sentinel. The brothers' upbringing along the frontier had given them both a fundamental education in field dressings. The wound was long and deep. He had already lost a lot of blood. "Let me bind it," said the Demon Master.

He cut at the bottom of the Sentinel's tunic, then sliced

away a long length of cloth, fashioning a rude bandage. The man lifted his arm above his head, obviously in pain, but seemed slightly more comfortable once the makeshift bandage was in place.

Laromendis returned and said, "Nothing followed." He looked at the Sentinel. "They neglected to send you the recall, as well, I see."

"There was no recall," said the Sentinel. "The demons swarmed the hub and some of us counterattacked to hold them off while others ran to draw them away so the galasmancers could shut down the portals." He pointed to blood and gore splattered on the walls. "We tried to reach this location, but I and two others were cut off. The rest of the Sentinels and one galasmancer came here to use this portal. My two companions perished, but I've been making my way here." He paused. "I really didn't think the portal would still be open. But . . ."

"You had to see," finished Laromendis.

"I had to see," agreed the Sentinel.

Gulamendis said, "It appears that those who got here also didn't get through. That's what's left of them."

The Sentinel said, "But they got the job done." Catching his breath, he continued, "My name is Arosha."

Gulamendis introduced himself and his brother, then said, "Sorry to hear about the sudden evacuation; nice to know it was necessity that shut this place down before the recall and nothing personal."

The warrior looked confused by the statement, but Laromendis said, "Never mind." He glanced at the doorway into the huge room. "We need to think of something very quickly because eventually . . . ?" He looked at his brother.

"Those fliers and most of the smaller demons won't trouble us unless we wander right up to them, but the more powerful ones . . . they'll sense we are here eventually."

The warrior looked at him and said, "You know demons?"

"More than I care to reveal most times," he said, "but I think I know how we can avoid them, for a while longer."

"If only we knew how to open this damn portal," said Laromendis.

Gulamendis said, "Something occurred to me."

"What?" asked his brother.

Gulamendis looked at the bodies on the floor and pointed to one, dressed in a robe, and said, "Arosha, is that the galasmancer?"

The Sentinel's knees weakened, and Laromendis helped him sit. "Yes, and the others are the rest of my company of Sentinels."

"Then he didn't have time to escape."

"Obviously," said Laromendis to his brother. "Your point?"

Gulamendis went to the body of the fallen portal builder and pulled a demon corpse from off it, then turned over the red-drenched robed figure. The elf clutched a yellow stone in his hand, so firmly Gulamendis had to pry it from his fingers. Holding up the faintly pulsing stone, he said, "He didn't destroy the portal! He only pulled the power crystal from it." He pointed to the empty hole where the crystal was placed. "When the demons got done with everyone, they saw an empty room with two sticks. Obviously none of the really intelligent ones have been here yet, else they might have also realized the portal isn't destroyed, just turned off."

He considered the situation as he looked at the glowing stone in his hand. "If we stick this back in the base, with the right starting spell, the portal should open, and we can get home!" He reached down and pulled a small bag from the dead elf's belt and quickly tied it to his own.

"It wouldn't do any good," said Arosha. "For the time being, anything that comes through a portal from this world will be killed the second it steps through."

"Lovely," muttered Laromendis. "Now what?"

Gulamendis paused, then said, "We go someplace else."

"Where?" asked his brother.

"Sorcerer's Isle," said the Demon Master.

"How do you propose to do that?"

Gulamendis said, "When I was there I was shown one of their rift gates. There are wards there that act as a beacon." He realized he was now at the edge of his knowledge. Looking at the Sentinel, he said, "How much do you know about portals?"

The wounded elf smiled slightly. "I've been watching galasmancers play with those things long enough to have a fair idea of how they work. I can recall the spell that activates them if a crystal is in place, but I have no magic."

Laromendis said, "We do, and I've been through enough of these things for the Lord Regent that I probably know the spell as well as you do."

Arosha asked, "Do you know how to find a different portal? I could help you tune this to one of our other portals, but I don't know if I can find one that we didn't build."

"Here's what I know," said Gulamendis. "According to the human Pug, what they call rifts have an affinity and if there is a rift in existence and you create a second rift, it will tend to follow the first."

"Tend?" asked his brother in a skeptical tone.

"If you have a better idea, I would welcome hearing it," said the Demon Master.

"You can activate this gate's destination?" Gulamendis asked the Sentinel.

"Yes," said Arosha. "That's the easy part. Setting a different destination than the one already cast is the hard part. I think I've seen it done enough times to have a sense of how to do it, but only to a few other portals, as I said, the ones we've built, and they are all now closed. If I open any of them from this end . . . they'll all be guarded and worse."

"What's worse?"

"The portal could be buried under rock, at the bottom of a lake . . ." The Sentinel shrugged, though it caused him to wince. "I can only imagine what would happen if you stepped through into solid rock."

Gulamendis said, "Do you know the way to E'bar?"

The Sentinel said, "This one is already set for the new city." He slowly rose and said, "It was to be where the last of us fled. But as I said, if we step through archers will be waiting to fill us with arrows before we say a word."

Gulamendis got a thoughtful look and then said, "We change . . . something."

"Something?" asked his brother.

"What?" asked the Sentinel.

"Set it for almost E'bar. If Pug is correct, a new rift should form, somewhere nearby."

"How nearby?" asked the Conjurer.

The younger brother fixed Laromendis with an exasperated look and said, "I will settle for the same planet."

"As long as we don't end up in the middle of the sea . . . or under a mountain . . ."

"Can you do it?" asked Gulamendis.

Laromendis nodded. "Setting magic imprints on objects, enchanting them, is a lot like conjuring an illusion—it's just moving energy over the surface of something, rather than in thin air."

"Tell me what you need," said Arosha. "I can adjust this for you—I know how to do it." The Sentinel indicated he needed help reaching the portal controls and the Conjurer put his arm around the wounded elf's waist and helped him reach it. Laromendis shot his brother a concerned expression and with a slight shake of his head told him the Sentinel was in worse shape than at first thought. He helped the guardsman stand before the controls, and felt blood drenching his arm where he had held him.

Runes were set in a large patter, and several glowed

with a faint light. "There's magic in the device, independent of the gate power." He pointed to the crystal Gulamendis held and said, "That will get the gate open . . ." He glanced around and said, "Let me study this while you look for another stone. The galasmancer should have it."

"What stone?" asked Laromendis.

"It may be purple or blue."

Laromendis did as he was asked and a moment later came up with a purple crystal, half the size of the yellow one his brother still held. "What is this?"

"This is what will close down this portal after we go. The gate will be useless and the demons will have to find another way to E'bar."

"How does it work?" asked Laromendis.

With a slight smile, the pale Sentinel said, "I pull out the yellow crystal, put this one in, hit any mark on the controls . . ."

"And what?" asked Gulamendis.

"It explodes."

Both brothers were mute.

The Sentinel said, "We all know I'm dead within minutes. This way is quickest and I serve the People. I can barely stand. You'd better go now, or I won't be able to close the portal after you. Good fortune."

Laromendis started to say something, but couldn't find words. He nodded.

The Sentinel put the yellow crystal in a small depression in the surface of the control panel and it began to pulse with a stronger light. Laromendis repeated the spell he had heard many times, closing his eyes to focus his energies on controls designed to easily receive them. Then he opened his eyes and nodded.

Arosha struck all the runes but one and held up his hand. "I've put in the runes for E'bar but one and . . ." He started to sway on his feet, but gripped hard on the edge of the panel. "Pick any rune save that one."

Gulamendis didn't hesitate, just reaching over to blindly pick one and push it. A faint hum was followed by a sudden increase in the pressure in the room, as if they had a huge influx of wind, then a faint thumping sound. A grey void, with colors shimmering across the surface, like oil on water, appeared between the uprights of the portal device.

"Go, quickly," said the Sentinel, and the brothers hesitated but a second, then stepped through. Certain death was their reward if they remained, and if death waited on the other side of the portal, what was the difference? But a chance awaited and they took it.

Suddenly they were underwater. There was a moment's disorientation and both brothers had to use all their focus and willpower not to gasp in lungs full of water. It was dark on all sides.

In a lucid moment, Laromendis understood they were not too deep, as he had experienced the pressure of water diving for shellfish as a youth. He blew out a slight breath and felt the bubbles rise up his face. In the gloom, he knew which way was up. He grabbed his brother's arm and pulled and they both swam furiously to the surface.

They were less than ten feet below the surface, but it felt as if it were a hundred. They broke above rolling combers and found themselves spitting out mouths full of seawater.

Gasping for air, Gulamendis said, "We aren't dead . . . yet."

Looking around, his brother said, "We have time. I have no idea where we are."

Gulamendis said, "This isn't Home."

"How do you know?"

"Demons. I can sense them."

"How many?"

"A lot."

The chop of the seawater was relatively mild. The peak to trough was roughly six feet, so they tried to time their exploration to looking in circles as they crested on the rising water.

"Lights!" said Laromendis.

"Where?" asked his brother as he slid down into a trough and began to rise again.

"That way," said his brother.

"I can't see where you're pointing. It's as dark as a cave here."

"You're right." He got close to his brother's face and could barely make him out. There was a faint shine on his face, and he turned to look for the source.

High in the night sky rose a single moon, a slivered crescent, obscured by a heavy mist. "Fog," said Laromendis.

"Then we'd better make for those lights before they get obscured again," said Gulamendis. He felt his brother's hand on his shoulder and felt himself being moved in a specific direction. He didn't need any more convincing and began swimming in the indicated direction.

Both brothers were not particularly powerful elves, but that still gave them more strength and endurance than humans or the lesser elves of Home. And both had spent years near the ocean, so they were both good swimmers. Both had depended more times than they cared to remember on what they could bring in from the sea if they were going to eat.

"Listen," said Gulamendis as he paused.

"What?"

"Breakers."

"Good. I'm starting to get numb and was desperately hoping we saw lights on land and not a passing ship."

Saying nothing more, they both set out toward the sound of breakers.

Minutes later the two exhausted, chilled elves heaved themselves out of the surf and trudged ashore in the dark. The beach was broad and welcoming, which they both counted as fortunate. A sudden crash into rocks would have almost ended their escape.

"Where do you think we are?" asked Laromendis.

"I have no idea, but with a little luck I might deduce something. We know the worlds taken by the Demon Legion, and if this is one of those, we might be able to come up with another means of reaching home."

"You always were the one to look on the bright side of things; it's odd how you ended up spending so much time in caves as a child."

His brother tried to chuckle, but couldn't quite work up the energy. "There!" he said suddenly, pointing to lights that dotted the side of the hill above them, then were again consumed in mist.

"Torches, I think," whispered Laromendis. Without another word they started moving up the beach, cautiously in the dark. Like all of their race, they were far better equipped to see in the dark, their night vision rivaling that of most cats, but no matter how acute their eyes might be, they still needed some light and there was very little.

Instead the land was shrouded in a murky haze, and they had to work their way cautiously on a path that led upward, perhaps a game trail. Movement was slow, as the way was littered with rocks and bramble.

Gulamendis kept his voice low and said, "There are a lot of demons nearby."

His brother whispered, "We need to get off that beach. If there are demons around, we need to find a place to hide until we can get some idea of what to do next. You were the one who told me some of those fliers can see in the dark."

"Thanks for reminding me," the Demon Master whispered in return. "Not many, and none of them like to fly in fog. Too easy to run into something unyielding."

They reached a small switchback and continued up the hillside. As they got to higher ground the fog thinned and a few minutes later they broke clear of it. The sky on the other side of the cliff they climbed was aglow, and they crouched instinctively against any sentries.

Looking back the way they came, the trail vanished a few yards below them into a low-lying bank of heavy mist. Both brothers had lived on the coast enough to recognize the heavy marine air that would roll in at sundown, only to burn off by midmorning. Natural barriers like this cliff face could hold it in place if it wasn't thick and even when it was, it wouldn't extend very far inland.

Reaching the top of the bluff they saw no sign of any other living thing, but both moved with a hard-won, exhausted caution. Neither had much left for a fight or a dash. Besides, where would they flee? Back down the trail in the fog to a beach they knew nothing about?

The bluff swept away on either hand as they came to a cut at the top of the trail and found themselves on tableland. Even without fog, there was little light as the sliver of moon provided only faint illumination.

Scrub and a few scrawny trees dominated the landscape, giving them a tangle of shadows and patterns of dark grey and black, and their only sense of those shapes was provided by the distant glow in the sky beyond.

"Demons?" asked Laromendis quietly.

"No closer," answered his brother.

"I suggest we just sit and wait for dawn."

Gulamendis squatted on the ground, then slowly put his legs out. After a moment he said, "No," and rose quietly.

"No, what?" asked his brother, on the verge of sitting.

"You rest. I'll stay awake."

"Why?" said his brother, though obviously he didn't care to argue much.

"You spent the last three days spinning illusions while I just pointed a wand now and again. We both know I have no control over demons as long as the demon captains or lords are present, and even if I could command one, there are dozens running around.

"No, you need rest more than I do, and if we need talent tomorrow, it will be your conjurations, so you need to be rested. If we can find a place to hole up tomorrow, then I'll sleep."

"You have no idea how long until dawn. The sun could have set an hour ago."

"I have no idea how long night is on this world, either, but it doesn't matter. Sleep and I'll keep watch."

Not wishing to argue any more, Laromendis put his head down on his arm. It wasn't the first time he had been forced to sleep on the ground, but right now he welcomed the hard soil beneath him as if it were a soft feather mattress.

Gulamendis was as exhausted as his brother, despite his claims otherwise, but struggled to stay alert. The sense he had of nearby demons made it far easier, and while he knew he flirted with the edges of exhaustion, he still managed to stay alert.

Hours dragged by and the Demon Master shivered while his clothing dried on his body. He wondered how his brother had fallen into slumber so quickly, then laughed silently at the thought; had he the opportunity, he also would have been fast asleep on the ground.

He studied the sky. He knew little of the sky on any world, really, as it wasn't an area of interest, and the idea that he might recognize a constellation or other astral sign and discern their location wasn't more than an idle thought.

He moved and hummed absently, to keep awake while his brother slept. He wondered at the strange course of events that had brought him here, and in a strange way made him closer to Laromendis than they had ever been.

As children they shared certain interests in things magical, and as initiates into the Circle of Light, they shared the early training. But when the Regent's Meet had disbanded the Circle and, according to rumors, conspired to murder some of their more powerful members, the brothers had gone their separate ways for years.

Later they discovered that on several occasions they had almost run into each other, one time living on opposite sides of the same island for the better part of a year, though Gulamendis had been high in the hills in a cave, as his brother wryly pointed out, while Laromendis had been down in the island's sole town working as a laborer while the purging of the Circle had continued.

Only the Demon Legion's onslaught had put off the further persecution of the remaining members of the Circle. Gulamendis was certain others still hid, but most had answered the call of their people, and had been welcomed back to Andcardia when the Regent's Meet granted amnesty.

Except for the Demon Masters. It was fate that spared Gulamendis, for only days before his arrival at the Regent's court his brother had "volunteered" for the mission to seek out a refuge for the Taredhel should the demons overrun their capital.

Gulamendis had spent some time in a cage but had been allowed to live; most Demon Masters hadn't been so fortunate.

The sky lightened and blacks resolved into greys and lighter greys. The Demon Master waited until he could see enough of the trees above them to chance moving, and woke his brother.

Laromendis came awake instantly, but it was clear he was still exhausted. He glanced around and nodded. Without comment the two elves moved into the woods.

The trees were scrawny and parched, and both brothers knew that fresh water might be a problem. The brush was dry and cracked when stepped on, so both moved slowly and with care.

Finally they reached a small clearing, an extrusion of stone that formed a ridge, and on the other side the land began to once again fall away. They peered over the stone and Gulamendis whispered, "Merciful ancestors!"

As far as the eye could see ranged fires, organized in rank and file, so a crisscross of lines of flame defined areas. Around the fires rested figures, and the Demon Master tugged at his brother's sleeve.

They moved back away from the edge into the relative shelter of the trees. The light from the fires had been what had illuminated the sky the night before, and now they saw that it wasn't a small fire close by, but many distant fires that had pierced the gloom.

"It's the Legion," whispered Gulamendis.

Laromendis said, "Where are we?" As soon as he asked, he knew it was a stupid question, for his brother had no more knowledge of their whereabouts than he did.

They exchanged silent looks, and both knew the same thing; they were on the world being used by the Demon Legion as a staging ground. The demons below were unlike any they had seen or fought, all bearing arms, organized, and resting before invasion. There was a calm that was so unnatural for demons it was frightening, and from the organization witness, they would be moving soon.

Finally Gulamendis said, "There's one good thing here."

"Really?" asked his brother, eyes widening.

"If they're here, and if they are going to invade Home, that means they have a way to get there."

"A Demon Gate?"

"They must," said the Demon Master. "We just need to find it and get through it before they do."

His brother shook his head. Words failed him.

CHAPTER 7

QUEG

Trumpets sounded.

James Dasher Jamison, Baron of the Prince's Court, Envoy Extraordinary of the Kingdom of the Isles, occasional diplomat, and full-time spy turned to his companions. Pug, Magnus, and Amirantha were dressed as scholars, in light tan robes and sandals.

"One more time," he said.

Pug smiled, but Magnus and Amirantha looked annoyed.

"One more time," he repeated. "These stories must be the first thing you think of should you have to answer unexpected questions.

Pug looked at his son and the Warlock, and said, "I am Richard, a historian from the Royal Court of

Rillanon. I have been there for years." Pug had spent enough time in the capital city over the last hundred years that he could easily describe most of the famous aspects of the "Jeweled City," and its recent politics had been a constant discussion among the four of them as they sailed from Krondor to Queg.

"I am his first student, Martin," said Magnus. "I am recently to the capital and am still finding my way around." Unlike his father, Magnus had spent relatively little time in Rillanon, so the identity chosen would serve. "I originally came from Yabon." He knew that area very well.

Both father and son looked at Amirantha who said, "I am Amirantha, a scholar from the distant city of Maharta. I have a royal patent from the Maharaja of Muboya, courtesy of General Kaspar, First Minister to the Maharaja, commissioning me to learn all I can about the nations of Triagia, and am collecting histories toward that end."

"Try to look a little more enthusiastic," said Jim.

"Shouldn't we get up on deck?" asked Magnus.

Jim smiled. "Quegan protocol dictates we keep them waiting at least another five minutes, ten is better. Quegans are an odd people. They tend to self-aggrandizement, to the point of considering the Imperial Keshian Court degenerate, and see themselves as the true inheritors of all things grand and imperial. They would be a silly people if it wasn't for that irritatingly large navy they insist on sailing all over the Bitter Sea. That gets them a great deal of respect they otherwise wouldn't enjoy. Their position as something of a balance shifter here in the west keeps them more or less at peace with their neighbors, but should the cause arise where the Free Cities, Kesh, and the Kingdom could get over their own differences, we'd happily obliterate this island." He said the last with a cheerful expression.

"But then you'd have a war over who got the island," said Amirantha with a wry expression.

"Oh, I'd happily argue to just let Pug and some of his

compatriots sink it." He looked at the magician. "You could manage that, couldn't you?"

Pug shook his head and deemed not to answer.

"What we have now is a short time of it. The Imperial Archivist is at our disposal, but only for three days. I need you to discover what you need in two, because if I must break in and steal something, I need to plan it the day before we leave." He sighed. "While I have little problem robbing the Quegans, I do have a problem with starting a needless war, especially when we may need to be fighting a far more dire one soon. So, try not to do anything overtly suspicious. The Quegans are suspicious by nature, and you will be watched, so always remember there are eyes on you, ears nearby, even if it doesn't seem that way. Once we leave this cabin, we will be living our roles as nobles and scholars. If you have any questions, now is the time."

No one did, as they had rehearsed their various roles for the seven days' sailing time from Krondor to Queg. The necessity of having to arrive in public by ship had given them a great deal of time to review their plan.

"Well," said Jim, standing, "I think we've kept the Quegan nobles standing in the hot sun long enough. Let us go and be diplomats."

Pug and his two companions followed Jim up on the deck and found the sailors of the Kingdom ship *Royal Dolphin* securing their vessel. A long gangway had been run out to the dock below, and Jim paused dramatically at the top before starting his descent. Pug had not visited Queg in over a century and more than anything he was amazed at how little had changed.

The City of Queg, capital of the island nation of the same name, was really two cities. Below were the docks, poor quarter, and every manner of industry given to dirt, blood, filth, and ofal: the tanners, dyers, slaughterhouses, fish markets, and forges. The air hung heavy with smoke, soot, odors that assaulted the senses, and noise to deafen.

The streets were thronged with workers, traders, and fishmongers, though few travelers came and went; Queg was not considered a hospitable nation.

The upper city rose up on the hills behind, dominated by the Emperor's palace. It shined in the sun, for it had been faced with white marble over the years, and this "gleaming jewel" of a building could be seen for miles out at sea on clear days. It was also, Pug judged, as fine an example of excesses and bad taste as one might find anywhere on Midkemia.

A delegation of Quegan officials waited on the dock, none of them looking especially pleased at the duty before them, but all affecting broad smiles and a forced air of conviviality that was less than persuasive. They wore the traditional white togas of office, all lined with a single band of color over the shoulder and along the hem. Those trimmed in red were city officials, while those in gold represented the Emperor. As only one person had gold trim, Jim presented himself to him. "I am Baron James, of the King's Court in Rillanon, and these are my companions."

The official said, "I am Lord Meridious, Chancellor of the Imperial Archives, and given responsibility for your visit." He was a round-faced man, but broad of shoulders and under his fat heavy muscle was evident.

Jim shook the man's outstretched hand and said, "I thank His Imperial Majesty for his courtesy and willingness to allow scholars access to your archives. Especially in light of the abrupt nature of the request."

"It *was* a bit odd," agreed the Chancellor, "but his Imperial Majesty is always anxious to keep harmonious relations with our neighbors and it seemed a small favor to ask."

Jim turned and motioned to his three companions. He introduced Pug, Magnus, and Amirantha. Looking overawed by the presence of such a great personage, all three magicians managed a fair imitation of a self-conscious bow.

"We have litters ready to bear you to the palace," said the Chancellor.

Jim nodded and with a tilt of his head indicated the others should follow. They walked down the docks, between two lines of Quegan soldiers, four with herald horns that had been sounded when the ship had arrived. Now they merely stood motionless in the hot sun awaiting the order to return to barracks.

Reaching the quay, they found four litters awaiting them. The various city officials, who had not uttered a word, retired to their various offices and the Chancellor indicated a litter for Jim to enter. Pug motioned for Magnus to take one of the litters as he would share the other with Amirantha.

The litter bearers were all uniformly muscular young men, wearing only the heavy linen skirt of their craft, and heavy-soled, cross-gartered sandals. Their bodies were oiled with flower-scented oils so their perspiration would not annoy their passengers. They picked up the litters and were off at a good pace, while two soldiers marched ahead clearing the streets of the citizens of Queg.

Amirantha kept his voice low, and in neutral tones said, "So, this is Queg?"

Pug smiled. He nodded. He knew as Amirantha did the chance was good they were being listened to by more than one of the bearers, who would almost certainly be a Quegan agent. "Yes," said Pug. "Does your master know much of this place?"

"A little," said Amirantha, going along with the pretense that he represented the Maharaja of Muboya. "One of my tasks was to learn as much about the Kingdom's neighbors as I could, despite being tasked to study your nation. Queg was once part of Great Kesh, true?"

"Yes," said Pug, assuming the Quegan agent listening would not be particularly attentive to a history lesson he knew as well as Pug did. "A great revolt in the south of the

Empire of Great Kesh, among the client states known as the Keshian Confederacy, caused the Empire to recall her legions from the north. They abandoned all the lands west of and south of Yabon. The Kingdom pushed out of Yabon into what is now the Far Coast, but the former Keshian cities on the shore of the Bitter Sea repulsed the Kingdom's conquest and formed the Free Cities.

"Queg was unique as it had served as a naval yard to the south, and as garrison here, and while the Legion left, the navy refused to depart, as their families and lives were here. Kesh was too busy fighting in the south, and by the time that rebellion was crushed, Queg had achieved independence and controlled the Bitter Sea." He paused as if thinking. "The people who lived here came from a relatively small province of the Empire, I believe called Itiac." He knew better than that; they came from a province called Itaniac, but he wanted to have whoever listened think he was not an expert on the history of the island nation. "I want to study some documents from that era and before, as our Kingdom history is full of holes and many misunderstandings.

"Our relationship with Queg has not always been as good as it should be, and as a result there are many mistaken notions about this place and its people circulating in the Kingdom of the Isles. I will take some pride in correcting those misunderstandings."

"Well, it's all new to me," said Amirantha, playing along. "Whatever I learn will be useful for my reports home. Perhaps my master will wish to send a trade delegation here; you say the Quegans build good ships?"

"Among the best," said Pug, knowing that was shading the truth. The Quegans built fearsome war galleys, but they were coastal-going vessels not meant to be more than a day or two offshore. They had nothing that could cross so vast an expanse as the Endless Sea to the west of the Straits of Darkness and reach Novindus. Still, flattery always appealed to those who thought it was sincere.

Amirantha and Pug chatted about nothing particularly significant as they observed the city through which they passed. The docks and more disreputable inns and businesses gave way to a series of broad streets that were obviously occupied by middle-class to well-to-do businesses, many several stories tall, with the owning families occupying the top floors. Beyond that was a green belt of parks that was the absolute boundary between the lower and upper cities, for on the rising hillside large homes with sprawling yards and fountains gave way to even larger estates surrounded by high walls and sturdy gates. Most were guarded by soldiers wearing private livery, all attempting to outdo their neighbors in terms of ostentation. As opposed to the Imperial soldiers dispatched to meet them at the docks, these guardsmen wore highly polished chest guards and helms of steel. Some were painted in bright colors, while some affected gold trim and ridiculous plumes of feathers or dyed horsehair. Certainly the guards looked stout enough to keep vagabonds and rabble from disturbing their masters, but one glance from Amirantha to Pug revealed what the Warlock thought of these "fighting men," should real trouble visit this island.

Upward they traveled, until they reached the Imperial district, the buildings that surrounded the Emperor's palace and offices. These were apartments and villas set aside for the functionaries and officers of the court, and all the buildings had been faced with white marble. "Centuries ago, this part of the city was like that below, buildings of stone and wood, but an emperor—his name is lost on me now—decided to make this the most beautiful city in the world, so he started hauling white stone from a massive quarry to the south. Over the years this entire district has been finished to match." He looked at Amirantha with an expression that communicated that what he said next was for the benefit of whoever eavesdropped on them. "It is said Rodric the Fourth, known as the 'Mad King,' was so envious he commanded his city of Rillanon be likewise finished in stone, but because he could have none of this fine white marble, he was forced to settle for a less than satisfactory riot of colors." The truth, as Pug knew, was exactly the opposite. The palace had always been faced with white marble but it was only after Rodric had begun the beautification of Rillanon, a task mostly completed by his successor, King Lyam, that the Emperor of Queg, by name Jumillis, had gone into a frenzy to likewise beautify all the Imperial district. The only reason he had stopped at the Imperial district is that the quarry ran low on marble, and what was left was harbored against the need for stones to repair weather and other damage.

Pug sat back silently for a moment; remembering King Rodric whom Pug had met on his first visit to Rillanon returned him to a dark and reflective mood he had managed to avoid since being sought out by Jim and Amirantha. Rodric was a sorely troubled but basically good man, driven mad by an illness no one could cure. Only lucid at the end of his life, he had named his cousin Lyam King and saved the nation from a bloody civil war on the heels of twelve years of fighting with the Tsurani.

That put him to thinking of all those he had lost over the years: Kulgan, his old teacher, and Meecham, Kulgan's companion; Father Tully, one of his first and wisest teachers; Princess Carline, whom he once thought he loved; and Laurie, one of his closest friends as a man, who wed the Princess. Laurie had died too young and left Carline a widow far too long. Lord Borric . . . He sighed and Amirantha looked at him with a questioning expression. Pug held up his hand to indicate it was of no importance, yet with the sinking feeling in the pit of his stomach, he knew it was. Katala, his first love, his first wife, lost to a wasting sickness no magic or art could cure. His first two children—William, his son, and Gaminia, the daughter of his heart—both lost at the end of the war with the Emerald Queen's army. And now Miranda and his youngest, Caleb.

Pug pushed aside deep and dark feelings and chided himself for not getting over his black moods. He knew from the day he had bargained with the gods that this would be his fate, yet he still resented it.

The litters arrived at the entrance to the palace, saving Pug more dark reflection. He glanced over and saw Amirantha studying him. Without saying anything, the Warlock made it clear he understood Pug's mind had been elsewhere.

The three left the litters and immediately were taken to quarters while Jim was escorted to a reception in the Emperor's Court. As part of his retinue, they could have been with Jim had he insisted, but Pug had decided there was work they could do, even from closely guarded quarters.

Once they were alone, Pug nodded to Magnus, who went to a chair in the corner of their quarters and sat. Pug said to Amirantha, "These Quegans seem like hospitable enough folks."

Amirantha looked around the room, a large antechamber for entertaining and casual conversation; there were two doors each on the right and left walls as they entered, and a large vaulted window opposite the door to the hall. Amirantha said, "Lovely view," and Pug joined him.

"Yes," said the magician, as they looked down on one of the Emperor's many gardens. This one was dominated by a large pool in which several people were swimming or lounging near it.

Amirantha's eyebrows rose slightly when he realized the bathers were all nude, and he said, "Ah, is that the custom here?"

Pug said, "The Quegans are Keshians by ancestry. The Imperial Court of Great Kesh is in a very hot climate, on table lands overlooking the Overn Deep in the heart of the Empire. Their attitudes toward dress are very different than those of us from the Kingdom. We are a cold-weather people most of the time and dress accordingly."

"I see," said Amirantha. "I pass no judgment. I just find it . . . interesting."

"Ah," said Pug with a smile. "Don't let it be a distraction."

"Unless the librarians are pretty young women wearing no clothing, Richard," he said, using Pug's false name, "I think I shall be fine."

Pug laughed, but his eyes were still searching every inch of the room. They assumed they'd be spied upon as a matter of course, but didn't know to what extent. It could be something as simple as someone at a listening post in a nearby room, overhearing what was said through a simple sound chamber, a tiny tube of metal behind a tapestry or a decorative plant, or it could be a very complex magic scrying spell. That was what Magnus was attempting to determine.

Pug looked at his son, who opened his eyes and shook his head once. No magic they could detect was at play. "I think I'll lay down for a while," said Magnus as he stood up and moved to one of the nearby doors.

Pug nodded agreement and went to another. Opening the door, he found a small but well-appointed room with a simple free-standing closet, a clean bed, one window looking down on a tiny patch of flowers, with a window opposite—another guest apartment from what Pug could tell. He saw no movement through the window and assumed that apartment was empty.

Pug closed the door and lay down, gathering his thoughts.

Since Miranda's and Caleb's deaths, any attempt at reflection seemed to plunge him into morbid introspection. He had fought certain battles within his entire life; losing Nakor had begun the struggle, but the death of his wife and son had defeated him.

Still, there was work to do and he had to pull himself back from a deep cauldron of self-pity and rage toward the gods that shackled him. He had made this bargain, he reminded himself for a countless time; he could have left this life after battling Jakan, the demon disguised as the Emerald Queen, but elected to return and continue the struggle. His price was to watch all he loved die. . . .

He sat up. Something tickled the edge of his mind.

Standing, he hurried to the door leading into Amirantha's bedroom and quietly knocked. When the Warlock opened the door, Pug held up a warning finger before his lips, then motioned the Warlock to follow him to Magnus's door. He knocked lightly again, and when his son answered made an encircling motion with his hand. Magnus nodded and motioned for them to enter.

Once in the room, Magnus motioned again for the two other magic users to stand close to him. He closed his eyes a moment, then said, "We are shrouded. It is a very weak enchantment, as it might alert anyone watching closely."

"We're being spied upon by magic?" asked Amirantha.

Pug said, "My son has certain skills even beyond mine. As you can sense demons, he can sense the practice of magic, even to the point of understanding the spells and countering them." He looked at his son with pride in his eyes. "It's a rare gift."

"It's a poor scrying spell being used, easily defeated. But the longer I maintain the illusion that we're talking about which books to examine tomorrow, the more likely it is someone may discover my counter-spell. So, what is it?"

Pug said, "Amirantha, I need to ask you something. We have spoken so much about what we know of demons and what we don't know, occasionally a question gets set aside and we just forget to revisit it.

"We spent so much time speculating on what happened to Maarg at Shila, we never got back to something you wished to discuss." Then he said quickly, "You were surprised at the demon captain Jakan seizing the Emerald Queen's body . . ."

"Demonic possession is rare," said Amirantha, also speaking softly and quickly. "And it has been limited to a particular sort of creature . . . I think of them as spirits or ghosts as much as the demons we face. The idea of a powerful demon lord, one of the great captains, or one of equal strength . . ." Amirantha shrugged. "I really don't remember what I wanted to ask at the time. Mostly I am confused by it."

"Why?" asked Magnus.

"It's not typical of their behavior. Piecing together what you've told me, and what I learned from Gulamendis, I'm just now beginning to get a rough idea of demon society, if it can be called that. Rather, how things are done in the demon realm. It's chaotic by our standards, yet it has its own rules and boundaries. This demon possession by a powerful, magic-using demon . . . it doesn't fit in."

He looked around, appeared frustrated. "This really is something we can't speak of in a short time, but it's good you brought it up. If you don't find this one tome we're seeking, do be alert for any other references to demon encounters or lore. It might provide us with additional insights."

Pug nodded. "We'll talk more when it's safe to do so."

They parted company and Magnus dispelled the illusion he had conjured in the counter-spell and they waited quietly in their rooms until they were summoned for supper with Jim.

The meal was sumptuous in the Quegan fashion. Four long tables were established in a square, with just enough space between the corners to allow servants to move inside the open area bringing trays of food. Each guest was free to pick that which appealed to them or wave the servant past. Behind them young men and women moved with large vessels of wine and a very light ale.

The servants were uniformly attired in a simple tunic

that fell below the knees, cinched at the waist with a double cord. Pug thought of them as boys and girls as they were all young, none looking older than late teens, or early twenties, and all were exceptionally attractive.

The nobles were all minor palace functionaries. Only the Imperial Chancellor was of note; he was there as a concession to Jim's diplomatic rank. Normally a Kingdom Baron wouldn't be entitled to so lofty a host, especially one sent on an academic mission with little political or military significance, but it was probable that the Quegans suspected Jim of being more than he appeared. Jim's own spy network wasn't the only one operating in the Bitter Sea, and no doubt he had attracted Quegan interest over the years as much as he had Keshian interest.

The other nobles were all mid-level functionaries, and Pug had been paired with a very attractive middle-aged woman named Livia, who reclined on the large settee employed by the Quegans for dining. She waved away a servant holding a tray of candied fruits and said, "Too sweet. I like simple foods, I confess."

She wore the traditional Quegan toga, which clung to her well enough to promise a full healthy body. Her features were strong yet feminine, and she had deep, dark brown eyes, and a tiny touch of grey amid her auburn hair, worn loosely to her shoulders. While Pug had little interest in dalliance, he still found her attractive and interesting. She was introduced to him as a fellow academic, an archivist assigned to assist him and his companions the next day. Pug was certain that she'd prove helpful, just as he was certain she was charged with observing everything the three visiting academics did and would report back. What he didn't know was if she was an archivist playing at being a spy or a spy playing at being an archivist.

"Really?" said Pug in a noncommittal tone as he selected a ripe pear lightly coated in honey and sprinkled with crushed almonds. He bit into it and said, "Unusual, but very good."

"You get bored with . . ." She sighed. "I'm not very good at this sort of thing. My parents were very minor nobles, ragged cousins of some very important people. I was not likely to marry well, so they secured me a position here in the palace."

Unsure what to say, Pug merely nodded. Then he asked, "Do you enjoy it?"

She seemed less than enthused, but said, "It can be interesting. Occasionally someone such as yourself arrives to disrupt the monotony."

Pug smiled as if flattered. He was now certain she was a spy, sent to seduce him and discover if there was anything more to him than the story provided by Baron James of the Prince's Court in Krondor. He glanced at where his son reclined, and saw that a somewhat younger and equally attractive woman had been paired with him. Amirantha was paired with a very academic-looking gentleman, and Pug held a grin in check. Amirantha had revealed himself to be something of a lady's man over the time Pug had known him, while Magnus . . . Pug occasionally worried about his last surviving son. Magnus had been terribly hurt by a young woman when he was barely more than a boy, and had retreated from becoming involved with women since then. Pug was certain he occasionally succumbed to his more fundamental needs—he was injured, not dead—but while he might have enjoyed the company of a courtesan in Kesh or a better brothel in Roldem, Magnus had avoided several advances by young female students at Sorcerer's Isle over the years. It would have worked out better for the Quegan intelligence apparatus had they placed the academic gentleman with Magnus and the pretty woman with Amirantha.

Pug turned his attention back to Livia and asked, "Seriously, do you like working in the archives?"

She shrugged. He had touched on something and wondered just what preparation for this visit she had been given. If she was a Quegan agent, she would have some knowledge of the archives, but would hardly be an expert.

She said, "To be truthful, it's a boring calling. Once in a while I get something to read that is interesting, and I don't mind those hours. My task is to write a one-paragraph précis of the work, assign a location within the archive, and ensure that my entry is copied into the main codex of the archive." She fixed him with a calculating gaze. "I could return to your quarters with you, if you'd like, to discuss some of the more esoteric volumes in the archives. Some are quite . . . revealing."

Pug held a smile in check and merely inclined his head slightly, as if thinking about the offer.

"Unless you prefer to stay for the orgy?"

Pug's eyebrow lifted slightly. Of all the nations in this part of the world, he had visited Queg the fewest times, and had forgotten that some of their customs were radically different from the Kingdom or even Great Kesh. Now he remembered why all the servants would be young and attractive. The after-dinner orgy was a staple of grand welcomes for foreign visitors and certain holidays. He had no moral qualms about other people's behavior for the most part, but his own feelings demanded intimacy be limited to a committed love.

Not having to feign his feelings, Pug softly said, "I just recently lost my wife."

Livia's eyes widened. "I'm sorry. Was it sudden?"

"Very," said Pug. "It will be a while before I'm . . ."

She reached out and touched his hand lightly. Her tone remained bright, but her expression was solicitous. "If I can do anything, please."

Pug admired her persistence. He sighed. "Someday, I'd like to return and then, perhaps." He slowly rose. "Now if you'll excuse me, I think I shall retire before the . . . festivities commence."

"Of course."

"I look forward to seeing you in the morning," he said. "Until then."

Magnus and Amirantha both had noticed him stand up and were watching. Pug made a slight inclination with his head toward his two companions, indicating they should leave as soon as possible. Jim was deep in conversation with a noble but Pug knew he missed nothing.

Pug retired to his quarters and found wine, sweets, nuts, and cheeses waiting, and sat heavily in a divan before the window. He hadn't eaten much at the supper, and wasn't particularly hungry now, but he did feel like a sip of wine. He picked up the carafe and then closed his eyes. He had learned a spell years before, one that would cleanse the wine of any drug designed to incapacitate or poison. He doubted this was necessary if the object of the exercise was to aid a seduction, but caution was the byword on this journey.

A few minutes later Amirantha appeared. Laughing slightly, he said, "You and Magnus get the pretty girls, but I get the scholar who wants to ply me with questions about Muboya!"

"Well, that is logical," said Pug. "Most people love to talk about their homes and the Quegans view all outside this island as potential enemies."

"I told him plenty," said the Warlock, sitting down in a chair on the other side of the room. "Some of it was even true."

Pug smiled broadly at that one.

Magnus entered and with a raised eyebrow said, "Orgy?"

"It's a local custom," said his father.

"Maybe we should come back?" quipped Amirantha.

Both father and son looked at him with a narrow gaze,

one of the few times a resemblance was evident. Magnus was tall and pale, while his father was short and dark, but that look was identical.

After a half hour of idle conversation, they decided to retire. As they stood to enter their respective rooms, Amirantha said, "I wonder if Jim stayed."

Pug smiled. "As ranking noble, it would have been something of a political incident for him to leave."

Amirantha sighed. "I noticed he did keep that one very pretty serving girl at hand." Shaking his head slightly, he said, "It's heroic what that man does for his King."

Pug chuckled and Magnus laughed as they both closed their doors.

CHAPTER 8

FORTRESS

Sandreena signaled.

The two Knights-Adamant she had recruited— Brother Farson, who had been arriving in Krondor as she prepared to leave, and Brother Jaliel, who was already in Durban when she arrived—reined in their horses. Her newfound rank gave them no option but to change their current plans and follow her. She indicated they should stay while she slowly urged her horse on.

To a parched, desolate desert fortress she had led them. Abandoned by Great Kesh's Empire centuries ago, apparently, for almost nothing here looked like a fortification. A few large stones that were once a wall, a single foundation of a gate that was half-buried under dust, and some stairs leading down into a labyrinth of tunnels and storage rooms. So little was left aboveground you could ride past a hundred yards on either side and not notice that once the Empire had thought this pass worth defending.

The two Knights were told only what she felt she needed them to know until they reached this point. Using the documents left her by Creegan, she had followed an ancient trade route out of Durban, south into the Jal-Pur, then southwest into the foothills. Those would eventually rise up in the west as the Trollhome Mountains, but here they were merely a landscape of tablelands and rising hills. Whatever the name of this once proud fortress, it was known to the desert men as the Tomb of the Hopeless. To the south of this position was a valley with the even less appealing name Valley of Lost Men.

Before leaving Krondor, she had gone over the maps in the Order's keeping of this region, and none showed either the fortress or valley. She took it as a matter of trust that Creegan wouldn't have insisted she read the report if he hadn't wanted her to act on it, and she was equally certain that he expected her to do exactly what she was doing, run off and take matters into her own hands. Simply put, there was no one in Krondor besides herself to do so. She knew Creegan had a relationship with Pug and the others on Sorcerer's Isle, but in rushing off to Rillanon to become the Order's leader, he neglected to leave her any hint about how to contact them. She suspected there were some others, like whoever gave her the messages in Durban in the first place, who were Kingdom agents of the Conclave, but she had no idea how to identify and contact them, either.

She remembered the young man who had fetched her from Ithra after she had almost died in her first encounter with the Demon Legion's agents on Midkemia. Zane was his name. But she had no idea how to reach him. Frustrated that Creegan put this on her alone, she pushed down her concerns to deal with the matters at hand.

Farson and Jaliel were reliable, but neither of them had been named on Creegan's list, so there were things she could not tell them. All they knew was that this was a special undertaking at the Father-Bishop's request and that secrecy was paramount. Though how secret could it be when three Knights-Adamant of the Order of the Shield of the Weak all rode out of the city together at sunrise into the desert? They had headed due east then turned south and circled around to the ancient caravan trail. Sandreena did not know if the Imperial Keshian Intelligence Corps was following, but she was certain they knew she and the others had left. When they failed to appear at the usual oasis in a few days, they might send someone out to track the three knights. She was hoping earnestly that by then, whatever business brought her here would be finished and they would be heading back to Krondor.

It was near sundown when they reached the edge of the ancient fortress. While the carnage that had taken place when the report had been written had been weeks before, the scene was no less grisly. The corpses were now bones, picked clean by scavengers and the drying heat and blowing sands. But enough connective tissue remained that a few skeletons hung from the makeshift gibbets around the edge of the clearing. The piles of ash contained the contorted forms of those who had been burned alive, and everywhere bones riddled with arrows lay in the open. Hundreds had been slaughtered here for some unknown dark purpose.

Sandreena called out, "You can come up now!"

The two other Knights rode into the ancient fortress and Jaliel said, "Goddess! What manner of butchery is this?"

Farson looked at Sandreena and said, "Sergeant, if you don't mind my saying, this is a little more than you usually find in any mission, secret or otherwise. Are we to know what is going on?"

"I'll tell you what I know," she said. "There is a very dangerous, evil man named Belasco, who consorts with dark powers. He has won over followers and they did this." She decided to omit that most of the dead were fanatics who had gone willingly to their death. It was an unnecessary detail not needed for these two to do their duty.

"Sergeant," said Farson, "what happened here?"

"I only have a rough idea, but it appears a cult of death worshippers have appeared."

The two Knights exchanged glances, and Sandreena knew exactly what they were thinking. A death cult was more the province of the worshippers of Lims-Kragma or perhaps even Sung the White, but not usually a concern with the servants of Dala.

Sandreena said, "Father-Bishop Creegan is concerned that they may be abducting local villagers as sacrifices."

It was not a complete lie, for she could imagine that might be part of Creegan's concerns, but left it at that. For whatever reason the Conclave of Shadows had made alliance with the most important man in the martial order of the worshippers of Dala, and perhaps it was simply that Pug didn't have anyone else to call upon. Certainly she knew there were few around who had as much experience with demons as she did, for she had destroyed more than her share. Still, for not the first time since departing Krondor she wished that the Goddess—or at least Creegan—had given this promotion to someone else.

"Are you both carrying wards?" she asked.

"Against what, Sergeant?" asked Jaliel.

"Necromancy, demons, and anything else you can think of?"

Both Knights patted their hip bags, in which they carried their wards.

"Good," she said. "We have no idea what we're going to find down there."

"Down where?" asked Farson.

She pointed south. "Down there in the Valley of Lost Men."

Farson's expression communicated how much he liked hearing that, but he remained silent.

"We'll rest up for the night, then head down at dawn."

Without further comment the men tied their mounts and then began untacking them. Sandreena unloaded a small bag of grain off the back of her mount then took off the saddle. Each Knight carried a brush and began currying their mounts once they had been secured and untacked. Sandreena took it upon herself to fill and fix nosebags for all three horses; the two Knights thanked her. All three knew that they needed to start back within two days, else the horses would begin to starve. There was no grazing or fodder anywhere between their present location and Durban, just arid tablelands, hills covered in thorns, and the odd dry desert plants that would bloom briefly after a rare rain, but otherwise were dried and dormant. It was hard to believe that any of this area needed defending.

One mystery that presented itself—and Sandreena was surprised no one else had brought it up, either Creegan or the author of the report he had her read—was why in ancient times had Kesh built a fortress here in the first place? The Trollhome was, as the name implied, the residence of creatures best avoided. Mountain trolls were smarter than their lowland cousins, who were little more than animals, but the desert was an effective barrier against them troubling anyone. If she knew where the caravan route had originally ended, perhaps then it would make sense, but as far as she could judge from all the old maps she studied before leaving Krondor, the route ended in the valley below.

As she brushed she mused over what might be down there. An ancient gold mine or source of some other wealth would dictate the route ran east, eventually terminating in the city of Nar Ayab, then on to the capital city of Kesh. She deduced whatever had been moving along the route, it had been going from Durban to this location. Maybe, she speculated, this was the terminus and the reason for the route was a quick supply from the nearest Keshian city. Which would mean the only reason for this fortress would be to keep whatever was down in that valley in that valley.

She finished and broke out her own rations, saying, "Cold camp," to her companions. They were both veteran Knights and a night without a fire was nothing new to them. They understood there was a possibility someone or something out there was watching.

The three ate in silence, then when they were done eating, Sandreena said, "Jaliel, first watch; Farson, last." They both nodded, but each silently thanked her, for as leader she was taking the least desirable watch. She lay down using her saddle as a pillow and with years of habit ingrained in her, fell asleep within minutes.

Dawn came hot and dry, which was no surprise, but with an early wind. The wind was a blessing and a curse, a blessing in that it would kick up enough dust that it could prevent them from being seen should hidden sentries be posted along the trail down into the Valley of Lost Men, and a curse because if it was blinding enough, Sandreena and her companions could lose the trail and find themselves taking a very quick route down to some unyielding rocks below.

Sandreena spoke loudly, to be heard over the rising wind. "How many demons have you faced?"

Farson said, "Two, Sergeant."

Jaliel said, "Seven, Sergeant."

She said, "Jaliel, you'll bring up the rear in case we get jumped from behind." To Farson she said, "Do not do anything unless I tell you. Demons can be very tricky sometimes and let one of us lead." He nodded. Both Knights knew that she was right; she hadn't asked how many demons they had defeated, because if they hadn't defeated all they had faced, they wouldn't be here alive.

Sandreena realized Jaliel had faced down two more than she, but hers had been particularly nasty and without Amirantha's aid . . . She silently cursed herself for a fool at the sudden stab of feelings from thinking of him. He was a miserable excuse for a man, a charmer with no substance and his words were honeyed lies. Still, he knew more about demons than any man she had ever met, and right now she'd put aside her urge to strangle him in exchange for his ability to control the monsters.

"Grab a tail," she instructed.

Farson moved up behind her mount from the side— against an unexpected kick—and gripped the warhorse's tail. The mare snorted, but she had been through this before. Jaliel did likewise with Farson's horse, and the three slowly began their descent from the platform down into the Valley of Lost Men. This way no one would wander and missteps would be kept to a minimum.

The wind blew blinding gusts of dust and small objects, pieces of plants, dried insect carcasses, a powdery grit like chalk or ash that coated the skin and matted hair. Twice they found large outcroppings of rocks to shelter behind as the wind picked up in intensity and the howling in the air made even the well-trained horses paw the ground, nicker, and snort. Sandreena patted the nose of her mount in reassurance, but she was hardly in a position to reassure anyone, even her mare. The impulse that drove her to undertake this mission now looked like an impossibly vain idea. Still, each time she had been visited by doubt she returned to the same conclusion; there was no one in the temple save herself and Creegan, and two other Knights, their whereabouts unknown, who could possibly follow up on what that mysterious Kingdom agent had reported.

Necromancy and demons were not usually involved together. Demons took too much delight in devouring anything living to leave something around long enough for a necromancer to use his arts on the recently dead. As demons devoured whatever they killed as a matter of course, that didn't leave much for the dark magician to work with.

Still, from her studies Sandreena knew there was a great deal of energy, albeit black and evil, in the dark arts, necromancy most of all. If someone was harnessing death magic to control demons— She left the thought unfinished; she really did not know what it meant, and wished again for five minutes to talk to Amirantha, then she'd strangle him.

She became aggravated with herself as much as she was with the Warlock. Of all the times to start thinking about that bastard!

The wind began to shift and then started falling off. Sandreena knew the desert wind in these hot tablelands was unpredictable. But in the relative lull, free from the worst of the stinging sand and blistering dryness, they would better be able to see trouble coming.

She motioned for the others to fall in and started down the trail. The wind came in gusts and swirls, but now she could see her way down. The path was roughly the equivalent of the one she had followed up to the fortress from Durban—it was ancient, eroded by wind and the occasional flash flood, and rarely used. Yet there were moments when the wind died she could see signs that this road had been recently used. A large number of horses and wagons had come this way, and by the look of it, heading down into the valley, not out of it. Silently she wondered who was behind this and what were they playing at.

Durban was a pest hole on the Bitter Sea, and the Governor profited hugely from looking the other way as smugglers moved contraband into or out of the Empire. It was a fact of Imperial Keshian life, and no matter how many times the Empire sought to reform that office, the reality of greed, opportunity, and distance from the capital melding in that miserable city asserted itself. Still, even by Durban standards, a lot of wagons and men had been coming this way for a while.

Sandreena estimated at least a hundred dead left to rot up at the ancient fortress, perhaps more, and that much movement across the desert should have caused notice. Whoever was behind this thing they were investigating had managed to keep the Imperial guards from noticing, which meant the Governor or someone highly placed in his service was looking the other way intentionally, either due to bribery or fear . . . or both.

As they descended down the winding trail, following long switchbacks that took them slowly down the mountain, the wind died. As they turned from one trail to the next switchback, it was as if a curtain of blowing sand and dust was pulled aside.

"What is that?" demanded Farson.

"What, indeed?" said Sandreena as Jaliel moved forward and halted.

"Good Goddess!" He exclaimed.

"That" was a massive structure being erected in the distant heart of the valley. The outline was vaguely like that of a massive fortification of some type, forming a nearly perfect circle around something. It was apparently a circle, but from this distance detail was lost. Four towers were rising, one further along in construction than the others, and it was clear they would arch over and touch the center of this . . . whatever it was.

Farson said, "I'm not an engineer, though my da built siege engines for the King, so I've seen a bit. Those towers"—he pointed—"can't . . . well, they can't do that, arch over and touch."

Softly Sandreena said, "I won't mention it to them."

"To whom?" asked Jaliel.

"Whoever's building that monstrosity."

"I suddenly feel like we should be seeking cover," said Farson.

Glancing around, Sandreena said, "I will be happy to oblige as soon as you show me some."

They stood on an exposed mountainside. If there were sentries on the wall of that distant construction, the three on the trail were still too distant to be noticed, but if there were sentries at the bottom of this long trail down, or anywhere nearer, they were not visible should anyone look in their direction.

Sandreena pointed to a depression down about a dozen yards below the trail. "That's a stream bed when there are rains, if I haven't missed my guess," she said. She turned off the switchback and carefully led her horse down the loose rocks and scrub, looking at each step for treacherous footing. When she reached the indicated gully, it quickly deepened. Reaching the bottom, she halted. "We leave the horses here and tonight we get as close as we can to investigate."

"Leave the horses, Sergeant?" asked Farson.

"The thing about switchback trails is there is no cover and those below can just sit there and start shooting arrows at you like swinging targets in the marshaling yard." She glanced upward. "We have three trails above and five or six below." She looked at the two Knights. "Farson, I want you to lead the horses back up to the top." She pointed to a notch directly above where they crouched. "Wait up there. Untack them, clean them, water them, and wait until sundown. Then tack them up again and be ready to ride at a moment's notice." She sensed he was about to object, but cut off anything he might say. "You have the most critical duty. If we are not back in a day's time, by sunrise tomorrow, you assume we are dead. You must get back to Durban and take the fastest route to Krondor, by ship if you can, or trade the three horses in for fresh mounts and then get to the Temple."

She realized there was only one man at the Temple who was on that list. "Brother Willoby, in Father-Bishop Creegan's office. Find him and tell him what we've found. He'll know what to do."

Brother Farson said, "What have we found, Sergeant?"

He pointed in the general direction of the distant construction. "I don't even know if I can describe what we're seeing, let alone divine its purpose."

"It is an invasion point," said Sandreena. "Can't you feel them?"

"Who?" asked Jaliel, his dark brown eyebrows knitted in concentration or worry.

"Demons," said Sandreena. "The place below is crawling with them if my skin is any indication."

Farson said, "Sergeant, I feel a little . . . on edge, but . . . I just don't feel it."

"Me, neither," agreed Jaliel.

Sandreena studied them both for a moment, then turned her attention back to the task at hand. "You have your orders," she said to Farson, and he nodded. Slowly he turned the animals around and she knew he didn't relish the idea of leading three horses back up that trail. She watched closely for any sign they might have been observed, while the returning Knight-Adamant tied her horse's reins to the saddle ring of Jaliel's, then that mount's reins to his own. "See you tomorrow, Sergeant; Jaliel," he said as he led the three horses back up the shallow gully and started the tedious climb back to the top of the ridge.

"Now what?" asked Jaliel quietly.

"We wait," she answered, looking at the sky. "Best if we rest. You try to sleep. I'll stand watch."

The more experienced of the two Knights she had recruited nodded, not needing further urging. It might only be morning and they might have a long day ahead to wait out, but years living in the wilderness had taught him to take rest when it was offered.

Left to her own thoughts, Sandreena crawled up so she could rest her arm on a big boulder, then her chin on her arm and study the distant construction. Flickers of movement gave tantalizing hints of something going on, but she could make out no useful detail. She would have to be content to wait until darkness fell—a good nine hours or more away—and then creep down for a closer look. She offered a prayer to the Goddess, for them to remain undiscovered, because she had no illusions of making it back to the top of that long switchback being chased while they were on foot. Being undiscovered was their only hope.

So she settled in and prayed, and waited for the sun to crawl across the sky, and she tried very hard to drive thoughts of Amirantha from her mind every time he intruded into her thinking.

Night came slowly, but after the sun set, they began moving carefully down the side of the mountain. The frustrating thing for Sandreena was that even as she got closer, she could make out less detail because of the failing light. Little Moon was the only one rising this early in the evening, and the smallest of Midkemia's three moons provided scant illumination. Middle Moon wouldn't be seen until just before dawn and Large Moon wouldn't rise until after dawn. Still, as they needed stealth, she would just as soon deal with having to get closer than trying to approach on a Three Moons Bright night.

Sandreena noticed that a small tower, barely two stories tall, had been erected near the base of the trail. Had they continued down earlier in the day, they no doubt would have been spotted by any sentry on duty. Sandreena used hand gestures, barely visible, to inform Jaliel they were going to circle even farther away from the trail.

The gulley down which they crept emptied out in a basin a hundred yards across, before running into a dry riverbed that moved around the base of the hills. A fairly large river must have flowed through here in ages past, though Sandreena found it hard to imagine this land lush with ample enough rain to fill a brook, let alone a river. Yet the evidence of erosion was under her feet, and currently hiding her from view as she and her companion crawled up the southern edge of the basin, to get a closer look at what was being fashioned in this once abandoned place.

Both Knights were battle tested and ready for any trouble, but both knew this was a reconnaissance, not elective combat. Something this massive, in a place this removed from any civilized authority, could only be the work of forces inimical to those authorities, and that made it a matter of concern for the Temple as well. And the stench of demon was so strong here Sandreena knew these were urgent concerns.

She rose up and studied the walls. Lights had been erected, large flaming braziers hung from chains attached to tripods evenly spaced along the battlement, for that was what this place was—a fortress. But one unlike any Sandreena had ever encountered or heard of.

"What is this place?" whispered Jaliel.

"No place good," answered Sandreena. "We need to split up. I want you to go that way." She pointed toward the southernmost end of the basin and moved her hand to indicate he should make his way along a line that paralleled the walls. The entire structure appeared to be circular, though she would need to get closer in better light to be certain. The curve of the wall before her suggested it, a massive circle of stone with a gigantic gate in the middle, with towers being erected.

She gripped him by the arm and whispered, "Go until midnight, then return here. If I'm not here, make your way to the top as best you can. If Farson has left for Durban, make your way to the Oasis at La-amat-atal, and wait for a caravan to get you safely to civilization. If you get there before he leaves, tell him what you see, and go with him to Krondor."

"Yes, Sergeant," he replied. "You?"

"I'm going to circle in the other direction, and I'm going to do my damnedest to be at the top of the trail before Farson leaves with my horse."

He chuckled and said, "Goddess be with you, sister."

"And with you, my brother," she replied.

He set off at once, moving surprisingly quietly for a man with armor and a shield strapped to his back. Sandreena waited a moment, not wanting too much movement in this area, and when he was gone from her sight, she set off up the side of the basin and onto the flat above. She crouched, though it was no easy feat with her shield on her back and her sword clutched in her right hand. She found a small stand of scrub brush between the lip of the basin and the watchtower. She prayed to the Goddess that whoever was stationed up there was watching for movement along the road and not for anyone coming up behind.

She would turn occasionally and glance at the far wall of the fortress—how she thought of this alien structure—and try to discern some more detail as to who was on the wall and what they were doing, but it was still too far. She came to an outcropping of rocks and knelt behind it, slowly raising herself up to observe the guardhouse. She sat down hard, barely believing her eyes. An elf stood guard in the guardhouse, and from his apparent size, she judged him to be one of the newly arrived Star Elves.

She sat down, her back to the rock, and felt completely confused. She sensed demon presence in huge numbers, yet an elf stood watch. Given their reputation for seeing in dim light, she counted herself and Jaliel fortunate to have made it down that gully undetected; certainly had they stayed on the switchbacks, even at night, the elf would have seen them a half mile away.

Now she knew she had to get closer to this structure and see if she could make any sense of what was occurring there. She waited until she saw the elf turn his back fully, to watch the trail above, and she hurried across what seemed a vast open space, moving as silently as she could, until she found more rocks behind which to shelter. Holding her breath so she could hear any hint of alarm, she waited.

Only the distant sounds of working coming from the fortress disturbed the silence of the desert night. Where was that wind when you needed it? she thought, then off she went, moving around the perimeter, seeking a place that would allow her to get closer to the construction.

Sandreena crouched below some empty wagons, their traces empty and no sign of the mules or horses that pulled them. She doubted those inside stabled their draft animals; most likely they ate them. This had all the appearances of a one-way enterprise, with the destination before her. She felt as if she might scream from frustration, but fear and caution combined to keep her focused and silent. There were so many questions plaguing her, but all she could do was creep around in shadows and observe.

A massive gate had been erected, but currently it was open, allowing for tantalizing glimpses of the inside. Her mind reeled at the image of dwarves, humans, elves, and even a troll, all laboring under the watchful eye of demons. They were using mortal beings as slave labor, by all appearances, something unimagined in the annals of all the demon lore she had been exposed to. Now more than ever she wished Amirantha was here, and not because he had broken her heart and she wanted to punish him; she needed him to make what sense he could of the tableau before her.

A demon overseer hove into view, and he paused, staring in her direction for a moment. She felt her heart jump and she held her breath. She had never faced a demon as formidable in appearance as this one. He had the head of a deformed ape, with two upswept ears, a grotesque parody of an elf's. He wore a massive chest piece with a human skull set in the middle like a heraldic device. The shoulders were covered with black steel spaulders that swept up and ended in gold-tipped points. His legs were covered in black armor. He wore a circlet of gold with another skull in the brow, and he carried a massive sword pulsing with an evil red light in his right hand.

He seemed to sniff the air, then after a moment turned away and shouted something to one of the humans. The human bowed and hurried off.

Atop the walls workers scrambled up wooden scaffolding to hoist large stones to raise the massive arching columns. Now that she was closer, Sandreena could see that these rising columns were being installed with great care and she could see their placement was being closely watched. Two men in robes watched and when the stones were in place, both began to incant. The sound of their words was lost, but the feeling that visited her as she watched the construction filled her with cold fear.

Something gigantic, impossible to understand, and to no good purpose, was being fashioned here by demons, who were overseeing mortal workers and mages. None of this made the remotest sense to her, and she knew her cause would be better served for her to start back now, to make sure what little she had seen was reported to Father-Bishop Creegan. This report could not wait for a message, even by fast ship or swift rider, but rather she would presume a voyage to Sorcerer's Island. Pug and his confederates had devices that would get her to Rillanon in days instead of weeks, and the island was far closer to Durban than Krondor, and a great deal closer than Rillanon. Besides, she thought in passing, the last place she had seen Amirantha had been on that cursed island.

Yet her curiosity tugged at her, for she didn't think she had seen enough. Still what more could be gained?

As she mused, she heard footsteps approaching from behind, and by the time she was turned, the dwarf warrior was charging her. There was something in his eyes that warned her there was no time to be spent on discussion. He carried a short sword and swung it with deadly intent.

Sandreena managed to roll out of the way, come to her

feet, slipping her shield off with a single motion and reversing it so she could slip her arm through the straps on the back, and had her sword up just in time to block the dwarf's following strike.

The shock that ran through her arm as she took that blow made her realize this was no mean swordsman she faced, but an experienced dwarven warrior who was offering no quarter. She had never faced one before, not even in a practice melee, and their fortitude and prowess were renowned. She knew she could not wear him down; he could fight until she collapsed from fatigue and then dance on her grave. She certainly could not overpower him, and she doubted she could disable him. Her only hope was a quick kill.

Two strikes and the dwarf hesitated, and Sandreena saw his eyes were slightly unfocused. More, she was nearly overwhelmed by an unexpected realization. She had fought in more than a score of life-or-death battles, and three times those against men whom she was trying to subdue. She had experienced every type of male body stench, and a few females', and thought nothing of it, but there was something here she had not anticipated: this dwarf stank like a demon.

He sent a skull-crushing overhand blow at her and overextended slightly. In that moment, she noticed a talisman hanging from a leather cord around his neck. It was a foul thing with red glowing stones for eyes and that's where the demon stench originated.

She danced away and rather than take his head from his shoulders—the opening was there—she turned her blade and struck him with the flat of her sword on the side of his head. It was like hitting a tree bole and the shock that ran up her arm nearly numbed it to the shoulder.

The dwarf barely blinked and came straight at her. She hesitated only a moment, then leaped to her left, right into the dwarf's next blow, but rather than take it anywhere vital, she crouched under it—no mean feat against a foe barely taller than five feet—then came up behind him.

Before he could turn, she reached out and snatched at the leather thong holding the talisman in place. She ripped it from him and tossed it away.

It was as if she had struck him between the eyes with the hammer he was holding. He stumbled, half-turned, then fell backward, landing on his rear. He sat in the dust, blinking as if blinded by brilliant lights, then let out a long sigh. His eyes finally focused and he looked up at her and said, "What . . . who are . . . ?" He looked around, and Sandreena followed his gaze.

No one on the wall had witnessed the confrontation, but more workers were coming into view. Instead of coming to his feet and alerting the others of an intruder, the dwarf crawled toward her, reaching up to grab her by the leg and hissed, "Get down, for the gods' sake!"

Sandreena kneeled, but kept her sword pointed at the dwarf. "You going to keep trying to kill me?"

The dwarf looked confused. "Kill you? Woman, I don't know who you are, but if you're not working for them"—he pointed toward the fortress—"then you're my new friend."

"Who are you?"

"I'm Keandar, son of Kendrin of Dorgin."

She nodded, motioning for him to crawl with her back under the shelter of the wagon. Dorgin was the dwarven city closest to their current location, a tiny city-state on the border of Great Kesh and the Kingdom of the Isles.

"What is this place?"

"That's a long tale, one I would prefer to recount as far away from here as possible." He glanced under the wagon and said, "Some of my kin are in there, and I mean to get back to Dorgin, tell the King, and return with every war-hammer we can raise."

Sandreena knew it would take more than even a small army of dwarves to deal with what was forming here, but decided that debate could wait. "Can you tell me what is going on in there?"

"Aye, some," he said, "but only a bit. I was a guard, mostly, though those of my people with skills—the engineers, smiths, and mongers, and the stonemasons—they were given jobs inside. But we spoke a little while we ate, when we ate."

"Come on," she said, glancing at the position of the Little Moon. "I have a horse and we can ride double, but it's some distance from here and we need to reach it by sunrise."

"Sunrise?"

"Else one of my order will be taking it back to Durban without me."

"Ah," said the dwarf. "You're not alone?"

"No," said Sandreena. "There are two others."

"Well, let's have a leisurely chat after we're miles from here. You lead, I'll follow."

Sandreena nodded once and crouched, then scampered from the wagons to the first pile of rocks, and began the long return to the gully that would take her past the guardhouse. When she reached it, she turned to Keandar and said, "We need to slip past that guard."

"Why not just go there and quickly kill him? It's only an elf."

"We may have them after us when you don't turn up," she said, "but we most certainly will if they find a dead sentry in that post."

He sighed, as if he were disappointed, then said, "Very well. They don't keep close track of us, mostly because those things they make us wear . . . it saps our will and makes our minds . . . muddled."

"Tell me about it later," said Sandreena, and Keandar nodded. To herself she muttered, "If there is a later."

Dawn found a very nervous Farson waiting in the designated spot, all three horses tacked up and ready to ride. He had his sword out as Sandreena hove into view, and was about to strike when she called him by name.

"Sergeant?" he asked, looking at the dwarf.

"This is Keandar of Dorgin. If anything happens and I fall, you get him to Sorcerer's Island."

Farson's eyes widened. "Sorcerer's Island? Sergeant, no one goes . . ."

"Sorcerer's Island."

"But Krondor . . ."

Firmly, she said, "Sorcerer's Island." She looked around, then asked, "Jaliel?"

Farson shook his head.

"We wait until the sun clears the horizon, then we leave without him." She knew he was probably lost; even coming from the other side of that fortification, had he been close to being on time, they would have encountered each other in the gully or on the upper trail. Still, she honored her word to him to wait.

And they waited. The sun rose, and when she could see it full above the horizon, she said, "Goddess, watch over him." She took the reins of Jaliel's mount and handed them to the dwarf. "Do you need a leg up?"

The dwarf grinned. In the morning sun his hair and beard looked especially red and his eyes were a glinting blue. He was, like most of his race, barrel-chested and broad of shoulders, with powerful arms and thick legs. "I'm short," he replied, "not a child."

His vault into the saddle was impressive and he took the reins in hand like a practiced rider.

Farson and Sandreena mounted and she took one last look around, half-hoping to see Jaliel come into sight. Then, taking a deep breath, she said, "Durban!"

They turned their horses and rode to the north.

CHAPTER 9

WAR

Gulamendis leaped.

The lizard scuttled away, but not before the Demon Master seized it and with a single motion, bashed it hard against the rocks. He hurried back to the cave where his brother waited. A small fire burned in the back and the Conjurer was huddled before it, trying to stay warm in the early morning chill.

The nights on this world were bitter cold and the days scorching hot. The sun had just begun to rise on the seventh day of their being stranded on this alien planet. They had found fresh water in a small stream down the side of the hill, and there were lizards and birds they had contrived to catch, subsistence, barely, but despite being filthy, tired, and hungry, they were still alive.

About the demons they were more puzzled than when they'd first arrived. They had rested a day, then ventured to look down upon the massive army twice since then. Both times they had proceeded cautiously and avoided detection. Something was stirring down in that valley, but they were uncertain of what it was. Had this been an elven army, they might have guessed its behavior, but demons organized in this fashion was outside their experience and knowledge.

The brothers barely spoke, as they had talked out everything they could about this situation over the first few days. They knew they had not ported into the demon realm, as they would have perished in minutes had that been the case. They might not be on the world they called Home, but they were in that same sphere of experience. Despite the less than hospitable surroundings, the air was breathable, the water drinkable, and the wildlife edible. Though one of the reptile varieties they had encountered had induced severe stomach cramps and other unpleasant reactions.

Gulamendis held out his hand as he reached the back of the cave where his brother waited.

"Lizard," said Laromendis dryly. "How unexpected."

His brother ignored the quip and started cleaning the small carcass with his battle knife. It was a clumsy tool, but a few days' practice had given him some ability to not totally destroy their supper before it was cooked. After cooking, it would provide less than a few ounces of meat and a tiny bit of fat, but it would be enough to keep them alive another day. They had both slowly gained back enough strength that they could mount a single defense should they be discovered, but neither had the energy for a prolonged combat.

So lying in wait was their current tactic, but both really knew they had a limited expectation for survival. They quickly devoured their meal and Gulamendis said, "The thing I find the most annoying about this, at the moment, is the need to walk down to the stream every time I get thirsty."

"Then don't get thirsty," replied his brother. "Or find us a damn jar or bucket or something to fetch water back."

"I suggested using your boot . . ." said the Demon Master, in a weak attempt at humor.

His brother made a face indicating what he thought of that notion. "How long can we sit here wondering?" asked the Conjurer.

"I don't know," said his brother, on the border of exasperation. "There is so much here that makes no sense to me."

Laromendis had heard this all before, from the first moment they had spied the demons over the rise, but asked, "Perhaps if you outline, one more time."

"To what end?" asked his brother, now showing his frustration. "Everything I know of demons is wrong, or at least flawed. Both that human Warlock, Amirantha, and I lost our ability to trust our conjurations. The rise of the Demon King made it uncertain we could trust any creature we summoned to not turn on us. Or to vanish back to their realm and report what we saw.

"More, until we got here, our experience with the demons has been that if they were not confined by magic they were out of control. The attacks on our people on *every* world taught us they were a horde of monsters, unrelenting, unforgiving, but without any sort of strategy save to assault, assault, assault."

"We saw those captains on Andcardia," reminded his brother. "They were giving orders."

"It looked like they were herding livestock, directing the flow of a stampede, not directing a coordinated attack." He sighed. "But that camp . . ." He shrugged in resignation. "I can't explain it. I have no idea who is commanding them, but they are unlike any group of demons I have ever heard of, let alone come in contact with."

His brother said, "I understand. Someone has changed the governing laws of your art, without bothering to tell you." Starting to rise, he said, "Let's get something to drink and then we can decide if we want to watch the demons do nothing tonight." As he started to rise, the ground suddenly heaved beneath them as a loud explosion echoed outside.

Laromendis was knocked back on his rump while his brother said, "What was that?"

Both looked up at the ceiling of the dark cave, barely illuminated by the light coming through the entrance, fifty feet away, as dirt came showering down on them. "Get out!" shouted Gulamendis. "This thing is collapsing."

They staggered as the ground under their feet shook and reached the entrance amid a shower of dirt and loose rocks. Once outside they looked around, as Laromendis said, "Earthquake?"

Another distant boom, followed by another lurch in the ground, and Gulamendis said, "I don't think so."

They could see nothing, but quickly realized all the noise was coming from the other side of the ridge. Motioning for his brother to follow him, Gulamendis tried to half climb, half crawl up the shaking hillside. As they neared the crest, they could hear the sounds of battle ringing in the distance, punctuated by more ground-shaking explosions.

Peering over they could see only chaos.

Smoke and dust filled the air as thousands of demons were roiling out of their encampments to meet the on-slaught of . . . more demons.

"What is this?" asked Laromendis, not bothering to keep his voice down. Everywhere they looked demons of all stripes and fashion were engaging others. The oddest quality of this mad scene was that the demons who were already encamped wore armor of a roughly uniform fashion—dull silverfish breast armor and helms, some with spaulders or pauldrons, others with no shoulder protection. Some wore greaves or boots, while others—those with massive feet ending in claws—went barefoot. But it could be quickly ascertained they fought under the same banner. And that banner was raised high atop a long pole in the center of the camp, a massive black cloth with a red design upon it, impossible to see in detail at this distance.

The attackers were likewise armored in a haphazard fashion, but their armor was a uniformly dark blue-grey color and they flew no banner in the field. Still, they were clearly holding the advantage in surprise and ferocity.

Even without armor and weapons, demons were lethally effective fighters; with arms they were even more terrifying. The slaughter was without pause, and on every hand demons went down in screams of pain, fountains of smoking blood, and body parts sailing through the air. It was butchery in every sense of the word.

Gulamendis replied, "I have no idea. A demonic revolt, by the look of it."

"There," said the Conjurer, pointing across the valley to the ridge opposite the one they hid behind.

In the distance, Laromendis could see what had caught his brother's attention. Atop the ridge rose a massive figure, dwarfing those around him. Still it was impossible to make out details at this distance. But enough could be seen to make it clear that group atop the distant ridge was orchestrating the assault on the demon horde encamped in the valley below.

Fliers from below rose up to meet those already overhead, and the two elves now saw the source of the massive concussions and explosions. The attackers' flying demons were carrying large objects that they released on the ground forces below and when they struck the ground, a massive amount of energy was released, throwing a tower of earth, smoke, flame, and bits of destroyed demons into the air. The early assault must have included assaults on positions closer to where the brothers hid, for these impacts were less severe.

Down three gullies from outside the valley a stream of attacking monstrosities came flooding. They rolled into the encamped army, caught up in the throes of panic, and the slaughter began in earnest.

"What is going on?" asked Laromendis.

"Can you conjure enough cover if needed for us to remain unseen?" asked his brother.

"Not for long."

"If what I think is happening is happening, we won't need long. Come, we must hurry."

The Demon Master headed off at a trot, staying just below the ridge and following it around the rim of the valley. Occasionally the ground shook, but the air assault ceased as the two opposing forces became entwined in hand-to-hand combat. Every so often, Gulamendis would peer over the edge, then motion for this brother to follow along.

They reached an outcropping of rocks, from which they could observe what went on from a better vantage, and Laromendis asked, "Do you recognize any of them?"

By them he meant those demons perched on the rim of the valley. Now they were close enough that Gulamendis could make out some details. The demon in the center was massive, perhaps twenty or twenty-five feet tall, with gigantic wings folded behind him. He might have been a true flier once, or the wings might just be for a more impressive visage when he unfolded them, but the Demon Master doubted the creature could truly fly without magic. On either side waited demons of a type Gulamendis had never encountered before, black-skinned monstrosities that were roughly half human from the waist up and some sort of lizard creature below. Long tails dragged behind and they were constantly watching in all directions.

"I think those two," he said softly, pointing to the half-lizard demons, "are guards or companions of some sort." He made a small circular motion with his finger as he pointed. "The rest are battle demons, but I've never seen them standing motionless, and never have seen them wearing armor and bearing arms."

He kneeled and said, "We're seeing something very new here."

"What?"

"I'll tell you when we have a little more leisure," said Gulamendis. "The big one is either the Demon King, Maarg, or someone who looks a great deal like the description Pug gave me."

"Didn't Pug also tell you Maarg was found dead on some other world?"

"Well," said Gulamendis, "there's dead and then there's dead. I've been dispatching demons back to their own realm for years, and have even destroyed a few in this realm, but I can't really say if they died or just went back where they came from in a messier fashion." He glanced back over the rocks. "If I'm right, we should find a way out of there down behind those monsters."

"We'd better move, because this battle is going to be over soon, and I don't want to be here when the victors start looking around for more things to chew on."

The Demon Master nodded. "Be ready to make us look like rocks if needed."

"I'll try," answered his brother.

They moved slowly, checking their progress every ten yards or so, and then suddenly Gulamendis halted his brother. "Something's not right."

"What do you mean," asked the Conjurer.

"I can sense demons all over this valley. It's like a throng shouting at me, but from ahead . . . nothing."

"Nothing?"

"If I close my eyes, there are no demons up on that ridge."

Laromendis peeked over the rise and studied for a moment, then said, "Something is odd."

"What do you see?"

"Be silent, but watch for a few minutes, then tell me what you see."

The two brothers ventured another look at the demons on the ridge, now less than a couple of hundred yards away. Even from this distance the forms were massive and could clearly be seen.

The Demon King stood with his arms crossed over his obscenely large stomach, his face a mask of evil glee as he glared down on the struggle with burning red eyes. Suddenly his hand shot up into the air and he motioned, as if urging his followers onward, but no more reinforcements were coming. "Why is he signaling the attack when it is almost done?" asked Laromendis.

"Because he's not signaling an attack. Come with me," said Gulamendis as he crouched and hurried along just below the circling rocks that shielded them from sight.

They scurried along, keeping out of sight as best they could, then when they were closer than Laromendis felt comfortable with, Gulamendis said, "Look, brother!"

They peered at the assembled demons and saw the Demon King signal the attack again. "What—?" Then Laromendis closed his eyes. "I'm a fool. It's a conjuration."

"A very good illusion, from what I can tell. Anyone else, even you, dear brother, who can't sense demons, isn't going to get close enough to see that this is all a trick of lights and magic."

"But why?"

"We can ponder that later," said Gulamendis. "We need to find a way home, or at least somewhere away from here. Those demons came from somewhere else, and why they were lured here to be slaughtered by their own kind is a matter for another time; right now we need to see if there's a gate of some sort down that side of the mountain."

He hurried, unconcerned about being seen by the illusions nearby, and Laromendis followed. The fatigue of days

of privation were offset by the excitement of possibly finding a safe route off this desert planet, and they moved as
beings possessed.

As they moved below the illusions, they found a wide
trail, and realized it was freshly trampled by thousands of
feet. "Well, now we know the attacking army is real," said
Laromendis.

"Demons can't be fooled that long," said his brother. "I
thought you'd have discovered that when they started ignoring your conjurations and started attacking us."

"I thought perhaps in a melee, with blood and screaming demons on all sides, they might not have the facility to
judge if there was enough demon stench in the air," said the
Conjurer as they descended quickly down the trail, almost
running.

"Point taken," conceded his brother. "Still, you're the
Conjurer. Could you create the illusion of an army on that
scale?"

"No," said Laromendis, his breath beginning to come
hard. "No one could. It would take a dozen as good as me,
I think. And then it wouldn't endure long. That's a great
deal of magic being used. To achieve it for a long period at
this level, it would take a hundred better than me."

"Well, let's hope whoever's behind this monstrous betrayal is too occupied with whatever he's doing up there—
or whatever they're doing up there—to notice the two of us
slipping away."

Suddenly the hair on their arms stood up and both slid
to a halt, dust rising from their sliding feet.

"What's that?" asked Gulamendis.

"A barrier . . ." Laromendis reached out and drew his
hand back. "It doesn't hurt, but it's not particularly pleas-
ant, either."

"What is it?"

Pushing with his fingers, Laromendis said, "I think
it's . . ." He stepped forward.

And vanished from his brother's sight.

"Laro!" shouted the Demon Master.

Abruptly a hand reached out of the air and grabbed him by the arm, yanking him forward.

"Where are we?" asked Gulamendis.

Wherever it was, it wasn't the desert world upon which they had stood only a moment before.

They stood in an empty marshaling yard, in a massive black stone fortress. Walls thirty feet high rose up on all sides of an open area two hundred yards across, by a hundred deep. Above them rose a keep unlike anything they had seen. If the castle created by the Black Sorcerer had been designed to warn away passing ships, sight of this fortress would have scared the sailors to death.

The sky above was a canopy of black clouds, so thick it was impossible to tell the time of day, or night. They were lit from below by an angry red light from a series of volcanoes that surrounded this place. Lightning exploded across the sky in the distance, and moments later was followed by peals of thunder that could be felt.

"Where are we?" repeated Gulamendis.

His brother grabbed his arm and pulled him into the relative shelter of a shadow where a tower rose up to form a corner with the wall behind them. In the distance a large figure walked out of the entrance of the vast fortress that rose up across the yard, and even though it was three hundred feet distant, they could see it for what it was—a massive battle demon, perhaps a dozen feet tall. It moved with purpose, but rather than attacking them, it moved at an oblique angle to their position, seemingly intent upon some business. Like those they had seen on the world from which they had fled, this one wore armor and carried a massive two-handed sword strapped across its back.

"Is this the demon realm?" asked Laromendis.

"It can't be," answered his brother.

"Why not?"

"Because if it was the Fifth Circle, we would be almost certainly dead by now. Everything we know about the Fifth Circle says we would die within minutes if we weren't protected by strong magic."

"Kosridi," said Laromendis.

"Yes," said his brother, referring to the tales they had learned about the human magician Pug and his allies traveling to the Second Circle. "On the other hand," said Laromendis, "who is to say the laws within the Fifth Circle are the same."

"I'll argue theory later," said Gulamendis. "Despite what we just saw, I'm not getting very much . . ."

"I can't sense any demons."

"Another illusion."

Gulamendis slapped the wall of stone behind him and felt the palm of his hand sting. "What do you think?"

Laromendis closed his eyes for a moment, touched the wall, then said, "If it's a conjured fortress, whoever did it has the powers of a god."

"Let's see if we can find a place to hide while we decide what to do next," said Gulamendis.

Setting off along the base of the wall, staying as deep in the shadows as they could, the two elves who stood seven feet in height tried to make themselves as small and inconspicuous as possible.

"This may not be the demon realm," said Laromendis, "but the air is choking."

"All that smoke and ash in the air," whispered his brother.

"Who builds something like this in a place like this?"

"I have no idea," replied Gulamendis. "Over there." He pointed to a small building that appeared to have been constructed after the wall. It appeared to be a simple wooden structure, a shed or storage room.

They crept along. There didn't appear to be anyone at hand since they spied the one demon crossing the marshaling yard, but they had no idea who might be observing them from any one of the hundred or so windows in the keep above. It reared high overhead, at least a dozen stories, a massive malignant black presence against the evil red-and-grey sky above.

"Fliers!" said Gulamendis, pointing above the top of the keep.

In the sky a dozen black specks appeared against the red glow and then vanished, only to reappear a moment later, growing larger. "They're coming this way," said the Conjurer.

"Let's see what's in here," said Gulamendis, opening the unlatched door.

Inside the hut sat sacks and boxes, arranged in a roughly organized fashion. When the door was closed, they were plunged into darkness.

The building was a rough construction, and there were cracks between the boards. The brothers peered through them and suddenly large winged demons descended into view, landing in the marshaling yard and assuming a rough formation, two lines of six each.

"They are waiting for something," said Gulamendis.

"What?"

"I don't know."

"What do we do now?" asked Laromendis.

"Well, as going anywhere is out of the question for the moment, I suggest we just sit here quietly and watch."

Thinking of nothing else to say, Laromendis fell silent.

Hours passed with nothing of significance occurring in the courtyard, and after a while the sun rose high enough to give faint illumination; like others of their race, the two elves were able to see in light that would challenge a cat.

"What have we here?" said Laromendis, almost absently, pulling down a sack from a large shelf on the back wall. The bag fell open and red round fruit fell out. "Apples!" he said.

Gulamendis didn't hesitate, but grabbed up one of the orbs and bit deeply. It was not the freshest he had ever eaten, but the dry cool storage had preserved most of the fruit's flavors and his stomach almost heaved from the unexpected treat.

"What's in the other bags?" asked his brother as he bit down into his second apple. He began a haphazard examination, opening bags, using his heavy knife to pry off the tops of boxes, and as he went, the brothers both began to wonder.

The boxes and bags contained provisions and clothing. The clothing was human-sized, too big for dwarves, too small for the Taredhel, and certainly not of a fashion for the other elven tribes.

"What is this?" wondered Gulamendis.

"I don't know, but have some of this," said his brother, tossing him a hunk of dried meat.

Gulamendis bit greedily into the jerky and began chewing. "What is this place?"

"You know more about demons than anyone I know; what do you think?"

"Demons eat everything when they see it. They suck life from the living, and then go after whatever's left." He made an encompassing gesture and added, "They don't store fruit, or dry meat. This is not demon food."

"Then who does it belong to?"

"Let's get some rest and eat and then we shall go and find out," suggested Gulamendis.

Laromendis said, "I don't have any better idea. Eat, then let us rest, and if no one disturbs our repose, we'll venture out after dark and discover what we can."

"As you said, I don't have a better idea."

They sat and began eating.

The day passed slowly. Twice they held themselves ready to fight as a company of demons marched by, but no one seemed to show much interest in this unexpected pantry. The two conjectures they had arrived at to explain this storage shed were that the original builders of this monstrous fortress were mortals, not demons, and the place had been overrun by the Demon Legion, or that the demons had it built for reasons yet unclear. Given the size and look of the place, the latter seemed a more reasonable conjecture.

The sky darkened and again the massive fortress fell quiet, and finally Gulamendis said, "We need to explore."

"Why?" said his brother, already knowing the answer. "Very well," he conceded before Gulamendis could voice his argument. "I know, we can't stay here forever, even if there's enough food for it."

His brother smiled and nodded, pointing over his shoulder in the general direction of the fortress. "If there's any way out of here, off this world to one that will lead us back to Home, it is in there."

"These are the times I wish we'd spent less time learning magic and more times learning how to sneak about unseen, like our forest cousins."

"It's a difficult choice," said Gulamendis. "We can skulk about, or you can enchant us to look like something else, but then we'd reek of magic to anyone sensitive to that."

"What's you're best guess, Demon Master?"

"With this bunch, I have no idea," he admitted. "They don't act like any demons I have ever encountered . . ." He fell silent a moment, then said, "Neither those camped in the valley nor those attacking remotely resembled the monsters we faced on Andcardia.

"It's as if we've encountered an entirely new breed of demon."

"What of their look?" Laromendis asked.

Gulamendis shrugged. "Before all this, I thought myself

familiar with demons, but I have seen more creatures new to me in the last few days than I have my entire previous life. Demons tend to a type, battle demons are large and powerful, but they can look like bulls or lizards or bulls and lizards, or lions or . . ." He shrugged. "Fliers tend to be small, but we've seen some very large nasty ones I've never encountered until we were on Hub. I've even seen demons in magician's robes." He sighed. "I wish that human Warlock was around to talk with; he knew a great deal, as did his friends Pug and Magnus."

"If we get Home, let's go visit," suggested his brother, dryly, "but until we do, turn our attentions to the matter at hand; illusions or skulking?"

"Skulk," said Gulamendis. "Save your energies for other conjurations."

"Skulk it is," said Laromendis, carefully opening the door.

The marshaling yard to their left was empty and the shortest distance to the side of the massive keep was directly across from them. "If someone's watching from one of those windows above, we will be seen," said Laromendis softly.

"It's dark," said his brother. "If we hurry—"

Not waiting another moment, Laromendis dashed out of the large storage shed and his brother exited, pausing only to close the door behind, then set out after his brother at a full run. It was not a vast distance, less than fifty yards, but it felt like they were exposed to view on every side for the longest time.

Hugging the keep wall, they paused, listening for any sounds of alarm. When none was forthcoming, Gulamendis said, "Now what?"

"That way," said his brother, pointing to the rear of the keep.

"Why that way?"

"Would you rather try to walk in the main entrance?"

"Point taken," conceded the Demon Master, and the two elves hunkered down and moved toward the rear of the keep.

Reaching a tower, they moved around its base, until they were looking at a large rear yard, half the size of the marshaling yard. Laromendis whispered, "I see steps leading down to a basement door, and a broad flight of steps leading up beyond that."

"Down," said Gulamendis. "Let's sneak in through the basement."

"Have you wondered why there are no guards?"

"I presume they're all too busy obliterating other demons on wherever it was we were before we came through the portal to here."

"One can hope, but I still find it odd we only saw that one lone demon and those two small patrols," Laromendis observed.

"Count it a blessing and move on!" hissed his brother.

They made a dash for the steps leading down and found themselves before two large doors. The latch was unsecured, and Laromendis gently pulled the nearest door open just enough to peer through. "It's a long, dark stairway," Laromendis whispered.

"Is there anyone there?"

"Not that I can see." The Conjurer slipped through the door, his brother following.

"This is the height of madness," said the Demon Master.

"If I push you back to the wall, do not move. I'm going to make us look like part of the stones."

As plans went, it didn't seem a particularly brilliant one, but Gulamendis didn't have a better one so he said nothing.

They moved down a very long tunnel that took them deep into the basement of the keep. When it finally ended, in a large chamber, Gulamendis judged they were at least three stories below the surface. The chamber had four doors, the open one through which they had just stepped, two other open doorways with stairs leading up, and a barred, heavy wooden one across from them.

"That one," whispered Laromendis.

His brother gave him a tiny push from behind signaling agreement and they quickly crossed the open room. The door had a small, barred window, and they peered through it. "It's a dungeon!" said Gulamendis.

Through the small window they could see a long hallway, with cells on the right with floor-to-ceiling bars. On the other side three large heavy wooden doors, like the one through which they peeked, were evenly spaced.

In the barred cells they could see a dozen captives, humans, dwarves, and elves. The last were lesser kin to the Taredhel, being of similar stature to the two brothers. "What is this?" whispered Laromendis.

"Demons don't take prisoners," whispered Gulamendis back.

"What now?"

"I have no idea."

In a dungeon beneath an impossible keep, on a world unknown to them until the day before, created by beings also unknown to them, the two elven brothers stood motionless, crippled by having no idea of what they should do next.

CHAPTER 10

Demon Lore

Jim groaned.

The festivities had lasted far too late for him to be welcoming the dawn, yet Pug, Magnus, and Amirantha had come into his room at first light, pulled aside the draperies, and insisted he awake.

"Water," Jim croaked.

Amirantha picked up an earthen pitcher on the night table next to the huge bed Jim occupied and filled an earthen mug with water. He handed it to the noble who took it and drank. Then Magnus noticed a large lump moving in the bed next to Jim. Magnus poked his father with his elbow and pointed, and Amirantha followed the gesture.

"Ah," said Pug. "We will wait in the antechamber until you get composed."

"Thank you," Jim said, his voice still gravelly from the previous night's debauchery.

Once outside they retired to a divan against the wall and sat. Pug said, "I should have thought of bringing a powder for this sort of thing."

"Which?" asked Magnus.

Lowering his voice, Pug said, "Years ago, before I met your mother, I had occasionally indulged in a little too much wine. A healing priest from the Order of Killian had this powder that one mixes with water to banish the effects of too much drink the night before—very effective. And, it turned out, easy to make. No magic involved; just the right mix of herbs and tree bark—"

The door opened and a very attractive young woman slipped out quietly. With a very slight smile she barely nodded at the three men and hurried across the room, to the hall door. She was dark of hair and eyes and wore the garb of a servant, though she was barefoot at the moment.

"Wonder where she left her boots?" asked Amirantha. "Wonder if she remembers where she left her boots?" he amended as he laughed.

Magnus seemed less than amused. "We have some serious work here for the next few days," he said.

Amirantha put his hand on the white-haired magician's shoulder and said, "You sound disapproving. If Jim wishes to go through the day with his head pounding and stomach turning, that's his prerogative. We had a good night's rest and once we've eaten, we'll be off to do our work. The state of his health isn't a matter for concern today, is it?"

Magnus shook his head and said, "Sorry. I worry too much."

"Takes after his mother," said Pug, and Amirantha was struck by the fact that this was Pug's first reference to his late wife that didn't contain a note of sadness. He hoped that was a sign the magician's black moods were behind him. Too much depended on Pug's leadership in the coming fight.

A few minutes later, Jim appeared, looking far more composed than any of the three had expected. He smiled and said, "We dine," and led them to the door leading out of the apartment he occupied.

As if anticipating his need, an Imperial servant waited to guide them to a small alcove overlooking one of the seemingly endless gardens within the palace. Rather than lying on a divan to eat, they sat upon large cushions around a low table. A variety of foods was provided, several Kingdom dishes like fried cake and savory sausage, as well as the more traditional sweet Quegan delicacies. To everyone's delight, a large pot of steaming Keshian coffee sat alongside a near boiling pot of water and an infuser with one of the more exotic teas from Novindus.

Jim ate like a man who had starved for a week, and when he noticed the others staring at him, he said, "I worked up an appetite last night."

"Apparently," said Magnus with a slight smile.

"You scholars can slight the Emperor's generosity if you wish, and I don't denigrate your reasons, but it would have been an insult had I left the festivities too early last night."

"We noticed," said Amirantha. "She was very pretty."

"Very smart, too," said Jim. "I managed to get out of the orgy by getting off in a corner with a particularly attractive server, which given the differences in our cultures, my host assumed had something to do with Kingdom modesty."

Pug began to smile. "She was a spy."

"Of course, and if I get back this way any time soon, I'm going to do my best to turn her." As if to himself he said, "Though if she won't turn, I'll have to kill her and that would simply be a waste." Looking at his three companions, he said, "It was a certainty the Quegan intelligence service would have several agents watching us."

"The young woman seated with me?" asked Pug.

"No," said Jim. "She is what she says she is: the minor daughter of a very minor noble, who if the Emperor can't marry off to some minor functionary"—he waved his hand at Pug—"will have to marry off to some distant cousin, and this Emperor would rather save himself even that modest dowry." Looking at Amirantha, he said, "That voluble fellow who bent your ear last night, now he is one of the service's best men. I doubt you even know how much you told him."

"Only the truth," said Amirantha. "The questions he asked about my homeland were obvious, but it was equally obvious after a while that I knew little he would find useful. He asked about the Maharaja's army, and I said it was big. I had no idea how big—which is true—just big."

Jim grinned, and took a drink of coffee. "You have the makings of a good spy, Amirantha."

"I gamble," said Amirantha. "I expected anyone asking a lot of questions could read a lie, so I find limited truth works well in those situations."

"Ah," said Jim. "We must play cards sometime."

"What are we doing today?" asked Magnus, already knowing roughly the plan, but not the details.

Jim chewed a mouthful of juicy melon, then swallowed. "I meet with functionaries until midday, at which time I dine with a few minor nobles—the Emperor and anyone of rank are done with me—and then I'll come find you in the archives.

"You three will be about your business and someone will see to your midday meal. After we dine tonight, we'll discuss the next day's work."

They all understood that meant stealing the Great Book of Demons should they locate it, but no one spoke of it.

They finished eating and when they were ready, servants came to escort them to their different destinations.

Pug, Magnus, and Amirantha were led through a series of long hallways and across several large galleries and

141

gardens, until they started down a long tunnel which they took to indicate they were heading into a portion of the palace excavated from the very soil under the palace.

When they emerged into the sunlight, they could see they were now on the back side of the rolling hills that supported the palace, looking down at a far less populated portion of the city. There were still ample houses and estates nearby, but below there the jumble of merchant and poor houses was minimal. Instead they could see an ancient wall beyond which a vast rolling series of hills, atop tablelands, were dotted with farms.

They trudged down the long road to another entrance, this one into a long and low façade with a dozen large windows, but most of the building had been constructed back into the hillside. "Gentlemen," said the servant, "we are here."

He turned and left, and the three magic-users exchanged glances.

"We are here," echoed Amirantha mirthfully.

Pug smiled, nodded, and indicated they should enter.

Once inside, Pug saw a long hall and off to the left a gallery illuminated by the sunlight streaming in from the tall windows. Two long tables trisected the room, and around them were arranged chairs. Opposite the windows were the end-caps of a half dozen shelves, each with books arrayed so that the spines were out.

A woman sat waiting and seeing the three men enter, she rose and crossed to them, a smile on her face. "Richard, how nice."

"Livia," said Pug, bowing slightly. "I believe you met my companions."

"Yes," she said, "albeit briefly. Martin, Amirantha. It's a pleasure to see you once more."

Amirantha's expression broadened. "As it is mine," he replied. "I was sorry I didn't have the opportunity to speak with you last night. Perhaps . . . ?" He let the question hang.

She glanced at Pug as if gauging his reaction, then said, "Perhaps. Now, what may I do to help?"

Pug said, "Martin and I are commissioned by the King of Isles and the Prince of Krondor to investigate certain discrepancies in our relative histories, especially looking for accounts of the period after Kesh's withdrawal from the region, but prior to the Kingdom's expansion westward through Yabon."

"I think I know where to start you," said Livia. Looking at Amirantha, she said, "And you?"

"I have a different charge, from my master, the Maharaja. At this point, I would be interested in subjects of a mystical nature."

"Mystical?" she said, as if not quite understanding.

"Our faiths are much the same as yours, but apparently there are some differences. Our gods have different names, and slightly different aspects."

"How odd," she commented. Then realizing she sounded judgmental she quickly amended that by saying, "I mean, it's odd that there are differences, not that your view is odd."

"I took your meaning," said Amirantha with a broad smile. "It might help my understanding if you could show me anything on . . . non-faith tales of magic and spirits, ghosts, and demons, let us say. Sometimes the tales of the villages and towns give us more insight into the beliefs of a people than the official records of the government or temples."

"I'll see what I can do," she replied. "Let me get you two"—she said to Magnus and Pug—"situated, then we"—she said to Amirantha—"will start looking for folk stories and legends."

With a smile and a nod, Amirantha conveyed he was amenable to this, and for a reason he couldn't quite put his finger on, Pug found himself annoyed.

They moved off down the hall, toward the rear of the archives.

Amirantha stood with his mouth closed only by conscious will. The term "jaw dropping" had entered his mind as he stood looking at a mountain of tomes, books, scrolls, and codices. There was one table in the far corner of the room, and no chair.

Livia said, "I'm sorry, but for the sort of thing you're looking to find, this is the most likely spot." She gently touched his arm, which he found both reassuring and distracting. "My people, as you will no doubt discover, are predisposed to three, no make that four, issues. Glory, both military and commercial, comprise two of the four. The third is self-aggrandizement, for I will confess we are a vain culture. Lastly, pleasures of the flesh, which you would have discovered had you remained at the banquet last night."

Amirantha tried to appear disinterested. "I've been to an orgy before, Livia."

"As have I, and like you I left before it began, but what I'm trying to say is, if it's not wealth, war, vanity, or lust, it's in there." She pointed to the massive mount of writings.

"So what you're saying is that Richard and Martin"—he used Pug's and Magnus's false names—"are likely to find only officially blessed histories where they are researching."

"No, they are finding the only histories not fed to the fire. However, there may be one thing or another in this mess that might provide them with a clue or two about what really happened in years past. However, for your research, any discussions of folktales, myths, superstitions, reports of encounters with the gods—not sanctioned by the temples, of course—or anything else you might find intriguing, it's in there." She again pointed to the mass.

Amirantha was silent a moment, then said, "I have three requests."

"What may I do to accommodate you?" she said with a clear double meaning as she studied the still-handsome Warlock.

He smiled his most charming smile and said, "First, could you arrange to have a pot of hot water and some tea brought to that table over there? I will not risk spilling anything on these old volumes, but I do prefer to refresh myself from time to time."

"Of course. What else?" she asked, touching his arm again.

"Could I have a ladder?" He inclined his head toward the mass and said, "It would be better for whatever is in there if I took the volumes off from the top down. A small ladder, ten feet tall or so, should serve."

She laughed, and he found the sound of it and her look delightful. "Of course. I'll have that sent along at once."

"Could you provide me with a servant, to haul books aside if I don't wish to look at them, and have him bring along some writing implements and paper or parchment as I wish to take notes."

"Of course," she said, though he noticed at once her manner was cooling.

Understanding a moment was slipping away, he added, "Perhaps I should have said four things. Would you dine with me tonight?" He quickly added, "Assuming Lord James doesn't insist on the three of us dining with him, of course."

She hesitated only a moment, not wishing apparently to appear too anxious, and said, "If your sponsor doesn't require your presence, I would enjoy supper with you."

She turned and in a playful fashion looked over her shoulder and said, "I'll have the tea, ladder, and servant sent to you at once." Her smile could only be called seductive, as she added, "And I'll come back later to see if there is anything else you need."

"Thank you," said Amirantha, fully enjoying watching her walk away. The long Quegan toga might run from shoulder to floor, but it hugged her curves in a most tantalizing fashion.

Taking his mind off the lovely woman, he turned and began to consider the prodigious task before him. Sighing, he reached out and took a book at random off the pile. He opened it and found it to be written in a language alien to him. Glancing around to ensure he was unobserved, he took from his belt pouch a small item Pug had given him before they arrived in Queg. He did as he had been taught and incanted a short phrase, holding the trinket to his forehead, then put it away. When he opened his eyes, the letters on the page seemed to swim, then come together in words he could read. Softly to himself, he muttered, "I should have met these people a hundred years ago!"

Now able to read this ancient Quegan text, he began to read softly aloud. "'On the matter of the stars and their locations in the heaven by seasons . . .'" He read another page, then put aside the amateur astronomy text and looked around. To no one he said, "You know what you want is at the bottom of that pile, don't you?"

"Sir?" came a voice from behind.

"Oh," said Amirantha, seeing two servants in the doorway. One held a tray with a pot and infuser, a cup, and a canister of tea, and the other held a short ladder. "Never mind." He pointed to the stocky man with the ladder and said, "Put that over there and climb to the top, and *gently* pull down the topmost book." To the other he said, "Put that on the table, please . . ." As the servant moved to do as he was instructed, Amirantha said, "And find me a chair for that table. Thank you." He turned his attention to the man climbing the ladder and the job that lay before him.

The day wore on, and Amirantha drank two pots of tea. Other than having to relieve himself three times before lunch, his morning was uneventful; there was nothing remarkable about his findings. He had chanced across a few interesting things, a treatise on higher consciousness and the gods—which he found more compelling for the absolutely blind leaps of faith than he did for any compelling evidence to support the hypothesis, but done in language both precise and elegant. He found himself admiring it despite it having no relevance to his current search.

There was one interesting account of a very bad famine, more family chronicles than he imagined possible; the Quegans were a self-aggrandizing people beyond his imagination. Even modestly successful merchants had commissioned family histories—most of which were far more fanciful than fact, he surmised. One particularly vivid but improbable tale concerned a merchant from the Kingdom city of Krondor who had contrived to build a fortune out of thin air, or so he claimed.

There were a couple of interesting finds, beyond their value as quaintly curious; a book of "dark spells" that had more truth in it than the author understood; anyone with a talent for magic would recognize elements in it. He put it aside in case Pug or Magnus might be curious.

Another work was a chronicle of a struggle between two temples, neither of which he recognized. The magic he used to read foreign languages did not make the understanding of proper nouns any easier. Someone named Rah-ma-to was named Rah-ma-to, and his only insight into that worth anything was context. He might be a local god, a local name for one of the gods he knew, or a farmer, for all Amirantha knew. Still, it touched on something of myth and magic, so he set it aside.

Other volumes were likewise curiosities, but nothing remotely akin to the information he was seeking. He wondered if Pug and Magnus were having any more luck.

Time of the midday meal was announced by the arrival of Livia. The charming Quegan woman seemed amused by the sight of Amirantha on his knees stacking books. "Are you finding anything?"

He pointed to a dozen volumes stacked over on the table next to the empty—again empty—teapot and said,

"Those look promising." He exaggerated, but he wanted to make this look like a worthwhile undertaking to bolster his need to return.

"I've come to take you to the archivists' quarters, where a repast has been provided."

He rose up and found his knees slightly stiff. Feigning more discomfort than he felt, he said, "I need walk a bit more, I think. Too many days of sitting and I'm turning into an old man."

She smiled as she slipped her arm through his in a gesture of familiarity. Amirantha had dealt with flirtatious women all his life and knew he had been judged and found appropriate enough to warrant further scrutiny. He considered the oddity of this culture's social constraints if a woman this attractive and bright might consider a foreign scholar of modest means a suitable substitute for a man of rank in her own nation; then he remembered women of her age who saw their child-bearing years coming to a close and reconsidered. She might be ready to marry the first man who asked.

He sighed and considered his need for pleasure and weighed it against possible injury to her.

"What?" she asked.

"I'm sorry," he replied.

"You sighed, and a rather heavy one at that."

He smiled. "Oh, just the amount of material yet to be considered is daunting," he lied. He would dismiss the servant after lunch. The pile was manageable enough now for him to sort through it, and now that he was becoming used to the manner in which Quegans recorded their personal histories, business records, and the other sea of useless trivial piled up inside the archives, he should be able to get through the bulk of this by supper.

"Perhaps you might stay longer?"

He smiled as he looked at her and saw that his instincts in this were almost certainly correct; this woman needed to find a husband and start a family. With a pang he realized that he didn't find the idea repellent, just impossible.

He shook his head. "As I understand it, the agreement between your Emperor and the King of Isles is three days, no longer. As I am but a companion to the official researchers . . ." He shrugged.

"I might talk to someone," she ventured.

"I live a very long way from here," he said neutrally, but she took his meaning.

She fixed him with a narrow gaze and pulled away ever so slightly. "You have a wife?"

"No, nothing like that," he said. "My work . . . consumes me."

"Ah," she said as if that explained everything.

They remained quiet until they reached the room set aside for their meal. A modest lunch by Quegan standards, but a small feast by anyone else's, was waiting for them. A moment after Amirantha had been shown through the door, Pug and Magnus arrived. Their escort and Livia withdrew, leaving the three of them alone.

"Anything interesting?" asked Pug as he picked up a stoneware plate and a long two-pronged fork and began putting cheese, meat, and fruit on his plate.

"Nothing worth being excited over," answered the Warlock. He pointed to a large pitcher of water then another with wine and his expression was a question.

"Water, please," said Magnus. "Wine with lunch and I'm asleep all afternoon."

Pug nodded, and Amirantha said, "Three goblets of water it is."

They assumed they were being overheard so they spoke in a fairly noncommittal fashion. They chatted and Amirantha finished his meal and said, "So, anything noteworthy?"

They knew he was asking if there was any clue that might help point him in his search under the massive pile of books.

Magnus said, "Quite a bit. It's clear that Kingdom records of the region are spotty at best."

That was a code phrase agreed upon telling Amirantha
they had found nothing that would aid his search.

After the meal, servants returned them to their respective areas and Amirantha felt a mild disappointment over
Livia not putting in an appearance. He cursed himself for
his appetites and willingness to construct reasons to do
what he wanted over the years, rather than what he should.
Since meeting Pug and his companions, many things had
left him profoundly changed in his view of the world in
which he lived: the scope of the dangers being faced, the
commitment and bravery of those undertaking the task of
confronting those dangers, and their generosity and selfless-
ness. But one thing had continued to leave him constantly
unsettled and troubled, and it had been something of minor
importance, he had once thought.

His encounter with Sandreena and Creegan had re-
opened old wounds, wounds he had not even admitted to
himself existed before that encounter.

To those like Brandos who knew him well, he was un-
apologetic about his bad behavior with women over the
years. He stopped a moment and considered the pile of
books still to be examined, yet he hesitated. His mind was
on the young Knight-Adamant from Krondor.

As a young man, like many young men do, he loved easily, or at least he had told himself it was love, but whatever it
was, he had felt strong attachments. But his life being what
it was, they never endured. By the time he found Brandos
as a boy scrabbling around the city streets, he had come
to not let his heart get involved. Women were creatures of
comfort, to be taken and then left behind, lest one became
attached and again faced loss in the end.

What he felt deepest was that he had cared a great deal
more for Sandreena than he had admitted, that the time they
had spent together in the oddly named little village north

of Krondor had forged something deeper than merely the physical or a liaison of convenience. He hated how he felt.

He forced aside this morbid introspection and cursed himself for a sentimental old fool trapped in a young man's body, and set about working on the volumes before him.

An hour into the afternoon, Amirantha began to sense something. He held a book in his hand and glanced at the title, then put it aside. He picked up the next and again felt the oddly familiar, yet nameless tingling. He cast aside that book and picked up two more. As he dug deeper into the pile, the sensation became more familiar, and more immediate.

It was demon.

He pushed his way downward, ignoring the damage he might be doing to ancient books—many of which were on the verge of falling apart due to improper storage in this very room—and felt the sense grow even more compelling.

His hand touched something and he recoiled as if experiencing a shock.

Trying to work as quickly as possible, yet not damage the object of his attention, he got the cover of the work clear and once he could clearly see the volume, his flesh crawled.

This volume was rife with demonic magic.

When he had at last cleared away the covered tome, he reached in and gripped it; the alien sense of demon magic assaulted him again, but this time he was ready for it.

He lifted the large volume off those below it and carried it over to the table. He gently put it down and studied it a moment before he touched it again.

He was almost certain the cover was skin; human, elf, or some other, he was unsure, but this book was bound by something that was once living and aware.

He opened the cover and let the magic spell Pug had given him serve him. The language may have been ancient and obscure, but he read it as easily as he did the first language he had learned as a boy.

Whispering aloud, he read the title page. "Greater Demon Lore."

Slowly he turned the first page and began to read.

After a few minutes his legs grew shaky and his stomach began to knot, but he kept reading, and slowly he sat in the chair offered and resisted the urge to run from the room screaming.

His mind rejected what he saw before him, but he kept reading for the rest of the afternoon.

From the moment they gathered at the end of the day to dine, it was evident to the others that Amirantha had something to tell them but was keeping silent lest they be overheard. When at last they were alone, Pug gave Magnus a questioning look. The younger magician nodded once, closed his eyes a moment, then said, "We have a few minutes; the magic they're using to spy upon us is poorly done, but if I counter it too much, someone may notice."

"What did you find?" Jim asked Amirantha.

"What we came for," he answered. "It is the Greater Demon Lore, and more."

"More?" asked Pug. "What is in it?"

"Apparently everything there is to know about demons," he said with barely contained excitement. "I consider myself a practiced Warlock; demons are my specialty. *I know nothing!*" He sat back. "There is more that I haven't finished reading, but I have read enough to already know something incredible is under way."

Pug glanced at Magnus. "Another minute, no more."

Amirantha said, "We can talk in detail later." He glanced at Jim. "After you steal the book."

Jim shrugged as if that would be a trivial issue; the library was not the Imperial Treasury. He could be in and out in minutes and have the volume secreted within his baggage before departure. As a diplomat, he would be spared any search of his personal items, and once at sea, the three magicians could pore over it to their hearts' content.

Amirantha said, "There is so much to consider." He paused, knowing they would have to keep silent in a moment. "The demons are so much more than we thought." He fell silent. "Much more," he repeated, then Magnus raised his hand and loudly said, "I found a recounting of the sea battle off of Questor's View, in the Fifteenth Year of the reign of Rodric the Third." Forcing a mild laugh, he added, "This account is quite different than what we found in the Royal Library at Krondor."

Talk turned to the mundane matters of academia and a few comments about the hospitality of the Quegans, all flattering, and each sat, quickly playing the role of innocent guest.

Jim considered the perfect timing to leave his quarters—without waking whoever was with him; he knew the Quegans would ensure he was not alone and whoever shared his bed was an agent. He could get out of his rooms, to the library, get the book once Amirantha gave him a precise description, and return in less than a half hour, perhaps as little as a quarter hour if he encountered no one along the short road from the place to the library.

Pug and Magnus shared the same thought: what had Amirantha found in that book?

And Amirantha sat silently, uncertain if he was even beginning to understand what he had uncovered and wondering if he was even capable of making sense out of it. For whatever he had imagined the demon realm to be like, if this book wasn't the total fabrication of a deluded mind, it changed everything he had ever thought he knew about demons and what his people called the Fifth Hell.

Amirantha placed the huge volume down on the table. Jim quipped, "Stealing it wasn't a problem. Getting it back without falling over was."

The tome was a foot and a half along the spine and half that per pages, about fifty or sixty pages of heavy vellum. It easily weighed fifty pounds—not a difficult load to carry, but impossible to hide. It was only as Jim observed that if the Quegans were expecting him to go skulking in the night, they thought he'd be pilfering state secrets or imperial treasure, not forgotten books.

They had left less than an hour before, and once clear of Queg's harbor and any observation, mundane or magic, Magnus had transported them to his father's study atop the tower at Sorcerer's Isle.

Amirantha looked as fascinated as a child opening a gift from Father Winter at the Midwinter's Festival. He pointed at it and said, "It should take me . . . only a day or two to determine if what is written in here is remotely true. If so . . ." He looked at Pug. "My newfound friend, the elf Gulamendis, he and I both came to our skills the hard way: trial and error. We may be among the few who survived that education, Pug, for I suspect a few lads and lasses who tried to conjure their first demon ended up with painful, deadly results.

"With this"—his finger poked at it for emphasis—"I would be twice the master of demon lore that I am now."

Pug said, "This sounds impressive."

"At the least you sound very enthusiastic," observed Jim.

Magnus shot him a sideways glance and then asked the Warlock, "Who wrote it?"

"I see no author named," replied Amirantha. "It may be stated somewhere in there; I only read a fourth of what was here before Livia took me back to call it a night.

"There are . . ." He caught his breath. "I don't know where to begin." He paused, then said, "My perception of the demon realm, what we call the Fifth Circle of Hell, is that it's a place of chaos, constantly shifting and violent, where the strong rise and take command." He let his voice drop. "It's so much more than that."

"They have . . . hierarchies." He held up his hand and could see he had both magicians' undivided attention, and even Jim was listening closely. "I, like you, thought that there was a demon king, Maarg, others before, perhaps after, but that he was simply the strongest, one who achieved his rank through combat, murder, terror, alliances with those seeking his protection . . ." He sighed.

"What is it?" asked Magnus.

"That's a slave class," said Amirantha.

"Slave class?"

"Like Keshian Dog Soldiers, trained killers, crazed, vicious, only good for one thing—fighting war. Even the imps are little more than criminals in their society."

"Criminals?" asked Jim, now obviously interested.

"They have a society," answered Amirantha. "They have builders . . . where did that hall you describe on the other side of the rift where Macros died fighting Maarg come from?" he asked Pug.

Pug blinked as if he had never thought of the question. "I saw it so briefly—"

"Yet you described it to me when you told me of Macros's death facing Maarg," said Amirantha.

"I thought it was some world . . ." He shrugged.

"One the demons had already conquered?" said Magnus.

Amirantha said, "I'll have to spend a few days studying this." He looked at Pug. "May I take it to my quarters?"

"Of course," said Pug.

Amirantha put his hands on the book, but instead of picking it up, he opened it to the very last page. That page was folded up, and as he unfolded it, the others could see that it had been tipped into the volume so that only a third of its length was attached to the spine, so that when it unfolded a four-foot-by-three-foot piece of heavy vellum was revealed.

"What is that?" asked Jim.

Almost grinning, the Warlock said, "Unless I'm mistaken, My Lord James Dasher Jamison, this is a map of hell!"

CHAPTER 11

ESCAPE

The brothers stood motionless.

Laromendis used all his arts to conceal their presence in the basement as a pair of demons escorted a handful of prisoners out of the cells. Only Gulamendis's demon sensitivity had alerted them in time. The quip of moments before became reality as they stood flat against the wall and the Conjurer made it look as if they were part of the wall.

The moments that passed were torturously slow yet eventually the door to the cell block was closed and the prisoners marched away. They had been a mixed group: four dwarves, two humans, and two elves. All were silent, sullen, yet not looking particularly fearful.

When the room was empty, Laromendis let the illusion fade. "What was that?"

"I couldn't understand the language," said his brother. "The demons are not speaking anything I recognize."

Since coming to this alien castle on this unknown world, they were confronted with one conundrum after another. The frustration that had gripped Gulamendis when he had first encountered the demon encampment on the previous world, raised to a maddening degree when he witnessed the assault by the rival demon faction, was now close to delivering him into near rage at not knowing what was occurring.

"We need information," said Gulamendis.

"Where do you suppose we get it?"

"I think our only choice is to go in there and talk to some of the prisoners."

"Are you mad?" asked Laromendis.

"Why? Do you think they might give us up to their masters?"

"If they think it will curry favor, perhaps!" argued the Conjurer.

"What do you suggest?"

"I think we try to find out more by ourselves. Let us get out of here and see what else we may discover." He sighed. "If we find no clear way home or at least a better sense of this place, we can always come back." He glanced around and said, "Besides, I'd rather strike up a conversation in there with our distant cousins when it's less likely we'd be surprised by guards."

Gulamendis inclined his head as he thought, then said, "Agreed. We might better be served to do it while the humans and dwarves slept. We can almost certainly count on our kin not to betray us."

"You have a better opinion of our people than I do, brother," said Laromendis. "Come on and stay close. If I have to suddenly conjure another illusion quickly, it's certain to be a small one."

"I shall be your virtual shadow," said his brother softly.

"Which way?" asked Laromendis.

"That way we came, opposite lie the cells. Across or behind? Let's go forward."

They set off softly and carefully, moving up the stairway that had been on their right side when they first entered the dungeon.

"Any other suggestions?" whispered Gulamendis.

"Keep still," hissed his brother, and they both backed down the hallway, ready to turn and run.

They had reached the top of the stairs and found themselves in a vast armory, and at the far end a group of demons were endeavoring to fit armor to what apparently were new recruits. With grunts and other guttural sounds, they communicated with them how to fasten the new chest-plates and helms. They were so intent on their task, they failed to notice the two elves who walked into the hall.

Gulamendis backed into the hallway as his brother tugged on his tunic. When they were back in the shadows, they turned and hurried down the stairs. When they were near the level of the entrance to the dungeon, they knelt and peered into the room. Seeing no movement, they hurried across the large expanse and paused. "That way," said Laromendis.

"This time a little slower, brother."

"Agreed."

They crept up the stairs.

Most of this huge keep was empty. The elves judged there was enough room for a thousand or more soldiers to be garrisoned in a host of now empty barracks rooms scattered throughout the massive structure. It was clear from this

The window was a vaulted affair, with a large cushioned window seat. They both could stand on it and peer through the dirty glass. "Can we open this? I can't see a thing," said Laromendis.

"It has a latch," answered his brother.

Gulamendis jumped down and his brother followed suit. The Demon Master tried the latch and found it reluctant, but it slowly released. He pulled on the window and found the hinges as reluctant as the latch. "No one has used this in a very long time."

Laromendis said, "Does any of that look familiar to you?"

Gulamendis looked and saw a dark and foreboding mountain range in the distance. The low light in the loft told him he was looking southward as the sun set behind the dark clouds. After a moment, Gulamendis said, "No, nothing."

"Can you see the fire peaks?" he asked, indicating the distant volcanoes.

"Of course," said Gulamendis. "Why?"

"See how that one massive one rises up on the right, while those other two look like smaller twins to the left?"

"Yes," said the Demon Master. "Does it mean something to you?"

"The Fire Twins."

"Could it be?"

"If you were miles to the south, looking northward . . ." said Laromendis.

"From the battlements of Can-ducar!"

"The twins would be on the right and the Fire Queen on the left!"

"How did we not know about this ancient fortress?" asked Gulamendis.

"We never got this far," answered the Conjurer. "Can-ducar was the northernmost fortification on Telesan when the demons appeared. We never occupied much of the world because of this foul smoke and ash. The only reason we had anyone here was for mining metals."

"Do you think that's why the demons have dwarven prisoners?"

"Possible," said Laromendis.

"Well," said his brother. "We have some idea where they came from, at least."

"Do we?"

Feeling defeat, the Demon Master said, "No. I mean, we know that portal in the wall by the gate leads to the world where we saw the demon battle, but we don't know where they came from originally."

Laromendis sat down in the gloom of the fading afternoon light. "We dare not light anything . . . assuming we can find tinder and flint, lest a light be seen, so we must wait until tomorrow to see if anything here is useful."

Gulamendis stood. "Help me get the door back on the hinges, just in case this is the one day they decide to investigate the top of the tower. Then one of us should go back to the storage shed and fill up a sack."

"I'll go," said Laromendis. "You were always the better scholar. See what you can make of this with what little light is left."

They quickly got the door back on its hinges and closed it to ensure it was secure. Then Laromendis left, closing the door behind and Gulamendis latched it shut. He looked at the many volumes on the shelves, wondering where to start, then he found his gaze drifting to one at the top, large and covered in leather. He reached up and when his fingertips touched it, he jerked his hand back. "Demon," he whispered. "Could this be—?" He pulled the book down and opened it. At once his vision swam and he recognized the writing, the arcane runic symbols of demon control. "Oh, my," he whispered as he sat down and began to read.

A short time later his brother returned with a sack full of food and said, "It's a good thing we vacated that shed.

When I got there some dwarves were leaving with food for the prisoners."

"Why didn't they find us last night?"

Laromendis shrugged and tossed an apple to his brother. "Perhaps they don't feed them every day." He started eating an apple as well and after a juicy bite, asked, "Find anything?"

"Yes," said his brother. "I think I may have found several important things."

"Such as?"

"Where the Demon Gate is that lets them into this realm."

"Really?" he seemed impressed. "What else?"

"Who or what may be at the heart of this madness."

Laromendis let out a slow sigh. "It's almost too dark to read. Finish that tomorrow." Elves were capable of seeing things on the darkest of nights, even if only starlight was the source, but without some light, reading ancient ink on parchment was beyond even their gifts.

"One other thing," said Gulamendis.

"What?"

With a broad smile he said, "I think I have found a way for us to get home."

Night dragged on and Laromendis repeated back what he had just been told to be certain he understood it. "So, this lair was the study of a human magician, by name Makras—"

"Macros."

"Macros, and he was the magician advisor to the local ruler."

"The King of Des."

"The King of Des. He discovered a portal, built by some unknown people in ages past."

"Yes."

Laromendis said, "So while experimenting with this device, he opened the portal."

"Yes, to a world . . . well, I will have to reread that part when the light returns."

Laromendis sat silently in the darkness a moment, then he said, "I'll skip the other parts. It's not the portal we came through to get here?"

"No, for he described its location as being in a nearby vale; I assume he meant nearby from where he was writing and I assume he was writing here."

"Well, let us say we can find this portal. How are we to operate it?"

"This is why I said 'I think' I have found a way home, instead of 'I know.' If there are controls we can use, I suggest we make for Home." Laromendis was about to object, but Gulamendis cut him off. "Not for E'bar, but for Sorcerer's Island."

"How?"

"I spent enough time near that portal in the keep on the island to . . . *I think*," he stressed, "I can contrive to get us there."

Laromendis was determined not to let his brother get his hopes up. "And what do we use for power?"

Gulamendis held up a small bag and even though his brother could barely see him in the gloom, he sensed his brother was smiling. "I took these from the dead galasmancer."

"Crystals?"

"Crystals."

Laromendis said, "As I don't have a better idea, can I suggest we leave now, take the volume with us, and read it somewhere far from here at first light?"

Gulamendis was loath to leave the treasure trove of ancient human magic behind, but saw the wisdom in getting out of this place when activity was at its lowest point. He took the volume and nodded once, and opened the door.

They moved purposefully but slowly down the circular stairs of the tower and at the base, looked down the long connecting hallway that would eventually lead them to the stairs back down to the dungeon, and then up to the yard. They made their way past silent doors and empty rooms and when they were once again in the dungeon, Gulamendis risked a hurried peek through the viewing window in the door to the cells. Prisoners were huddled together for warmth, all sleeping. There were no guards.

They moved as silently as possible and when they were once again at the low door that opened on the courtyard, Laromendis opened it a crack and peeked through. The three steps up to the surface were open and no one else was in sight.

They crept along the wall, staying as much as possible against it, despite being covered in darkness. With even a chance at freedom before them, they were loath to take even the slightest risk that they might bring failure upon themselves.

A quick stop in the storage shed and they loaded up with provisions. They were stymied for a short while when they reached the gate and found it bolted. They realized they had come in through a portal in the wall that emptied into the marshaling yard, and hadn't given any thought of getting through the gate. Logic dictated there was more than one way through the wall so a hurried examination of the defenses led them to a postern gate behind the keep. It was unguarded and they opened it and went outside.

"If I understand what it is we're looking for," said Gulamendis, "we need to start south."

"Toward the volcanoes and the battlefield?" asked his brother.

"Yes," said Gulamendis.

With a slight turn of his head to indicate acceptance, the Conjurer indicated his brother should lead the way. Into a very dark night two elves ventured, neither of them certain of where they where headed, but both knowing there was nothing good being left behind.

Dawn found Gulamendis and Laromendis sitting under the shelter of an overhang, eyes smarting from the acidic smoke that hung on the hillside like an ill-conceived cloud of suffering. The three volcanoes were belching smoke and ash into the sky on a regular basis, and at one point Laromendis had observed it would be just their luck to reach their destination when one of the three erupted, destroying the portal. He was uncertain if it would be fate's crueler irony to have them burned alive with the portal, or to stand on a relatively safe outcropping watching their last hope of escape go up in flames. He was inclined to think the second a more painful outcome.

His brother merely gave him a withering look and said nothing. As soon as he could, Gulamendis avidly began reading the volume he had purloined from the ancient keep. Finally he said, "As I understand this, these people, called the Edhara, were just beginning to experiment with portals. They had created the one we are seeking in a cave—I hope not too far from here—and had discovered a few relatively benign worlds. Then the demons found them."

"Found them?"

"Remember what Pug said about the nature of rifts?"

"Not really," said his brother. "I think that was a conversation you had while I was learning some things from that very odd creature from that world whose name I can't pronounce. The fellow with the blue skin and those things coming out of his neck, but whose illusions . . . they were stunning."

"From you, my not so modest brother, that is high praise," said Gulamendis.

"I'll grant him his due; he was very good."

"Rifts have a loadstone quality. As loadstones draw iron to them, rifts tend to draw other rifts. So if you have an established portal from one world to the next, if someone is casting about for a random destination, there's a better than average chance it will connect to a world that already has a portal on it."

"I wonder if that's why the galasmancer created Hub?"

His brother shrugged. "As the Regent's Meet didn't see fit to consult with me on the matter, I can only speculate." His finger stabbed a page. "From here to the end it's written very hastily.

"It reads much as the reports we had when our people first encountered the demons; massive assaults in chaotic fashion, no quarter asked or given, mindless wave after wave of demon of every stripe."

"Obviously something is different," said Laromendis. "Those demons we saw being slaughtered, and those in the keep to the north . . . they are nothing we've seen before."

"This is where it gets interesting," said Gulamendis. "Let me read: 'And then to our lord Hijilia came a herald of the demon kind, under a banner of truce, offering terms.' "

"A truce?" Thinking of the dozens of worlds overrun by the Demon Legion and the millions of Taredhel left dead on those worlds, he muttered, "We never got the offer."

"These Edhara didn't accept, in any event, vowing to fight to the end. The author of this chronicle began writing as if this was his last testament, and jammed in every detail he thought was important.

"The reason I think we might contrive to use the portal in the cave to get away is that was what the rulers of the Edhara were planning on doing. It's unclear to me if they managed to get away in time or if they reached the portal.

"The point is, if we manage to get out of here, and if we can reach Sorcerer's Island, and then E'bar, we have something vital to tell the Regent's Meet."

Laromendis was silent a moment, then said, "You mean we need to tell Tandarea."

Gulamendis fell silent also and then said, "It always comes back to that, doesn't it?"

"The Meeting cannot continue on the course it has been on for the last three hundred years, brother. The Circle of Light must be reformed, and all matters regarding magic need to be restored to it. Just a few months with those humans on Sorcerer's Island tells me that this is true; if you spoke to Magnus or Pug about their own history and learned of Pug's first attempt, the Academy at Stardock, and all the problems that created . . ." He took a breath. "Let's get home first."

Gulamendis said, "Let's. I think we can be there today if we leave now."

"In daylight?"

"Do you see anyone else around here?"

"No, but a few months ago there was a really massive battle taking place a few miles south of here," reminded the Conjurer.

"And as we abandoned this position, I doubt it's still in progress," said the Demon Master. "That would explain why there's only a small garrison in that huge fortress we just left, and why we were able to come and go as we pleased. They've gone somewhere else."

Laromendis stood up. "The thing that's annoying me most," he said, "is that there are still too many mysteries and odd goings-on. I'm a simple elf at heart; I make things appear out of thin air, and people give me things: food, gold, their daughter's virtue, a nice robe . . ."

"You have always thought like a brigand, and a brigand you are at heart." Gulamendis smiled. "Still, you're my brother and my brigand, and I shall stand with you."

For the first time in days Laromendis felt like returning his brother's smile. He clapped him on the shoulder and said, "As it should be. You may consort with the foulest of beings, but I shall be at your side to the end."

"Let us go."

As they walked to the south, Laromendis said, "A question I've been meaning to ask for some time now . . ."

"Yes?"

"Remember when that human girl, Sandreena, was saying all those things about Amirantha?"

Gulamendis laughed. "How could I forget?"

"Remember that part about a summoned creature named Dalthea? A female of extraordinary beauty, as I recall."

"A demon who looked like a beautiful human woman. Yes, I remember. He conjured a succubus and modified her to look beyond compare."

"Imagine a totally obedient beautiful female elf? Do you know that trick?"

Gulamendis, for the first time in almost a century, hit his brother in the arm.

Midday and the two brothers were getting closer to the volcanoes. The air was rich with the stench of burning ash and their eyes stung from low-hanging smoke—there was almost no wind today. That helped mask them from casual observation, but it also made their lungs and eyes hurt.

The landscape was now exclusively a rugged sea of basalt rock—large, relatively smooth patches of light grey to black sheets, interrupted by jagged outcroppings of upthrust stone. At times their weight would crack the rock below as they stepped on the relatively thin top of a bubble, occasionally releasing a cloud of noxious, sulfurous gas. Once Gulamendis dropped partway into a gas dome and his brother had to help pull out his right leg. The edges of the rock were sharp and they had to move slowly to avoid injury at almost every step.

"Who would want this miserable place?" asked the Demon Master.

"We did, for a while," said Laromendis. "Besides the crystals that come out of these volcanoes, there are huge deposits of metals on this world." He glanced around, as if gaining his bearings. "I spent a little time here, early on when I was exploring for the Regent's Meet, and the mines to the south of here, on the other side of our abandoned fortress . . . impressive is all I can say. There was copper, silver, iron, gold." He took a deep breath, then coughed. "How far?"

Gulamendis paused to read out of the journal just to ensure he was not making any mistakes. "If I understand this correctly, we climb that ridge there"—he pointed to the south, and Laromendis could see there was a high ridge about a mile away. He saw a notch that looked as if it might be navigable, as a long flow of basalt created a relatively smooth ramp leading up to it. "On the other side."

They moved slowly, taking their time, and an hour later made it to the top of the notch in the ridge. They surveyed the landscape and Laromendis said, "Gods and fathers!"

Before them spread out mile after mile of more twisted and broken rock. In the distance they could see gas plumes and steam vents, and they knew they were reading the outer boundary of volcanic activity. Since coming to this world, the Taredhel had witnessed two eruptions, neither of which was violent enough to threaten the fortification to the south, but large enough to prevent exploration in this region. Had they not occurred, the brothers speculated the Taredhel explorers would have found the human fortress to the north. Of course once the demons had reached this world, it was behind their lines.

"Where now?" asked Laromendis.

"Somewhere out there?" said Gulamendis.

"Can you be more precise?"

"No," said his brother as he started walking down the side of the solid lava flow.

CHAPTER 12

ALLIES

Sandreena galloped forward.

Farson and Keandar urged their lagging mounts to keep up as they started down the final hillside into Durban. Dust blinded those not seeking shelter as another hot wind blew hard out of the desert. Sandreena had been unrelenting, pushing the poor animals to the limits of their strength, knowing that three fine warhorses were most likely headed for the knackers when this ride was over, their health so compromised they would never again be fit for battle.

Still, she judged it a necessary sacrifice, just as she judged Jaliel's loss necessary. She prayed each night that the Goddess protect Her servant, and hoped that if Jaliel had been fortunate he was a captive and not a corpse, and that if the mystery she had discovered in the Valley of Lost Men could be further unraveled, he along with the others enslaved down there might be freed.

Durban was by any measure the most dangerous city on the Bitter Sea. The titular seat of Imperial Keshian government in the Jal-Pur desert and the Bitter Sea, it was effectively a city-state. Occasionally an Imperial edict would be handed down from the Emperor's Court in Kesh requiring reform, but for the entirety of its history, the city was a law unto itself. Strength of arms, gold, and power were the only means of safe passage in this city. Three ragged riders entering at a gallop would hardly elicit a second glance from the city watch and only those considering them as potential prey would cause anyone else to study them.

One look at the arms and surcoats of the two knights warned away potential predators that whatever profit might be squeezed from them in the slave pens, it wouldn't be worth the trouble. Sandreena got that third look, for despite the dark circles of fatigue under her eyes, road dirt, sweat, and filthy hair, her face was still beautiful. Still, she was armed and any Knight-Adamant of the Order of the Shield of the Weak would offer far better than she received in a melee. The other Knight and the dwarf would instantly be dismissed as far more trouble than they were worth. So the three proceeded through the city untroubled.

Sandreena pulled up before a stable near the docks and found the owner. A quick round of haggling got her enough gold to buy a boat. No boat owner in Durban would take anyone to Sorcerer's Isle, no matter what the price, so she knew they were on their own.

A quick stop in an inn for food, then they took possession of their craft. The boat was small, less than twenty feet, and should they encounter bad weather on their journey, it could mean a watery end. So Sandreena mustered up her meager sailing skills, and said a prayer to the Goddess, and they departed.

Sandreena had one gift at sea—she knew how to read the stars, and she had no doubt she could find Sorcerer's Isle. She dead reckoned her first day, going north by northeast, and would adjust that night. Farson and Keandar were both ignorant of boats and got a swift instruction in what she needed for this little craft. It would be cramped and uncomfortable and there would be no privacy, but they had had none on the road, so they were used to one another.

Little was said. They were all exhausted and Sandreena had gleaned all she could from Keandar with questions while they walked their horses or let them rest. None of them had slept for the last two days, and only one night's rest in the last four had been granted.

From what Keandar had told Sandreena, along with what she had seen, she knew this discovery was far beyond her ability to judge. Nothing she observed, nothing he had told her, made sense in any fashion, and right now she felt a driving need to bring order from this chaos.

Once in the boat, Sandreena ordered Farson to rest as best he could, and Keandar needed no urging to cross his arms, drop chin to chest, and lose himself in sleep. Sandreena knew her best choice was to somehow keep awake until nightfall and then wake Farson, give him two clear guides in the heaven to steer by, then she would give herself permission to rest. Her only concern now was the marauders that plied these sea lanes. By striking straight for Sorcerer's Isle she would quickly leave the coastal routes behind, with their attendant risk of pirates. Three armed warriors in a city with plenty of defensible positions from which to defend themselves—and the risk that the usually indifferent city watch might choose to take a hand—was one thing. Three armed warriors in a small boat come upon by a full company of armed men at sea was quite another. Sandreena knew that should pirates heave into view, she and her companions would be quickly bound back to Durban and the slave pens.

Sandreena stayed awake by sheer strength of will, and when finally the sun set and the stars rose, she nudged Farson. With a nod of her head she indicated they should let the dwarf sleep, though from what she saw, waking him might prove difficult.

She quickly gave him a brief lesson on steering the little craft. With a single boom sail and no jib, it only took her a few minutes to demonstrate the simple task of running abreast a following wind. She made it clear that if something proved too difficult for him, he should wake her at once. He nodded, and she pointed to a star rising directly ahead. "That will be your point of reference, that large slightly blue star. If you keep pointed directly at it, you'll eventually come north and we'll be sailing west of where we want to be. So in about three hours you'll see three small stars rise about the same place. They form a tiny triangle, point down. Put the bow of the boat between where they rise and that blue star until the blue star is over there." She pointed off to her left. "Once it's past the highest point in the sky . . ." She blinked. Then she yawned uncontrollably. "If it starts to go down . . ." She lay down. Closing her eyes, she said, "Between the blue star and the three until the blue star starts to sink, then straight at the three. You'll zig and zag, but we'll get there. Wake me when the eastern sky starts to brighten. I'll need a quick look at the sky to see . . . how . . . far . . ." She fell asleep.

Fortune, or the Goddess, smiled on them and for three days they had fair winds and Farson didn't sail them too far off course at night. Keandar had proven useful once he had gotten over an almost natural aversion to sailing; it seemed deep water and boats were not something his people found appealing. Still, once he had learned the basic mechanics of sailing the small craft, he seemed to enjoy it.

The food was gone and the water almost gone when the sharp-eyed dwarf said, "I see land!"

Sandreena motioned for Farson to take over the tiller, moved to stand behind the dwarf, putting one hand on the mast, and peered ahead. A few minutes later she saw a smudge on the horizon and said, "If we didn't sail right past it and we're looking at the coast of the Kingdom, that will be Sorcerer's Island." She glanced behind her and saw a darkening sky. "Just in time, it seems. I think we're going to be getting foul weather soon."

No one spoke as the smudge in the distance resolved itself into a dark spot, which in turn became a distant island. When the sky above began to darken, they could see cliffs and a castle on the eastern edge. "There's a beach to the west of that point," Sandreena said, and Farson nodded.

Sandreena said, "Beach landings can be tricky, so plan on getting wet." She had had them strip off their armor as soon as they had cleared Durban harbor, so she wasn't worried about either of her companions drowning a hundred yards off shore, then she thought to ask, "Keandar, do you swim?"

"Not a stroke," he said. "Never had much need to learn."

"I'll try to keep from swamping the boat."

"That would be appreciated, Sandreena," said the dwarf calmly.

She took the tiller from Farson and said, "When I tell you, move to the back of the boat."

She deftly moved the small boat so it pointed straight at the little beach, and when she felt the swell rising beneath the hull she shouted to Farson, "Take down the sail."

He did as ordered and Sandreena saw the canvas fall loosely just as a comber broke behind the boat, and suddenly they were hurling toward the beach. "Back!" she shouted, and they moved a few feet to the rear, tilting the bow up so it wouldn't plant in the sand. "Get ready to jump and pull us in." She waited. "Jump!"

The dwarf and Knight-Adamant were over the side into thigh-high water for Farson and chest high for Keandar, but four powerful arms hauled the boat safely into the sand. Sandreena let out a long sigh of relief. She had trusted in the Goddess to bring them safely here, but she had never been completely free of doubts. "Get your armor," she instructed as she picked up her gear.

On the beach she quickly rearmed herself and when all were ready, she led them up the small path that at first led away from the castle until it reached the top of the bluffs, where it split, one path heading into the heart of the island, the other toward the castle.

No one hailed them and no sign was given they had been observed in their landing, yet Sandreena knew that Pug would know she approached, or if he was not home, whoever was in charge would. She was tired to her bones, but energized by at last reaching her goal.

When she entered the courtyard to the ancient-appearing castle, she found a familiar face in the form of Jason, a young magician she had met on her previous visit to the island. "Sandreena," he said with a warm smile. "I am to see to your needs."

"These two need food, clean clothing, and rest," she replied, introducing Farson and Keandar. "I need to speak to Pug at once."

He inclined his head and with a wave of his hand summoned another young magician who had been standing at the door of the keep. He took Keandar and Farson in tow and led them into the keep while Jason said, "Are you certain you wouldn't rather rest, yourself? If you don't mind me saying so, you are looking a little in need of it."

She smiled. "I look like I need a lot of it, you mean." She shook her head. "No, talk now, rest after."

He turned and said, "Very well. Follow me, please." He led her into the keep and then across the main floor where she could see Samantha hard at work over a massive kettle of stew. The plump woman smiled and hurried over and threw her arms around Sandreena's neck, almost knocking her over.

Sandreena was so tired she could barely laugh, but she hugged her old friend back and said, "I take it this means Brandos is still here?"

"Yes," said Samantha. "And Amirantha."

"Good," said Sandreena, to Samantha's obvious surprise. "Good?"

"He may be a right bastard, but we need his knowledge. I've got to go. I'll catch up with you later." They hugged once more and Sandreena found Jason waiting. He led her through a door and up a winding staircase to a tower. "Through there," he said.

Sandreena opened the door, expecting to see Pug and perhaps Magnus and Amirantha waiting, but instead the room was now empty. "What?" she asked.

"Step through that portal," said Jason from behind.

That's when she noticed there was a tiny ripple in the air, like a distant heat shimmer. She nodded and walked into it.

Suddenly she was someplace else. The room was huge, well furnished, and there were two dozen people sitting around a semicircle of benches. Facing that semicircle was a table behind which waited Pug, Magnus, and Amirantha.

"Sandreena," said Pug, standing to welcome her. "We had word you were approaching the island."

She nodded, suddenly wishing she had taken up Jason's offer, for she was filthy, probably smelled like horse, sea-salt, and sweat, and now she stood in the midst of what was obviously a very important meeting. Pug motioned for her to take a seat at the end of the table, next to Magnus, and she complied.

Pug said, "That is all that we have for you now. Please

go back to your designated tasks, but be ready. The call may come any moment."

The score or more of people who were sitting in the semicircle stood, and several of them winked out of sight instantly. A couple of others vanished moments later, while still others filed out one at a time through another apparently invisible portal. Finally, Sandreena was alone with Magnus, Pug, and Amirantha.

"You have something to tell us?" asked Pug.

Sandreena nodded. "Creegan has gone to Rillanon, most likely to be named Grand Master of the Order. He left me in charge in Krondor and then left me with this report"— she looked at Pug with suspicion—"which I warrant you've already read."

"A copy," said Pug.

"There was no one else I could trust to go investigate, so I went."

"What did you find?" asked Pug.

"Very few answers. Many more questions. I'll tell you in detail, but first I need to know: did I just walk into a meeting of the Conclave?"

Pug nodded slowly. "The end of a meeting."

"There are more of you than I thought."

"More than we want people to know, even our friends in some cases. But it was necessary to call them here." Pug stood up.

"To brief them?" asked Sandreena, rising as well.

"No, to instruct them," said Pug. "Those you saw are leaders of groups we have hidden all over the world. But we must begin to marshal our resources."

"Marshal?" asked Sandreena, her fatigue making her mind sluggish and uncertain of what she was hearing.

"We're going to war," Amirantha said. "And it's going to be the bloodiest, nastiest fight this world has seen, in all likelihood."

Sandreena sat back down.

• • •

Gulamendis said, "It should be near here."

"How do you know?" asked Laromendis.

"The author gave travel time. I know how long it takes the average human to ride his mount—"

"What if he was on foot?"

Gulamendis threw his brother a withering look. "He mentions riding. I assume, given the abandoned stables back at the keep, it means riding horses."

His brother conceded. "Go on."

"I compensated for that, factored in how much this landscape has changed, and how long it would take us to walk the same distance . . ." With his hand he made an encompassing arc. "Somewhere, near here, we should find it."

"What exactly are we looking for?" asked his brother.

"A . . . portal." His tone sounded far less convincing than it had the last time he answered his brother's question.

"You do remember the one back at the fortress was invisible?" asked Laromendis.

The Demon Master pondered something for a moment, then said, "You're the master of things seen and not seen. Do you have any means to discern something invisible?"

"If I know what I'm looking for, perhaps."

"A portal?"

Laromendis looked embarrassed at realizing this was something he should have thought of. "It would help if I knew the general area."

Gulamendis indicated their immediate surroundings with a wave of his hand. "If I read this correctly, the portal should be somewhere close by. It appears that they removed themselves far enough from the fortress so that if something dire occurred, they would not endanger their ruler and his court.

"This blasted countryside has been ravaged by those volcanoes for ages, so something scorching a few more hectares of land would hardly be a problem."

"Then where would you logically place it?"

"Someplace close to an ancient road that once ran below our feet." He pointed to a non-volcanic hilltop close by. "That may be the only remaining landmark from before the recent eruptions, but if that's the hill mentioned in this journal"—he looked around—"we should be close. Where would you put a portal? By the road. Someplace flat. Someplace easy to observe from a safe distance . . ." He pointed. "Like over there."

Laromendis nodded and walked up a steep incline and then down a steeper one to a flat area dotted with a few loose rocks. He closed his eyes and extended both hands outward and downward. After a minute he said, "No. Nothing."

Gulamendis said, "Well, we might as well be methodical about this." He turned and looked for another observable location and pointed, then led his brother to examine it.

Three hours later they found the portal. It wasn't invisible. Instead it had been knocked flat by some geological shudder in past years. It was a large base very similar to those used by the Taredhel, with two slender bowed arms sweeping upward. They had to be careful getting it upright again, as there was no means to repair any damage they might inadvertently cause.

Laromendis said, "Do you think you can make this thing work?"

"I don't know," answered his brother honestly. "I can only try." He consulted the book several times, then said, "Look for a recess in the base."

Laromendis did so and said, "There's a very tightly fitted cover." He poked and prodded, and then the lid slid to the side. A faint humming filled the air. Inside they saw a glowing yellow crystal.

"It's still working?"

"I don't know," said Laromendis. "You're the one who read the journal."

"We've both been through those portals a dozen times."

"Yes," said the Conjurer, "but neither of us has programmed one."

"I did," said the Demon Master dryly.

"And almost got us both drowned."

Gulamendis knelt and inspected the base, then the two arching wands of wood that formed the boundary of the portal. "I feel energy, but it's very faint."

"Do you see controls?"

"I think here," Gulamendis answered. "Feel here." He pointed at a spot on one of the uprights.

Laromendis did and said, "I feel a depression . . . wait, a series of them."

"Try turning your hand sidewise."

"Fingers!" said Laromendis with delight. "You put your fingers in there."

"And one for the thumb, I am certain."

"Why?" asked his brother.

The Demon Master said, "Because few of the demon hosts have four fingers and a thumb, and most of those that do have long talons that would prevent their fingers from fitting!"

"Or they just designed it that way because that's how they create artifacts."

"Or that," agreed Gulamendis.

Laromendis moved his fingers around a little in the impressions and said, "I don't know how this works."

"There's nothing in the journal about how this device operates. Lots of discussion of what happened when they used it, but nothing as to how it's controlled."

"There are no markings, no devices . . . nothing to tell you if you've selected the proper alignment . . ." Laromendis looked defeated.

Suddenly Gulamendis said, "Think about where you want to go."

"Think?"

"You're the Master Conjurer. Conjure in your mind . . . that place where the dragon landed us on Sorcerer's Isle."

With no better idea, Laromendis closed his eyes and envisioned as best he could that exact location. Suddenly a shot of energy ran up his arm, causing him to jerk his hand away. "Ow!"

"What?" asked Gulamendis.

Shaking his hands a little, his brother answered, "Nothing. Just a little shock—unexpected. It's as if I touched metal on a very dry day." Tentatively he returned his fingers to the spots and said, "It's not bad if you expect it." Closing his eyes, he again tried to concentrate on the location on Sorcerer's Island where they had both been taken when reunited.

After a full minute he took his hand away and said, "No, something's not right."

"What?"

"If I knew, I'd be a galasmancer, not a conjurer."

Gulamendis sat, opened the journal, and began turning pages. "This is probably futile, but let me see if there is something I've missed."

His brother sat down a short distance away, content to wait and rest. While they had endured little in physical exertion except a long walk since escaping the battle with the demons, the stress and lack of sleep had taken its toll. Laromendis wished there was someplace more comfortable to sit than a rough patch of basalt. He ran his fingers over the fine-grain dark grey rock and then inspected the tips. There was a powdery dust and it glimmered with tiny fragments of crystal. He let his eyes wander the landscape, noticing a glint of light here and there as the afternoon sun reflected off exposed outcroppings of crystal or rhyolitic glass. Not too far from where he sat he could see a vein of obsidian running through the exposed face of the rock. Ages ago water began seeping though an interstice in the rocks, and at some point in time a portion of a hillside had slid away, leaving a veritable record of the geological history of this region. The mineral riches of this violent place had drawn the Taredhel here. He wondered if the demons had come for the same reasons, or if they had merely come because their enemies were here.

There were so many things Laromendis didn't understand, or even pretend to understand. From any perspective the war with the demons was lost the moment it was undertaken, for the band members of the Circle of Light were the only magicians with demon lore. Only those few who had avoided the wholesale destruction of the Circle centuries before or, like his brother, who had gleaned their knowledge in isolation from distant central authority had survived to come to the aid of their people. Not for the first time Laromendis was visited with a deeply bitter resentment over the Regent's Meet and their policies.

Perhaps Tandarae, the new Loremaster, was sincere and some progress could be realized in the policies of the surviving Taredhel, or perhaps it would take violence to change things. Laromendis closed his eyes a moment, fatigue washing over his soul, as he realized this was an academic consideration unless his brother could come up with a way home.

He turned his mind to wondering what they would do if Gulamendis couldn't activate this portal. Would there be any possible way home in the old abandoned Taredhel fortress, many miles to the south? Even if there was a working portal, would it take them back to Hub, or if they got to E'bar, would death be awaiting them as they stepped through the portal? For the first time in years he felt defeated.

"I have it," his brother said softly.

Laromendis sat up straight and said, "What?"

"I know why the portal isn't working."

"Why?"

Rather than saying anything, Gulamendis scooted over

a few feet to the base of the device and opened the base, revealing the crystal. He removed it, then opened the small bag on his belt and took out a crystal he had taken off the dead galasmancer on Hub. He inserted it into the receptacle and closed the latch. Looking at Laromendis, he said, "Now try."

Laromendis came to his feet, put his fingertips on the depression, and instantly was overwhelmed by images. He closed his eyes and said softly, "I see things."

Gulamendis said, "That shock you received was designed to let anyone operating the device know that the crystal lacked sufficient energy to make the device work."

Laromendis took his fingertips away and laughed. "Of course. There are no symbols, no markings, nothing else." He took a deep breath, closed his eyes, and saw tumbling landscapes. "It's as if I'm flying over . . . worlds. . . ." he said softly. "Desert, mountains, oceans . . ."

"Try to steer it. Like a ship at sea."

"I'll try." Laromendis first started by imagining he was halting and suddenly the image around him was motionless, as if he hung a few feet above the ground. It was a meadow, with trees that almost looked familiar but were just different enough to inform him this was not a world he knew. He willed his mind to take them to the vale near the burned out Villa Beate on Sorcerer's Isle, where he had been reunited with his brother.

There was resistance, as if the device did not wish to go somewhere not already known to it, or so far away, but suddenly there was a wrenching and he was apparently speeding among the stars. He felt an almost overwhelming sense of vertigo and his stomach knotted, but he kept his grip on the device and his eyes closed. Then he saw a world and it looked at first as if that world was hurtling at him, then abruptly it seemed as if he was falling toward it, seeing a vast ocean, with masses of land, and a sea with islands in the middle! Then he was heading straight for a small island, northwest of the coast, and he willed himself to slow down.

Fearing to open his eyes, he softly said, "I think I've found it."

His brother spoke in hushed tones. "Open the portal, Laro."

He willed the portal to open, imagining a way between the worlds, and felt a shock up his arm, not as he had before, but rather a physical vibration as the air made a loud whooshing sound and then a sizzle of energy. He opened his eyes.

"You did it," Gulamendis said softly.

Laromendis said, "This is amazing. This is a better portal by . . . many times, than our own. Or the humans', from what I've seen."

"The builders were humans," reminded his brother.

"The humans on Home."

"Home," said Gulamendis. With a look of profound relief, he said, "Let's go home."

He stepped through and Laromendis followed.

They were on another world and for a moment startled by a change in the air pressure; they had come from high mounts to sea level in a step and their sensitive elven ears protested. And the smells were different, from the acrid stench of the volcanic blasted lands to this green island.

And there was also the matter of a dozen determined-looking magicians forming a half-circle before them, with Pug at the middle.

Gulamendis held up his hands, palms out. "It's us, Pug."

Pug motioned for the magicians to step back. Turning to the two elven brothers, he said, "How did you do that?"

"We found a portal, ah, rift device on another world and knew if we turned up in E'bar, we'd be . . ."

"Explain that later," said Pug. "What I want to know is how you got the rift to open?"

Gulamendis looked at his brother, indicating he should answer.

"I just . . . told it to bring us here."

"And it did?" said Pug in amazement.

"Yes, is that so odd?"

"Very," said Pug, looking concerned. "I have placed wards on this island since the last attack, which is why I knew you were coming. We were merely a second or two in being alerted once the rift punched through our defenses. We located the source and were here as you emerged."

"Defenses?" asked Laromendis.

"You should not have been able to get through my barriers without magic of incalculable power."

The two elves glanced at each other and Laromendis said, "I know the portal . . . rift gate was better than what our builders have created, but I didn't think it was that much better."

Pug put out his hand as if reaching for the rift through which they had stepped and then, looking concerned, let his arm fall. "Nothing. It closed a moment after you stepped through. Where did you come from?"

Gulamendis gave a brief description of their travels and said, "If we can deal with the demons and get safely back to Hub, I can get you to Can-ducar on the world of Telesan, and from there I can find that portal again."

"That will have to wait awhile, but I will take you up on that offer. That design explains why a lot of things have happened over the years that shouldn't have, especially attacks on this island that do a fair job of ignoring my defenses."

"Could we go somewhere and sit down?" asked Gulamendis. "We are both rather tired."

"Yes," said Pug with a forced smile. "Forgive me." He motioned to the other magicians and said, "We'll meet you back at the keep." He put his hands on the shoulders of the two elves and suddenly they were in Pug's private study in the tower.

Laromendis said, "This is a prodigious conjuration, Pug. I'm impressed."

Pug smiled. "You are good at your craft. I have two rooms occupying two different locations and anyone who steps through the door without knowing how to control entrances comes here. My office. It is my office, and I do work here, but it is in a different location."

Laromendis glanced out the window. "The view?"

"Another illusion, reflecting what you would see if you were in the tower looking out."

"Again, impressive." Laromendis glanced around. "The other room, the one you enter if you do know what you're doing?"

"That is for another time. Please, sit."

The two exhausted elves did so, and Pug said, "I can see from your appearance you've been through a lot recently. I expect you'd prefer a hot bath, meal, and bed before any long interrogation, so I'll keep this brief and we can delve into all we need to know from one another tomorrow."

"That would be welcome, Pug," said Gulamendis. "But two things I feel compelled to report first: I think we've found something never encountered before; we discovered on the abandoned world of Telesan an ancient fortress, human or close enough to human I'm fooled, but the demons have occupied the fortress and are keeping prisoners."

Pug remained motionless, then nodded once and said, "I see."

"I don't know if you do," said the Demon Master. "Demons don't take prisoners. They eat everything they can and move on. It's as if they've somehow changed from what I know them to be."

"Isn't that a conclusion you and Amirantha reached after your pet demons betrayed you to Dahun and Belasco?"

Gulamendis said, "That was . . . Yes, we did, but that

was us being confounded at how their behavior changed. This is more that their nature has changed. They're becoming more like us."

Pug again nodded. His dark eyes studied both elves for a moment, then he said, "You said two things?"

"They seem to be at war with themselves." He described the attack by one army of demons, at the behest of the illusion of Maarg, upon another, and the surprising organization of the operation.

When Gulamendis was finished, it was his brother who said, "Right before we abandoned Andcardia, we began to notice demons in the field who were not simply throwing themselves at our defenses, but who seemed to be instructing other demons, organizing them in a rough fashion, sending them in waves against specific areas of defenders. I didn't think too much of it, well, because it wasn't my job to think of it, and I was very busy running for my life most of the time.

"This, however, was far beyond that. These were demons organized into units, camped as humans or elves would camp, with officers, pickets, what I took to be a command tent, and those who attacked came down the hill in multiple columns, coordinated by some unseen overseer—those demons we thought to be in command were illusions." He sat back, obviously bordering on exhaustion.

Pug was silent for a long time, then said, "We have much to discuss. But it can wait until you're recovered from your ordeal."

Gulamendis handed over the journal he was carrying to Pug and said, "You might find this interesting. I know I did, and I don't understand half the things he was writing."

"Who?"

"The author. I didn't see his name, but there is a glyph. I have a demon-taught spell of reading languages . . . I suppose you do as well. I think it's a human tongue." He sighed. "I don't really know what I'm thinking. He had a little tower, in which there were many books and scrolls, and he kept copious notes and journals. This was the one I found conveniently on the work desk, else I might not have noticed the information that got us to the portal we used to come here."

"Very fortuitous," Pug observed. "Please, if you don't mind, find yourself downstairs to the common room and feed yourselves. Brandos's wife, Samantha, has taken charge of the kitchen. She should have food for you. Then Jason will find you a place to sleep. I'll have water heated for a bath." He stood, then said, "Though where we'll find clothing to fit you . . . ?"

"We'll get by," said Laromendis. "We can wear these a while longer if we must."

"Perhaps some robes while your clothing is washed," suggested Pug. "In any event, please, go eat and rest and tomorrow we'll have much more to discuss."

The two elves left his study and Pug looked at the book handed to him by the Demon Master. He didn't even need to open it to know who authored this work. He recognized the symbol on the binding. But to satisfy himself, he opened it and saw the glyph on the first page. "Macros," he said softly.

Pug let out a long sigh. Did Macros live on that world and advise some alien ruler, or was this another of the man's false leads left for him by the Trickster God?

"Kalkin!" Pug shouted. "Is this your handiwork?"

Silence was his reply.

CHAPTER 13

ANCIENT HISTORIES

Pug held up his hands.

The others in the room fell silent as he said, "We have three issues here. What the elven brothers"—he indicated a considerably cleaner, well-fed, and rested pair of Taredhel magic-users—"have brought us is important and worth investigation, as well as supporting recent observations we've had regarding the changes in the Demon Legion's behavior.

"What Amirantha has brought to our attention"—he pointed to a massive volume lying on the table before him—"is still being closely examined, and maybe will give us a far more fundamental understanding of our enemy's nature and purpose."

He paused, then said, "But what is most imperative, what demands our first consideration is the information that has come to us from Lord James"—he nodded toward Jim Dasher, who had chosen to stand in a far corner—"and Sandreena." He inclined his head toward the Knight-Sergeant of the Order of the Shield of the Weak, who sat on the other side of Magnus at the table, just to his father's right.

"This construction in Kesh, in what is known as the Valley of Lost Men, is something I personally plan on investigating within a few days. Its nature and purpose must be determined.

"The dwarf Keandar, who came to us with Sandreena, was only partially able to help us understand what is taking place down there. He was a hunter, herdsman, and warrior, and was quickly made a sentry and given a patrol. All of his people who were smiths, engineers, miners, or with other like skills, they were taken away to someplace deep within the construction, and apparently were aiding the invaders in building the device."

From deep in the shadowed corner a voice said, "It's a trap."

Those at the table turned to see Lord James step out slightly and he said, "They made it too easy to find that festival of slaughter. The more I think on that the more it was them not caring if they were seen or them wanting to be seen."

Sandreena studied the way he moved and concluded it was likely he was the Kingdom agent wearing Jal-Pul desertman dress who had handed her the message she had delivered to Creegan. There was something about him that made her go on edge, but she couldn't quite decide what it was. She thought she had seen him before, but she had so little contact with the nobility she was certain that had she met him she would vividly remember where and when.

Pug said, "From what Sandreena reported, it's guarded."

Sandreena's attention was pulled back to the situation

before them and she said, "He may be right. I had little trouble getting close and it was only fatigue and carelessness that caused Keandar to discover me. Had I not torn off the magic token that kept him under control, I think I would have killed him; he's sturdy enough and a skilled fighter, but they're not feeding their prisoners well or resting them, and he was weakened.

"I don't know. They are undertaking something on a tremendous scale, Pug, for just a lure to a trap." She reiterated what she had seen for those in the room who might be vague on the details of what she had reported to Pug earlier in the week.

It was Gulamendis who spoke next. "I don't know if it's a trap, in particular, but it certainly is something neither Amirantha or myself can reconcile with what we know of demon behavior. It's far too . . . patient. This device Sandreena describes has been under construction for at least a year, probably two, given the amount of stone in those walls and the number of workers involved.

"Our own geomancers could do it in a fifth of the time, but, Sandreena, did you see any signs of magicians constructing anything?"

"No," she replied. "Three of the four arching towers are finished, and the fourth was halfway done. They were hauling stones up with a gigantic hoist atop a series of huge wooden platforms. And the workers looked as if they were ready to drop at any minute."

Pug said, "Jim, I appreciate your impulse toward caution, and I promise that my own experience with demons tends to put my instincts in harmony with your own, but we have one occurrence on this world that is clearly demon controlled, and we must go down there and put an end to it."

"May I suggest one more reconnaissance before you launch an assault? I can provide as much distraction from Krondor as you need for the Keshian court to not pay attention to an army of ten thousand mercenaries marching across two hundred miles of open country, but it would really be a benefit to our cause if we didn't get them all obliterated and have to inform Kesh that an infernal invasion is under way on their sovereign territory and, by the way, the Demon Legion is heading straight toward the City of Kesh."

"Then we'll make sure that doesn't happen," said Pug. "But your suggestion is in harmony with my own opinion; I will go with Magnus to look over this site." He looked at Amirantha and Gulamendis. "I would really find it useful if you two would accompany us."

"Of course," said Amirantha, and a moment later after considering the request, Gulamendis nodded as well.

Laromendis said, "We need to send word to the Lord Regent, as well." He did not look happy at that prospect, and Pug thought it best to ask him about this later, in private.

Pug said, "Given the time, we shall leave after the evening's supper. Sandreena." Then, turning to the Knight-Sergeant, he said, "Would you care to accompany us?"

Amirantha barely hid his surprise at the request, but said nothing.

"Certainly. If there's any way I can find out what happened to Knight-Adamant Jaliel, I will take it."

"Our first responsibility will be to evaluate the situation." To the others in the room Pug said, "Continue your duties, and make sure everyone is ready for whatever orders are issued." He motioned for a young magician to come to him. When the youthful-looking magician was close, he said, "Send word to Lord Kaspar and ask him to join us. Tell him we'll have him back to his palace before anyone notices he's gone. Thank you." The magician nodded he understood and departed.

"Let us adjourn and we shall send word after we have completed our reconnaissance."

The meeting broke up and Sandreena rose quickly from the table, first to put some distance between herself and Amirantha; she found the necessity of being with him in the name of duty acceptable, if barely, but would just as soon avoid his company if she had the option.

Besides, she was intrigued by this Kingdom nobleman lurking in the corner of the room, and decided it was as valid an excuse to get away from the Warlock as she could contrive. All too soon she would have to be conferring with Amirantha and his elven counterpart on matters of demon lore and, more important to her, how to eradicate them.

She caught up with Jim at the door and said, "Excuse me, sir, but have we met?"

With a slight smile, he nodded. "On the docks in Durban. I was the agent who gave you the package."

"Ah," she said. "Still, I have some other meeting in mind. In Durban I could not see your face, just your eyes . . ." She squinted slightly. "Something about your eyes."

"Well, then, a formal introduction: I'm James, Court Baron in Krondor, aid to the Prince at times, servant of His Majesty the King, and," he lowered his voice, "member of the Conclave of Shadows."

She glanced around. "Apparently I am as well."

"I heard about Creegan having to hurry off to become Grand Master of your order." He motioned for her to walk with him. The meeting room was in the lower basement of the castle opposite the pantry and kitchen, and he led her up the stairs to the central keep's great room. Here tables had been set up and the fire was burning, against the need to feed nearly thirty key members of the Conclave. "Walk with me outside?" asked Jim.

Sandreena said, "I could use some fresh air."

They stepped outside the central keep and found the marshaling yard relatively empty. Whatever activity the Conclave was undertaking, it was doing a masterful job disguising it. Against the remote possibility they were under scrutiny, anything relating to marshaling the Conclave's forces with their allies was happening somewhere else.

"You and Amirantha . . . ?" He looked her in the eye. "Something going on between you?"

"It's personal."

Jim took a slow, deep breath and looked away. He said, "I was going to have this talk with you tomorrow; I've already discussed it with Creegan and Pug. But now is as good a time as any."

She caught a glimpse of his profile as he stared into the sky a moment and for reasons she couldn't name she felt herself tense and her hand moved toward her mace. Suddenly his hand shot out and seized her wrist, his thumb digging into a nerve bundle and paralyzing her for a moment. She instinctively twisted her wrist before she pulled away, breaking his hold, but the damage was done. She could not get a decent grip on her mace with her right hand.

She switched to her left and her mace came up. "What did you do that for?" she demanded as she got into a defensive position.

"Your training," he said, backing away a step. "I didn't want to take the chance you'd leave my brains all over the sand before I had the opportunity to explain a few things to you."

"Such as?" she asked.

"Let's start with the first problem between us, though it is the least important. You've been trying to remember where we have met, correct?"

"Yes," she said, still on guard. The numbness in her right hand was wearing off and she tossed her mace deftly from left to right.

"I'm the bastard who sold you to the Keshian."

Her eyes widened. "You're Quick Jimmy!"

"Jimmyhand, Jim Dasher, yes, to all of them."

He could tell it was taking all her self-control not to lash out at him right then. Slowly she put her mace back on

her belt. "I can kill you later, if I must," she said softly, almost a hiss of warning. "Why? Don't tell me this was some
part of a great plan you and Creegan had for me. I was a
whore then."

"Creegan had nothing to do with it. He didn't know
you existed," countered Jim, crossing his arms over his
chest. "And it had nothing to do with the Conclave, at least
not directly. I wanted you in bed with that merchant, and
after a month or so, we were going to contact you and offer
you your freedom after you worked for us for a while."

"Freedom . . ." She paused to consider. "You wanted me
to spy on him!"

"Yes. He was well connected to members of the Keshian
Intelligence Corps, but he also had dealings with Kesh's
criminal empires. He was a smuggler as well as a trader."
Unfolding his arms, he put his right hand on his chest and
said, "I am also a man of many interests, and when I tell
you this, you will know that your life has forever changed,
once more. I am the Upright Man of Krondor, and I needed
my competition from Kesh neutralized.

"As fortune would have it, even though you didn't reach
Kesh and became a Sister of the Order of the Shield of the
Weak, I found other means to achieve my end." He looked
at her with a narrowing gaze. Her expression was one of
open shock. "You know what this means?"

"The Upright Man . . ." She put her mace away. "It
means I'm not leaving this island alive if I don't agree to
something."

He grinned. "Creegan said the Goddess had plans for
you that were better than mine, and I will not disagree. You
are far too intelligent to let you wither in some Keshian
lord's bed, or retire to some small town to start a modest
inn with the gold we would have given you.

"No, you are destined for greater things, Sandreena." He
took a folded parchment out of his belt and handed it to her.

She took it and saw the seal of the Order pressed into

heavy wax. She cracked the seal and unfolded the message. She read it. Then she read it a second time. Softly she said, "He can't be serious?"

Jim was forced to laugh at her response. "He said that would be your exact words. He knows you well, Sandreena. Or should I say, Mother-Bishop Sandreena."

"Me, in charge of the Order in the west?"

"You already are. As you no doubt realize, we of the Conclave have not done as well recruiting agents within the various temples. We have none in several of the temples, Sung, Astalon, and Lims-Kragma being the most difficult— it's that absolute mind-set, I think. I am as practical a man as you'll meet, and there are times when I feel divided in my loyalties between the Kingdom and the Conclave."

"Then why do it?" she asked.

"Because while I love my homeland, Pug is trying to save the world. It's hard to argue for the Kingdom's interest if the entire planet is conquered by demons."

She took a deep breath and said, "What if I don't want to be Mother-Bishop?"

"Well, you were wrong about not leaving here alive. You'll wake up on a beach somewhere near Land's End, and you'll have a vivid memory of your boat overturning in rough water and you not reaching Sorcerer's Isle. You'll also decide that rather than try again, you'll return to Krondor and seek out help there.

"After that, you'll continue as Knight-Sergeant of the Order while waiting for Creegan to send a new Bishop to run things in the west, and . . . ?" He shrugged. "Creegan will find another."

"Another?"

"You're not the only talented youngster in the Order, Sandreena. You just happen to be the one who is here now, and, well, you're a great deal more talented than anyone else we have around. Amirantha practically sings your praises when it comes to how you can dispatch a demon." Jim narrowed his gaze as if appraising her. "You always were one of the more striking women I'd seen. I remember you in the brothel and there was a reason you commanded the highest price. You've kept the core of that beauty despite the training, sweat, and pounds of muscle you've put on, but I'll tell you this much: he sees more in you than most men."

Her expression turned dark. "He had a pitiful way of showing me."

"Ah," said Jim with a single slow nod. "Now I see; more than he admits to himself. Very well; that's between you and Amirantha. Now, are you taking the commission or not?"

She looked one more time at the folded message, then said, "Of course I am. If I don't, I'll never get to go look for Jaliel."

Without another word, she turned and walked back to the keep. Jim stood outside, enjoying the cool breeze off the ocean and the relative calm. He knew there wouldn't be much calm after today.

Taking in a deep breath, shaking his head at how things turn out despite plans at times, he chuckled to himself at how well Creegan did understand his protégé, and he slowly returned to the keep, trying to savor a few more moments of fresh air before plunging back into the intrigues and murderous needs of the Conclave.

Pug asked, "Why can't you go?"

Laromendis said, "My brother and I are not well regarded by our people." He sat back in one of the two chairs before Pug's desk. The other should have been occupied by his brother, save Gulamendis was somewhere with Amirantha poring over a volume on demon lore. "To understand, you'd have to have some knowledge of the history of the Edhel."

"I know a little," said Pug, "from Tomas."

Laromendis nodded. "His memories from the Valheru,

the Dragon Lord." The elf's forehead furrowed in an expression of worry. "There are many things that I fail to understand, and that particular miracle is one of them, but what he remembers is what another being saw. It is not the only perspective."

Pug made a gesture with both hands indicating the elf should continue. "I will spare you a long story of our struggles and say that at the height of our power, the Taredhel had risen to heights no elf living on Midkemia could imagine. We were rulers of worlds, Pug. But with such a change in our nature came a price—arrogance. Few of my race would admit to it, but having spent some time on this world, scouting and encountering . . ." He took a slow breath. "Before I returned to Andcardia with word that I had found Home, Midkemia, I killed a member of your race; a cleric I had captured and after I obtained all the useful information I could from him, I simply killed him to ensure no one would know I had been there. I know travelers who've ventured too close to E'bar have been murdered. I know the Lord Regent has ordered raids against farms and villages in the Free Cities, letting blame fall on our cousins, the Moredhel."

Pug said, "This is disturbing news. Why are you telling me this if you know this will indispose me toward your people?"

"Because there are those of us within the Taredhel who do not agree with this course of action. Before I was born, all matters mystical, what you would have called priests, magicians, healers, and the like, existed independent of civil authority.

"Your friend Tomas is wed to the woman who we view as the unbroken connection back to the roots of our past, those elves primarily responsible for the cultivation and care of the holy groves, what we call the Stars. But real power for our people has resided with the Regent's Meet and the Circle of Light.

"When we first encountered the demons, the Regent's Meet ruled that all members of the Circle of Light had to sever ties with that organization and subject themselves to the rule of the Regent's Meet or suffer the consequences, which were imprisonment or death, the latter being the more usual consequence."

"For what reason?"

"Power. Pure naked power. The Regent has by tradition been forbidden to take the title King, because there always was this faint hope among the Taredhel that we would someday return here and reclaim the world." Laromendis sighed and shook his head slowly, as if in regret. "We never expected this world. We thought we'd find one in ruins, or perhaps in a primeval state, or even one occupied only by other elves, and we would assume our rightful place as their rulers.

"We even imagined a world where the Valheru were still in residence, and we were prepared to fight for our freedom. We have evolved. You've seen the other elves of this world, Pug, and you know that we are larger, stronger, faster, and more ruthless. Our magic dwarfs any that the Spellweavers of Elvandar can hope to bring against us.

"In short, the Regent doesn't want allies; he wants subjects. And of any voice to whom he might listen, mine is among the least likely."

"You were a member of the Circle?"

"Barely. My brother and I are young compared to the others of the Circle. I was a member less than ten years, Gulamendis not at all; Demon Masters are not well regarded, even among the most accepting of our people."

"Amirantha suffered the same regard," said Pug. "Or should I say lack of regard."

Laromendis said, "He is the first of your race I can say my brother has developed some affection toward; it's quite remarkable. As I said, we are an arrogant people." He sighed, then said, "In my case, I do not particularly care for your race, Pug, but I also do not hold you in any sort of disdain. If I were to admit my shortcoming, here it is, that I don't feel much kinship with anyone besides my brother. Perhaps that is due to our upbringing, but I feel much the same way toward the other elven races on Midkemia.

"But to return to the reason we are talking, I think you may have difficulty with anyone you might choose to speak to the Regent." He narrowed his gaze. "The only person I can name who might persuade him to mitigate his position regarding alliances with humans and dwarves—and that would be close to a miracle; dwarves have never gotten along with the Taredhel—that person is Lord Tomas."

"Why?" asked Pug, now intrigued.

"The Regent honors the Queen, but he doesn't respect her. The Eledhel are seen as rustics, simple, lacking the sophistication of the Eldar. The other Eldar, the ones who did not become the Taredhel, those are viewed with distrust, because they serve the Queen. The others?" He made a small motion of dismissal with his head. Pug knew he meant the Moredhel, Glamredhel, and others were just not worth discussing. "But Lord Tomas, the Regent cannot completely rid himself of our heritage. He fears Lord Tomas. As much as he would like to displace him and the Queen and proclaim himself King of all Edhel, raising the Taredhel to supremacy among the People, he doesn't dare think about the consequence of trying. You only have to see Tomas standing there in his armor, not even climbing up on the back of a dragon, to know that he *is* Valheru when he wants to be." Laromendis nodded slowly. "Yes, have Lord Tomas speak with the Lord Regent, and perhaps some good may come of it."

Pug was silent, then said, "Thank you, Laromendis. Both for the suggestion and your frankness. The truth is those few of your people I've met besides yourself and your brother strike me as being as you said they were."

"I have another name," said Laromendis, standing, as

he knew this discussion was coming to a close. "Tandarae, the newly appointed Lorekeeper of the Taredhel. He understands there are powerful beings on this world, and that having them as friends is a better choice than trying to conquer them. Were there a million of us here, the war would already have begun, I fear, but we have perhaps ten thousand or so who now cling to the legacy of the stars. It's both a sad time and a time for opportunity, Pug. Tandarae, keep his name in mind, and if you ever have cause to speak with anyone in the Regent's Meet, it would have to be with discretion, but he's the one."

Pug nodded. "I will remember. Thank you."

Laromendis left, and Pug sighed. He had much to do, but it seemed that at the top of the list now was a quick visit to Elvandar.

Amirantha was astonished at the insight and observational skills of the elf. Gulamendis had quickly digested all that Amirantha had come to understand out of the tome they had removed from Queg, and then in short order had drawn some conclusions from the material that left him doubting his own intelligence; they were obvious once they were pointed out. The elf was slightly arrogant at times, but for the most part was respectful of the work Amirantha had done and on more than one occasion had complimented him on a particular insight or conclusion. Amirantha was forced to either become increasingly annoyed with the elf's attitude or accept it for what it was; he chose the latter, because he was forced to admit that it was closer to his own manner and behavior than anyone else he had ever met.

He was taking a break from the work, leaving Gulamendis on his own, as the Warlock had given everything he had to give, and really was tired of reading, discussing, and wondering. He simply needed a few moments outside, in the fresh air, away from worry and concern.

That sense of freedom from worry and concern vanished a moment later when Sandreena's voice cut through the air: "Amirantha! I need a word."

As he turned to watch her approach, two things struck him simultaneously: the first was she still took his breath away, despite the martial apparel. All too well he knew how she looked without the armor, tunic, and trousers. The second was he knew it was going to be many more than one word. He recognized that expression.

Deciding it was time to say little and listen, he said, "Of course, Sandreena. What is it?"

She paused, looking at him, gauging his expression and manner, deciding exactly what to say next, then she blurted, "I've been made Mother-Bishop of the Order in the west."

He inclined his head slightly, smiled, and said, "Congratulations. Deserved without a doubt and I know you will excel in your new post."

She blinked, revealing that whatever she expected him to say, that wasn't it. Then suddenly she reached across and back-handed him across the face, knocking him to the ground.

Amirantha sat stunned for a moment, then reached up and put his hand to his now throbbing right cheek. Finally he said, "I wish you'd stop hitting me."

Her eyes shining with emotion, she hissed, "Just be glad you're needed; otherwise I'd have no compunction about killing you!" With that she turned and hurried off, back to the keep.

She passed Brandos coming out of the keep. He took one look at Sandreena hurrying by and then another at Amirantha sitting on the ground, and broke into a broad grin. Coming to stand over his old friend, he reached down and helped him to his feet. "You'd better do something to get that girl over you, or she's going to kill you."

"Any suggestions?" asked Amirantha, wiggling his jaw and hearing it pop in and out.

"Either kill her first or marry her are the only two that come to mind."

"Marry? She'd rather marry a demon. Not to mention she's just been promoted to Mother-Bishop."

"No wonder she's so cranky," observed Brandos. "Well, I guess marriage is out of the question. Unless you think you'd like temple life . . . ?"

Amirantha gave him a look that would wither flowers. "You wanted something?"

"Yes. Pug sent me to fetch you. Gulamendis seems to have found something in that book you stole . . . retrieved from Queg."

Amirantha put aside his annoyance, hurt, and confusion over Sandreena and followed his friend into the keep. Brandos took him to the entrance to the tower, and said, "Let me know if it's anything interesting."

"Things have hardly been boring around here lately," said Amirantha, moving quickly up the stairs.

Reaching the entrance to Pug's private study, he knocked once and heard Pug say, "Come in."

Amirantha entered and found Pug sitting at his desk with Gulamendis in a chair opposite him. Amirantha said, "You sent for me?"

"Yes," said Pug. "Gulamendis has interpreted a few passages that seemed to have caused you some problems, and we have, if he's correct, a very different situation than we anticipated."

"Really?" said the Warlock, sitting in the empty chair next to the elf's.

"Yes," said Pug. "I'll let him explain how he arrived at these conclusions, but in short, it seems that things in the demon realm are not what we imagined them to be."

"I suspect we understood that when Belasco subverted the demons we held in thrall and Villa Beata was sacked."

Pug visibly tensed at mention of the destruction of his home, where his wife had died.

"Sorry," Amirantha said softly. "No disrespect intended. What has changed?"

It was Gulamendis who spoke. "I want to go over this with you in detail, Amirantha, but unless I am completely misled by something I don't see, what my brother and I witnessed is one part of a very nasty civil war in the demon realm."

"Civil war?"

"We know Maarg is dead, but someone is keeping alive the notion that he's still around, still in command. But he's not. Pug saw his corpse on the world of Shila, and the demon king we saw on Telesan was an illusion; we can assume Maarg is dead. Even if he's returned to the demon realm, it will be some time before he rises to power again, if ever.

"That leaves us with two questions: who's pretending to be Maarg and why?"

"Three," said Amirantha. "Who's he fighting?"

"Four," amended Pug. "What has any of this to do with Midkemia?"

The three sat back, thoughtful, as they realized that for every question they had answered since the Demon Legion started threatening Midkemia, they now had two new ones.

CHAPTER 14

SLAUGHTER

Pug signaled.

Magnus followed Gulamendis's instructions and they found themselves suddenly standing in a vast chamber. The Oracle of Aal rose up above them, her magnificent dragon form made all the more impressive by the multifaceted layer of jewels that adorned her body, the result of a magic fusion that took place in a battle with a Dreadlord over a century before.

"You come uninvited, Pug," said the Oracle, though her tone was neutral; it was a statement, not an accusation.

"I face the unknown, Lady," answered Pug. "A great danger approaches, and I would know what you can tell me."

The Oracle was silent for a while, as if weighing the question, then spoke: "Too many futures, most of them dire, some ending life as we know it. Too many nexuses of possibility."

"Is there one thing you can tell me to enhance our possibility of successfully avoiding the most dire of consequences?"

"Two waves, the one you see and the one behind it. You remember, from your youth."

Pug was startled. No one knew of that moment, or at least he was almost certain he had never spoken of it. It was the day he had first spoken with his future teacher, Kulgan. He had fallen into a doze on the beach and was awakened by a sudden storm. He had been knocked over by a wave on the beach and as he was attempting to rise, one behind it swept him under. "I remember," he said. "It was a lesson I've remembered all my life."

"You must seek out the hidden wave. The wave before you is meant to distract, to bleed your resources and scatter your focus."

"Can you tell me any more?"

"Shadows hide deeper shadows. There is a void from which no light emerges, and into which none may see. Those who seek to destroy all you love lurk within." A deep sigh came from the massive figure and the Oracle said, "Seek more knowledge before you act, for once begun, this conflict can only end in complete victory or utter defeat."

Magnus said, "Not the first time we've been faced with that option."

The Oracle said, "Wave after wave, young magician, that you must realize. This struggle started before you were born, before your father was born, before even I was born. It is not apparent, but all is connected. Be cautious, be wise, seek more intelligence before acting is my counsel."

The massive dragon head slowly lowered to the floor and the men and women who had been standing in the shadows—the Oracle's companions—moved forward to meet any need she might have.

Pug nodded to his son and suddenly they were back in his study.

Magnus asked, "Father, did that help?"

"Somewhat," answered Pug. "I think before we run down to Kesh to look at Sandreena's big hole in the ground, we need to backtrack the elven brothers' route, and find that lost castle."

"What do we seek there?"

"As always. Knowledge. There are dwarf, human, and elven prisoners there, so we should free them. And there's a room full of books I wish to bring here."

"Books?" said Magnus. "What sort of books?"

"We won't know until we fetch them."

"Why are they important?"

With a wry grin, Pug said, "Because it appears this is another small den that had been at one time occupied by your grandfather."

Magnus visibly sagged. "Macros."

Pug reached over and pulled a book off the shelf, handing it to his son. "Look at the mark on the first page."

Magnus opened the volume and looked. "It's grandfather's glyph, if I read it right."

For a painful moment, Pug looked lost and he said, "I just wish I knew what your mother would say right now."

"Something scathing," said Magnus and he laughed.

Suddenly Pug laughed, too. "No doubt." It was the first time either of them had been able to laugh since Miranda's death and they looked at each other. They needed to put the past behind, for the coming struggle was approaching faster than either would welcome, and they needed to be at their best. Pug pushed aside a rising fear: is this where I lose my son? Ignoring that stab of near panic, he resigned himself to the fact the gods were exacting a price for returning him to this struggle, and it was a bitter price, watching all he loved die before him. But that didn't mean it would be now, or even soon.

"I think we need to find Gulamendis and start backtracking to that world with the volcanoes."

"Who else?"

"Amirantha and Sandreena, because we need all the demon knowledge we can bring to this, and Brandos, because we could use a good sword and he's faced his share of demons, too."

Magnus said, "When do we leave?"

"As soon as you gather them all here. No time like the present."

Magnus nodded and hurried out of the tower, and Pug sat in his chair, lost in his thoughts. Fear over his last child's fate threatened to rise up and instead of succumbing to it, he forced his mind to dissect the Oracle's riddle. The hidden wave. An enemy hiding in a lightless void. He could feel his mind almost comprehending something, but with the Oracle the mix of simple fact and metaphor often confused things.

He turned his attention to her predictions and waited for the others.

It had taken some time, but eventually they discovered the source of the brothers' last rift. Pug had spent the better part of an hour in the clearing where they had arrived, using his powers to seek out any lingering effects of the magic rift, and finding it after a tedious search. It was a faint trail, but there was enough of it that with calculations and patience he finally decided he could reach the point of origin.

"Everyone, stand back," he instructed. "Magnus, be ready to get us out of here if needed." Rifts could be very unstable and destructive and while no man living knew more of them and their nature than Pug, still he was cautious when constructing a new one to a previously unknown location.

Pug closed his eyes a moment, then with a quick incantation formed a rift.

Pug was pulled forward a step, as if seized by a massive invisible hand, then fell back, as if that same hand pushed him away. Brandos stepped forward and steadied Pug, keeping the sorcerer from falling on his backside.

"That was unexpected," said Pug.

"What, Father?"

He looked at Magnus and said, "That rift formed with a great deal more energy than I intended. It was as if someone was helping me form it." He turned to the others and said, "Best be ready for anything when we step through."

Pug led the way and stepped through. When the others came through they found him examining the gate used by the elven brothers. Brandos and Sandreena both coughed, as the air was thick with smoke and an acrid bite stung their eyes and noses. "Must have had an eruption recently," observed Gulamendis. "It wasn't this bad when we left."

Magnus came to stand beside his father and instantly understood what had his father's attention. "I've not seen its like."

"Neither have I. Look at this." He pointed to the impressions where fingers were to be placed.

Magnus put his fingers there, closed his eyes, then opened them wide as if he had been surprised. "Those controls . . ."

"Masterful," said Pug. "If this is one of your grandfather's designs, it surpasses anything I've been able to construct. If it's someone else's . . ."

"Who?" said Magnus quietly.

Amirantha said, "Wind is rising!"

Pug looked around. It was impossible to tell what time of day it was, as ash and smoke formed a canopy in the sky. The air was acrid with stench from the distant volcanoes, and a faint fall of ash covered everything in sight. It could be sunrise, sunset, or noon, and they wouldn't know. "Yes," he said, "I think you're right; there's been an eruption recently."

"None of this ash was here when we left," Gulamendis said. Glancing around, he continued, "At least the darkness will help mask our approach."

As if to accent his observation, a deep rumbling came through the ground as a hot tower of flame appeared above one of the distant cones. "I wonder how long this has been going on," said Amirantha.

"Ages, no doubt," said Pug. "These sorts of regions can go through very calm periods then suddenly become active again." He pointed to the sloping ground. "The lava flow fans out at the bottom of the cone and forms these relatively flat surfaces." He then pointed to the erupting volcano in the distance. "But a big explosion and this can all be lifted, dropped, broken . . ." He shrugged. "If we can, I want to take that gate back with us." He turned to Gulamendis. "But first, which way to the fortress?"

Pointing north, he said, "That way. About a half-day's walk."

"We'll get there a little faster than that." He motioned for them to stand close and join hands. Sandreena and Brandos stood beside Magnus, while Amirantha and Gulamendis stood beside Pug. They all joined hands and suddenly they were standing on a ridge that had been easily a mile north of their previous position. "Don't let go," Pug said, and another jump put them on a plateau. They could see the fortress rise up in the distance. "What's the best way in?" asked Pug.

"We came out the main gate," said Gulamendis. "It has a small door to admit people in and out without opening the big gates fully; there was no one in the yard; we just opened it, walked through, and closed it behind us. If no one's noticed, it still may be unlatched."

Pug nodded and said, "I think over there," and suddenly they appeared on a slope just below the ridge line opposite the main gate. Pug poked his head above and looked around. If anyone was on the wall or in the tower, the chance of them being seen on the other side of the slope was high, though Pug was confident Magnus and himself could deal with anything likely to come from a half-abandoned fortress. Still, it paid to be cautious and Pug's last encounter with a demon prince had almost cost him his life.

Pug studied the fortress for a long minute, moving his hand to indicate the others should remain out of sight. He saw no sign of movement anywhere. He waited and then conjured up a wandering eye.

The spell was one he rarely employed, for while useful for scouting areas he did not personally wish to enter, it was easily detected by any other competent magician and it tended to leave him with a splitting headache.

A tiny orb appeared before his face, and suddenly Pug's vision originated at the orb and his own eyes were as if blind. He sent the orb speeding across the clearing before the gate, the so-called killing ground, and over the wall and swiftly into the open doors of the main keep.

No alarm was raised. Pug let his magic vision race along halls and corridors, into rooms, and up towers. The armory stood empty as did the pantries. The keep was abandoned.

Pug let the spell end, opened his eyes, and said, "There's no one there."

He rose and led them over the ridge and down the slope. Pug stopped for a moment and knelt. He poked at what appeared to be a fibrous plant, knocked down by falling rock and ash. "This plant was nearly four feet tall . . ." He stood. "No one has cleared this area for a while. You don't provide even modest cover for an attacking foe."

Gulamendis said, "I suspect this place was abandoned years ago and only reoccupied by the demons recently. Parts of the keep we passed through had layers of dust on the floor."

"Tracks?" asked Magnus.

"We just didn't worry about them," said Gulamendis. "We judged that if no one has used those parts of the keep in years, they were unlikely to use them just after we left, and that if anyone came in after a few days . . ." He shrugged. "We planned on being far from here by then."

Pug said, "Logical."

They quickly walked to the door within the massive gates and Pug pushed on it. It swung slowly open. "Apparently they had no idea you had visited the area."

They slipped through the gate, staying within the deep shadows along the walls. Moving quickly, Gulamendis led them into the corner then over to the side of the shed. He glanced around. There was no hint of life.

He led them quickly to the ramp leading down to the door into the basement and found the door refused to open. He pushed, and despite his above-human-level strength, the door wouldn't budge. Magnus whispered, "Let me."

The younger magician moved to stand before the door and held up his hand. With a short motion and a single word, the door moved in balky fits and starts until it was open enough for them to see what blocked it.

"Bodies," whispered Magnus.

The stench of decomposing flesh rose up and even Brandos swallowed hard.

Sandreena said, "What happened here?"

"We won't know until we get inside," said Pug. He spoke in a normal tone, not evidencing any concern over being heard. "I think the demons have quit this place and decided not to take the prisoners with them."

Magnus waved his hand again and the door veritably flew off its hinges, back into the room. The large room that led into the dungeon cells and up to the kitchen was littered with corpses: humans, elves, and dwarves all piled atop one another. It was clear a good number of them were racing for this door, to escape, and were cut down from behind. The wounds were mixed, some smooth cuts, from sword or knife blades, others torn, ragged, as if made by fang or claw.

Once they had cleared a way though the piles of bodies,

Pug knelt and inspected the corpses. "Some of the clothing I recognize," he said softly. "I think this dwarf here is from Dorgin, perhaps a companion of Keandar's. That pattern in the weave of the tunic is common there. But these elves . . ."

Gulamendis said, "They are unknown to me, but then until we found Home . . . Midkemia, we knew only the Taredhel."

"I don't think they're from Midkemia," said Pug. He felt an undamaged piece of shirt on a dead elf and said, "I do not recognize this material. It's not silk or linen, but it's light and . . ." He stood and said, "Too many mysteries. Too many distractions. Where is the tower?" he asked.

"That way." Gulamendis pointed.

Sandreena and Brandos had both seen their share of battlefields, yet both appeared pale and shaken by the carnage in the room.

The light was faint and at the end of the hall, Magnus raised his hand, creating a bright blue-white glow that illuminated their surroundings more efficiently than a lantern. They reached the bottom of the tower stairs and moved quickly to the top.

The door was still unlatched and once they moved inside, Pug said, "I can feel it."

"Grandfather?" asked Magnus.

"Yes, though how long ago . . ." He shrugged. He reached up and pulled a book off the shelf at random and glanced at it. "I have a copy of this in my library."

Magnus came to his side and said, "I will look for anything that I don't recognize." He started with the volumes on the desk and quickly tossed those on the floor that were duplicates of those already on Sorcerer's Island.

Soon Pug had a small stack of books set aside. He was taking one off a low shelf when a massive upheaval in the ground below the keep threw them to the floor. Dust ground from between ancient stones rained down on them and the stones of the tower seemed to undulate for nearly a half minute. When it subsided, Brandos looked out the window and said, "Look!"

In the distance the biggest of the three volcanoes was shuddering and a wave of smaller shocks was rolling through the soil beneath them, causing the keep to feel as if it might shake itself apart. Then there was an explosion of titanic proportions, a massive upheaval of brilliant hot lava, and a funnel of white steam blowing straight into the sky like the gods' own teakettle on boil. All around rock, ash, and liquefied stone were spewing out and up at astonishing speed. Pug said, "In about one minute a wave of poisonous air hot enough to broil the skin from your bones will hit us. Grab those books!" Everyone grabbed an armful of books. "Stand close!" he instructed.

At the sound of wind rising to an earsplitting shriek, there was a sudden pulse of air in the room and less than six inches in front of Brandos's nose a grey void appeared. Without a word the old fighter leaped into it, while others followed, with Pug pushing his son through, and suddenly they were back on Sorcerer's Island. The hasty transport through the rift landed them hard on the ground, and Amirantha, Sandreena, and Gulamendis all lost their footing and fell. The others staggered a bit.

Pug let the books he held fall from his arms and turned. A wave of his hand dismissed the rift just as a pulse of super-heated steaming air came through, and Pug erected a shield that vented the scalding wet air around them.

Everyone could feel the heat suddenly dissipate before anyone was burned. It gave them all a queasy feeling at how close they had come to being boiled alive in their own skins.

Pug turned and said, "I think"—then his legs went weak. His son let go of the books in his arms and grabbed his father. As Pug was gently lowered to the grass, he muttered, "Damn. I so wanted to bring that gate back here." Then he closed his eyes and fell into darkness.

Pug awoke with a massive headache. He found his son sitting at his bedside and said, "How long?"

"All night and half the morning."

Pug sat up and felt light-headed.

Magnus said, "That was a prodigious feat, punching a rift through from that tower to the meadow where we left in so short a time. No wonder you passed out."

"We didn't have a lot of choice."

Magnus said, "That got me to thinking. Even if we know a world has a rift we've visited, it might be a good thing to send a vision orb through just to be safe."

Pug nodded. "I think you're right. Had we stepped through as that shock wave washed over the plateau rather than a half hour before, we'd all be dead now."

"Caution," said Magnus with a nod. "What next?"

"Look over what we've found, see if there's anything that has any bearing on what we're facing, then you and I and the demon experts take a journey down to Kesh to see what's being built down there."

"I'll have food sent up."

Getting out of bed, Pug said, "Don't bother. I'm in need of a lot of water and some food. I'll get some down in the kitchen. Have you been studying those books of your grandfather's?"

"Of course," answered Magnus. "There are a couple I've put aside for you to look at, but I think he made copies of things here and took them there, after he left this island, before you found him wandering around mindlessly."

Pug paused. "That would explain part of his absence. But what was he doing on that world, and who was he serving? And does it have anything to do with this coming demon host? I find it difficult to believe that Macros just coincidentally happened to visit a world that is infested with demons and left behind his library that we just happened to find when we were facing a demon army."

"With grandfather anything was possible." Magnus had never met his grandfather, but he had encountered a Dasati called the Gardener who had possessed the memories of Macros the Black—it had been a ploy by Kalkin, the Trickster God, and it had provided Pug and his son with useful information leading to saving Midkemia from a dreadful invasion, but at great cost: the utter obliteration of the world of Kelewan and most of the inhabitants. Even if the Dasati's memories had not been his own, his belief that he was Macros had given Magnus the opportunity to get to know his grandfather slightly.

Magnus went down to the kitchen with his father, and found Amirantha and Brandos waiting at a table, just finishing a meal. "Where are the others?" asked Pug.

Brandos said, "Gulamendis is studying that demon book you found on Queg, and Sandreena is busy being somewhere else." The last was said with a glance at Amirantha, who almost winced but managed to keep his reaction to the comment minimal.

Magnus said, "Anything interesting in the books we brought back?"

"Not really," said Magnus. "There are a couple of things that are probably worth a little study, but this was Grandfather's work from a long time ago, if I can judge these things. I remember the story you told of coming here after the Riftwar ended, and finding a letter from him about his library, giving it to you. What he took to Telesan were copies. Exact copies, so I think they were magic duplicates, not made by scribes. Perhaps if we had saved everything by considering the titles there we might get some idea of why he went there after leaving Midkemia and what he was hoping to accomplish."

"You have a better memory than most, Magnus," said Pug. "I can remember a dozen titles I tossed aside. Let's quickly draw up a list and compare them, and with those we brought back with us, perhaps we'll get some understanding of this previously unknown jaunt of your grand-father's."

Magnus made a slow exhalation, not quite a sigh, and said, "Again another reason to miss Mother."

Pug reached out and took his son's hand for a moment, squeezing it slightly, then releasing it. "I know." Both father and son knew that Miranda might have provided an insight into what her father had been doing on that other world. "One thing," said Pug. "More than anything else, Macros having lived for a time on Telesan—and from having his own quarters, in some station of importance—clearly indicates a connection between our world and that one. It seemed a little too coincidental that the brothers would flee from their Hub world and end up somewhere that just happened to be a former residence of Macros the Black."

"Kalkin?"

"Who knows what the gods are doing?" replied Pug. "I have long ago accepted the notion that I will never fully understand this struggle, our part in it, or just how much good we are accomplishing."

Amirantha said, "I'd say quite a bit, even if not intentionally."

Pug asked, "How do you judge that?"

"Your friend, Kaspar, he is doing remarkable things in Muboya and the region has never been this peaceful in my lifetime, and that's over a hundred years.

"You've got people from various nations around the world putting the safety of this planet ahead of their personal interests and their national interests. I am hardly anyone's idea of a good man, Pug, yet here I am doing my bit for the greater well-being of the world." He smiled slightly and said, "That's no mean achievement."

"Perhaps," Pug said. "There are times I wish it was worth the price."

No one at the table said anything. Amirantha and Brandos had both witnessed Miranda's death at the hands of a demon who had been feigning death and then leaped upon her back before anyone could prevent it.

Finally Brandos said, "So, if I might presume to ask, what's next?"

Pug said, "We—the same group as before—head down to Kesh and inspect that thing being built in the Valley of Lost Men. From Sandreena's description, I don't have a remote idea what they are doing."

Amirantha said, "Neither do I. Gulamendis and I have talked into the night about what we thought we knew of demon lore and what we are now discovering." He shook his head in wonder. "I am not ashamed to admit I have been humbled to discover how little I truly understood."

Brandos grinned and clapped his old friend on the shoulder. "That's a good start." He stood and said, "Well, if we're going off again, I think I should go spend a little time with my wife. She's starting to feel neglected and that's never a good thing."

Pug nodded, a slightly sad expression on his face.

A young magician came into the kitchen and said, "Pug, we've just had word from Lord Kaspar that he will be here in an hour."

Pug stood up and said, "Good. That means we leave after sundown. I wanted his military expertise."

Amirantha said, "Well, I think I'll leave Brandos and Samantha to their own . . . devices, and I will go find Gulamendis and see if he's come up with any new insights from his reading. A little rest before we go would be nice."

Magnus and his father were left alone at the table, while those in the kitchen were trying to ignore them as much as possible. Finally, Magnus said, "I wonder how Laromendis is doing up in Elvandar?"

Pug absently nodded. "I wonder, too."

Laromendis stood before Tomas, and despite his complete understanding of what had been told to him about the figure he regarded being a human transformed by ancient magic into the likeness of a Valheru—a Dragon Lord—he still had to fight the alternating urge to kneel or to run in terror. He wondered if he would ever get over that feeling, no matter how many times he had come to see him.

"Laromendis," said Tomas, motioning for the Taredhel conjurer to take a seat at the small table in the Queen's private chamber. "You wished to speak to me in private?"

"Yes, my lord"—Tomas held up his hand. "Err, yes, Tomas." He laughed slightly. "I may never get used to that."

Tomas smiled and behind the warrior's powerful visage a youthful humor seemed to peek out. "It took a while for a lot of people around here to get used to it, Laro. You don't mind if I call you that? I overheard your brother call you that."

Laromendis was startled, but the smile directed at him was infectious, even charming, and he said, "Why, no. I'd be flattered. He's the only one who ever did, but, please, feel free."

"So, why did you wish to see me alone?"

"Not alone, for I am certain you'll need to consult the Queen. I'm here at Pug's behest."

At the mention of his childhood friend's name, Tomas's expression became concerned. "How is he?"

"Well, I guess. He took Miranda's death very hard." The elf said, "I don't know how such things are with humans, I must admit, but I got a sense of a profound sorrow. Lately, however, as the matters that brought me here have arisen, well, I think he's coming out of his darkness."

"That's good to hear," said Tomas, adjusting the white tunic he wore when not armored. Even without the helm of gold and the white and gold armor, he was an impressive sight. Laromendis was one of the few beings Tomas met who was taller, yet the Star Elf was still in awe of the imposing Warleader of Elvandar.

"To the point, then," said Laromendis. "Pug asks if you

might be disposed to convey the following to the Lord Regent at E'bar: indications are that the Demon Legion may be arriving in Midkemia soon. Would he be willing to discuss a mutual defense?"

Tomas was silent for a moment, then laughed. "Why is he asking you to ask me?"

"Because I am not particularly in a position to influence the Lord Regent and, frankly, of all of those not of our race on this world, you are perhaps the only being he holds in . . ."

"Fear?" said Tomas with a slight smile.

"I was going to say respect, my lord."

Tomas inclined his head slightly, as if considering a question. "Your Lord Regent is a complicated person. He exhibits a certain deference to My Lady and myself, yet I sense he views us with some suspicion."

"He's is a proud being, of ambition for our people and himself personally, as well." Laromendis continued, "My brother and I have spent more time here than any Taredhel, so we begin to understand, at least a little, how profound the Eledhel ties to this world, this Home, are." He fell silent a moment, then said, "But even we have no doubt that our branch of this far-flung family is . . ."

"Superior?" supplied Tomas with a slight narrowing of his eyes.

"I was going to say more highly advanced." He glanced around the room, fashioned from within the living bole of a majestic "Star," as Laromendis's people called these magnificent trees. "There is a fundamental rightness here, Lord Tomas. Those who remained here kept intact an unbroken line of service, remaining in harmony with the most fundamental aspects of our world.

"We who fled the Chaos Wars took with us what we could carry, nothing more, and out of that humble beginning a ragged band of refugees conquered the stars." He looked Tomas directly in the eyes for perhaps the first time and said, "If we tend to be arrogant, we earned the right."

"I have lived the life of a human, Laromendis, and recalled the life of a Valheru; I have lived here with My Lady's people for more than a century and this I can tell you: power in and of itself is worthy of neither respect nor contempt. It simply is. It is how power is employed, for what purpose and toward what ends that ennoble or denigrate the wielder of power. When I don my armor, there are few beings on this world who can rival my abilities, Pug being perhaps the only one able to best me." With an unexpected smile, again recalling a boyish quality that was very unexpected, he added, "It's certainly a good thing he is my closest friend and ally." His smile faded. "But I have done things under the sway of my own power, back in the early days of coming to my station, that I know now to have been cruel, base, and completely unworthy of any rational being.

"I say all this to make it clear that while the Eledhel may appear rustic, or even primitive, to your people, they are hardly that. The Spellweavers' magic is subtle, but no less powerful than that of your people who raise up mighty cities by making the rocks flow and move as they wish. Those cousins of yours who reside with us, the Eldar, have much the same lore and magic as your own 'mancers, yet they choose not to reshape Elvandar, but rather to adapt to it."

He closed one eye and smiled. "Now, to the real reason you wish me to speak to the Lord Regent rather than carrying Pug's message yourself."

Laromendis was forced to laugh. "Primarily because, as I said, the Lord Regent respects you as much as any being not of the Taredhel. And, the somewhat less important, but very real disregard for my brother and me he holds—our crafts are not held in high regard by our people—and lastly, he most certainly thinks Gulamendis and I are dead, lost in the battle of the Hub."

"You've neglected to inform your people you survived," Tomas said.

"We're not entirely sure our being abandoned there was an accident of war. In fact, it may be it was by design."

Tomas said nothing.

"If I might be so bold, if you undertake the charge Pug sends you to consider, it would be useful if you could discreetly deliver a message to one Tandarae, Lorekeeper of the Regent's Meet. He would be the one most likely to let us know if we can return to be hailed as clever survivors of a hopeless battle or if we would be executed for desertion in the face of the enemy."

"That would prove a useful thing to know before showing your faces in E'bar," Tomas agreed. "Until then, what are your plans?"

"I would like to return to my brother on Sorcerer's Isle. He's quite enthused about the opportunities there to learn about our own crafts from people from other cultures. I must confess I am more dubious than he, but his enthusiasm about the things he has learned from a human Warlock named Amirantha is intriguing. And while my arts don't plumb the depths of dark mystery as his do, I am always looking to improve my craft."

"A wise choice," said Tomas. "Though you would certainly be welcome to stay in Elvandar should you wish."

Just then the curtain moved aside and Aglaranna, Queen of Elvandar, entered. "Greetings, Laromendis." Coming from court she wore a simple but regal gown of sky blue, trimmed in white at the collar and cuffs. Her only jewelry was the simple gold circlet with a ruby gem in the bow, which held back her mane of auburn hair.

Without thought, Laromendis stood, then took a knee before the Queen, bowing his head. "It is a joy to see you again, My Lady."

"Please rise," she bid him.

He did, but would not sit in her presence. He was as overwhelmed by the Queen as he had been the first time he had come to this court. In a real sense, she was as powerful a presence as her husband, but in a completely different fashion. Tomas evoked ancient fear and a need for obedience, impulses that could be battled and overcome. Aglaranna overcame the senses with her beauty and majesty. There was nothing challenging in her nature and that made her irresistible. Softly, the Conjurer said, "If possible, My Lady, Lord Tomas, it might prove useful if the Lord Regent could be persuaded to visit Elvandar."

"We have extended the invitation," said Tomas.

"Perhaps you should be a little more insistent, Lord Tomas." He studied the Queen, her nearly flawless and ageless beauty, her reddish brown hair and finely sculpted features. She possessed a beauty he did not find personally attractive in the females of his own race; he preferred a more robust-looking female, and by Taredhel standards the Queen was small, almost petite. Yet her beauty was something that transcended the merely physical, defied the logic of attraction; it was the same beauty he found walking in the sacred grove; if Home had a soul, it was Elvandar, and if Elvandar could be embodied in a single being, it would be the Queen.

"If you will excuse me, My Queen, Lord Tomas, I will take this clever device Pug gave me and employ it to return to Sorcerer's Island."

The Queen gave her consent, and the Conjurer removed the device from his belt pouch, thumbed a switch, and with a faint humming was suddenly gone.

Aglaranna looked at her husband and said, "What word does he bring from Pug?"

"Dire warning, and an attempt to reach out to the Taredhel and ask alliance."

She moved out of her chair to kneel before her husband, still almost girlish in her fluid grace. She rested her head on his knee, as a child might with a parent, and said, "What are we to do with our newly returned cousins?"

"That is the problem, my love," said Tomas, stroking

her hair. "They are not 'returned,' and I think they never will be. Like those of the Ocedhel who remain across the waters, they feel no need to come here.

"We shall endeavor to respect their independence, and we will try to be friends."

"Friends? You don't sound hopeful."

Tomas said nothing. He knew in his heart that since the coming of the Tsurani invaders, when he'd begun his strange and wonderful journey into the life he now lived, more than the army of the Emerald Queen, even more than the Dasati invaders, these Star Elves posed the gravest threat to Elvandar he had ever beheld.

CHAPTER 15

STRATEGY

Pug signaled for silence.

Kaspar, onetime Duke of Olasko and now General of the Army and First Advisor to the Maharaja of Muboya, said, "Pug has asked me to take over conducting this next bit of business.

"As I understand it from what Sandreena, here"—he indicated the newly minted Mother-Bishop of the Order of the Shield of the Weak; somehow Pug had contrived to get her a new cape and surcoat emblazoned with her badge of rank—"and what that dwarf Keandar said about his captivity, we have two tasks at once.

"The first is gaining intelligence, which has to take precedence over any other consideration. The second will be to effect any rescues if we may. Sandreena, explain how, if you please."

"If any guard or worker is wearing a talisman around his neck, something like a red wolf's skull on a black background, they are under some mystic control. They are compelled to attack anyone not wearing the same device." She looked around the room. "When I struggled with Keandar, as soon as I tore it off him, he regained his own volition. My suggestion is we find outlying sentries and quickly overpower and free them. They are not being fed well nor rested, it seems, so it should not be too difficult."

Kaspar continued. "If they're up to it, they can help us; if not, we shall direct them up the trail to the abandoned Keshian fortress and from there we'll arrange safe transportation back to their homes." He looked at two young magicians, Jason and Akeem, and said, "You will be up at that fortress and coordinate getting those wretches safely away."

"This is not a military adventure, and while it may look at first like a raid, it is not. From the description of that monstrosity they're building, if we are there longer than an hour, we are dead," said Kaspar. "Coming down that switchback trail prevents a fast assault by foot or horse, so we will approach stealthily, and if we have to leave in a hurry—" He nodded to Pug.

"Each of us will have a transportation sphere, set to bring you back here."

From the corner of the room a voice said, "I count eight of us going down there, Kaspar. That's either too many or too few."

Kaspar smiled. "Jim, I was wondering where you were lurking."

Out of the shadows stepped the head of the Kingdom's intelligence service and he was wearing an effective black cloak over dark grey tunic and trousers. "Too many, or too few."

"That's why we will split into two groups." He pointed

to Pug. "Pug, along with Gulamendis, Amirantha, and Brandos, will investigate whatever that device is, looking to discern its magical purpose, assuming there is one and it's not just a majestic monument to demonic vanity.

"I will take Sandreena to scout out the military aspects of the place, with Magnus there to provide any magical aid we might need. Feel free to join either group."

"I think I'll tag along with you, Kaspar." He grinned. "Keeps the groups even."

"Wise," said the former Duke of Olasko. "Given there is little difference in time between here and that valley, we leave at sundown. Get something to eat, some rest, and meet out in the courtyard just before the sun sets."

Laromendis entered the room as the group was disbanding, and came to stand before Pug. "Tomas says he will travel to E'bar and speak with the Lord Regent," he said.

Pug studied the elf's face and said, "And . . . ?"

Surprised the human could detect the subtleties of elven expression, he said, "I hold little hope you'll get any cooperation from the Regent's Meet. They're handpicked to agree with him. If the demons come, he will not help; he'll just order us to dig in and look for another escape route while the rest of you fight them."

Pug nodded. "Will you go back?"

Laromendis paused, as if thinking, then said, "They think my brother and I are dead; it might serve all our causes if they continued to think that for a while longer. I will stay here with my brother, if you will accept me."

Pug nodded. "Talk to your brother about tonight's expedition. I wouldn't mind you along to look for . . . anything the rest of us might not see."

Laromendis said, "Of course," and went to where his brother still sat.

Magnus came to stand next to his father and whispered, "What are we expecting to see down there?"

"Nothing I can imagine, and I can imagine a lot, my

son. Let's get something to eat then rest a little. I have a feeling it may be a very long night." The two magicians left the meeting room.

Amirantha sat alone on the steps leading up into the keep. It was late afternoon and he had eaten. Sunset was an hour or more away, but he didn't feel the need for rest. He just tried to keep his mind calm as he contemplated what they were to investigate in a few hours.

After the wet, cold weather, a series of storms, and little sunshine, this day had been a welcome respite, a balmy hint of spring and summer to come. Amirantha felt a deep mix of anticipation—the idea of discovery—and concern: the risks. It had been easy at first to throw in his lot with this bunch, the mad magicians and happy warriors who served an abstracted greater good.

Then he had watched Miranda die.

He had seen death before, even having lost those for whom he cared, but no small part of his view had always been that these were people fated to die eventually, so what mattered when? He realized with bitter self-loathing that this had been a facile apology, a not very well-considered reason why he shouldn't care. In Miranda he had come to know a woman of stunning ability, magic knowledge that rivaled Pug's and dwarfed Amirantha's. Moreover, she had been long-lived, older than he by a century, yet looked no older than advancing middle age. She could have expected another century or more, yet there she was, dying in a brutal, bloody, and sudden fashion before those around her could help.

Nothing in his life's experience had driven home to Amirantha the fragility of life more than that one instant. Pug, Magnus, himself, and other magic-users of considerable ability stood close enough to reach out and touch her, yet none could react quickly enough to keep her alive. It was like watching someone drown as you stood helpless on the shore.

It had left a sick feeling in the Warlock's stomach that had lingered. A year after and he still felt as if he should have been able to do something to help, for he was the Warlock, he was the master of demons.

A stirring caused him to turn, and he saw Sandreena standing behind him. He started to rise, and she pushed his shoulder, forcing him back down. Trying to regain his poise, he said, "If you're going to hit me again, please don't. I'm really very tired of picking myself up off the floor."

She smiled a sad smile and softly said, "Sorry. You bring out the worst in me."

He tilted his head slightly, and said, "It's a talent."

She surprised him by sitting down next to him. "I've given some thought to this situation."

He was about to ask which situation—the need to scout the demon site once more, her elevation to high office, or them finding themselves together—but in a rare attack of wisdom he said, "Really?" in as neutral a way as he could imagine.

"You find that surprising?" she asked accusingly.

He tried to remain even-toned. "I don't find it surprising you've thought about things, but rather that you'd speak to me of it."

"Really?" she echoed, her tone very confrontational.

He knew he was rapidly losing any hope of a civil conversation. In the time they had spent together he had found her a perplexing combination of a keen intellect and a tendency to impulsive behavior that bordered on the reckless. Her order taught a quick evaluation was necessary in determining which side of a conflict to come down on, but it seemed to have had the collateral effect of denuding her of the ability to take a moment and consider. He just nodded.

"I have been known to give consideration to weighty matters," she said, her eyes narrowing and her tone rising. "I only came to speak with you because despite the horrible excuse for a man you've become, you still know more of demon lore than anyone I've met. Besides, Magnus told me of your discovery in Queg and I need to know what you uncovered about the demons we face."

Amirantha studied her face for a moment, unsure of exactly what she expected of him; he decided his best course was to take what she said at face value. "Do you want to know what we've uncovered about demons in general or specifically what we think about the bunch we're going to go face down in Kesh?"

"I've seen the ones we're facing in Kesh personally, remember," she retorted with her eyes narrowing in anger. "Brandos says you and the elf have come up with all manner of new things about demons and you're barely able to contain yourselves you're so giddy from it."

Amirantha looked pained at the thought of being portrayed as "giddy." "Brandos tends to colorful characterization at times. In any event, what we've found is, if accurate, a completely different perspective on what is known as the 'Fifth Circle' of Hell.

"Demon summoners like Gulamendis and myself are self-taught for the most part, and occasionally we meet others with whom we can share what we know. In Queg I found a . . . for lack of a better word, a book, but it's more than that. It's a comprehensive examination of the Fifth Circle. The author was often viewed as a madman, and the work was thought a fabrication to perhaps thrill a rich patron or terrify the gullible, but both Gulamendis and myself find the work credible."

"Why?" asked Sandreena, her personal ire toward Amirantha set aside for the moment by genuine interest in what he had to say.

"The first thing I noticed was demon stench—the book reeks of it. Whoever scribed this work did so in the presence of demons." He got a faraway look and said, "It's almost as if it was the demon reciting facts and the scribe writing them down. The other thing is what he said about demon lore that was familiar to me and Gulamendis was both accurate and . . ." He looked at her. "We both know that in my time I have engineered any number of ploys to chivy confidence in the gullible to better separate them from their gold. A confidence often tends to the grand, and the weakness of a bad confidence is to overstate things. This work while sensational in scope and depth of subject is not overly given to grandiosity. If anything, it's a little dull and academic."

"Or exceptionally clever in execution."

"But toward what end? It's one thing to rush to some minor baron and claim a demon is running around his woodlands, and for a small price you'll spare the villagers of having their children devoured. It's quite another to spend . . . years writing this tome, and then what? Sell it? No, the author was earnest."

"What does it say that will help?" asked Sandreena, now genuinely interested.

"Our experience with demons appears to have been with only a portion of their population. There are many details I will skip, but here's one. Demons when summoned must be confined, else they run amok and devour everything they can. Or they flee into dark places and hide, waiting for their opportunity to venture forth, then they run amok and devour everything they can. That's the difference between the powerful demons and the clever ones. Occasionally we find a clever one with some talent for magic; they are especially difficult.

"Gulamendis and I both have skills which confine a demon's choices when summoned. They are called into a circle of power that limits their ability to move without our permission. When I summon one, it must become subject to my will or I return it to the demon realm. If it becomes my servant, then I can allow it to depart from the confines of the circle and allow it to roam."

"So it can run around the woodlands frightening the villagers so you can part the gullible baron from his gold?" Amirantha nodded. "Or perhaps put on a fetching visage and climb into your bed?"

Amirantha closed his eyes a second, then said, "I will not tell you I am sorry one more time, Sandreena. I did what I did and you have continued to punish me for it every time we meet. Enough!" His tone was sharp, but not loud. "Dalthea . . . you bury three lovers over a century and see if finding comfort with an immortal being with beauty and amorous skills doesn't become appealing."

"Three?" said Sandreena. "You never said . . ."

"And you never asked." He looked her in the eyes. "I thought us two strangers who chanced to meet in an improbable place, a village with the silly name of Yellow Mule, and thought us both seeking the comfort of the moment, both the body and the heart. I was a traveling mountebank who occasionally did real work with demons and you were the very serious young knight trying to do some great good in the world. I thought it but a passing thing, not what it turned out to be; I never meant to hurt you."

"You lied to me!"

"I lie," he retorted. "That's what charlatans do. We lie. We cheat. We do what we find in our own best interest." He looked out at the distant sky as if remembering.

"Then what brings you here?" she said, her eyes bright with emotion.

He let out a long sigh, leaning so he could put one arm on the step above him, and his shoulders sagged. "Honestly, I don't know. I look at the grey in Brandos's hair and realize that if he doesn't get himself killed in a brawl, in ten, twenty years I bury another person I love. And Samantha. I'm over a hundred years your elder, Sandreena. I was a man full grown when your grandmother was a baby. For all I know, I bedded her. I need something more than being a confidence trickster, a liar, and a cheat. I need something bigger than myself." He let his voice fall. "I thought I might stay with others like me for a while. Pug is older than I, as was Miranda.

"When I saw her killed, I realized that no matter how long or short our lives may be, we must do something with them." He shrugged and gave her a sad smile. "That's when I decided to stay and help. I can't undo those things in my past I regret, but I can strive to do better from now on."

She studied his face and remained silent, then finally said, "Tell me about these demons."

He realized that in some way she had just forgiven him, or at least agreed to forget how he had wronged her. What that meant was unclear, but at least he could turn his attention to the matter at hand.

"The demons that we conjure are from what can be called the outer precinct of hell, a region of sheer chaos and confusion. There, life is a nonstop struggle for dominance.

"But, if you think of the Fifth Circle as a disk, and the outer precinct as the rim, the farther toward the center you move the more organized it gets." He paused. "It's hard to describe, because if I make it sound as if demonkind resembles us in any way it's a false comparison. But we lack the understanding of their nature to truly describe their society.

"They have a King, or several, and a High King, whose name is not known, but under him reign Kings in each region. The King that we thought we faced was called Maarg, a being almost certainly gone, but whose legend someone keeps alive to keep some element of that outer precinct in a semblance of order.

"He may have been replaced by Dahun, the demon my brother and his mad followers seem to worship, or Dahun may be the ruler of a different region of hell.

"There are a thousand more questions than we have answers, but two have come to the fore: why are the demons fighting among themselves, and how can some of them exist in this realm without magic protection?"

Sandreena said, "I thought the act of summoning gave them the protection they required?"

"Yes, the circle of confinement is also a circle of protection and when they bow to our will, we protect them from quickly succumbing to this environment. But what of those demons we didn't summon?

"Pug told me of the demon he faced, who replaced the Emerald Queen—"

Sandreena interrupted. "The temple has long had dealings with demon possessions, Amirantha."

"Yes, discorporate demon spirits, but they are simply another type of demon, a minor creature of the mind that can take over a weak individual. But even that tenure is brief.

"No, this demon Jakan didn't possess the Emerald Queen; he killed her and took her place, with a conjured seeming, a likeness that even those closest to her couldn't penetrate."

"Impressive."

"Laromendis is considered a great Conjurer among the Star Elves and he says he could not do this for long. He said the ability to maintain the illusion for . . . months is a feat beyond imagining!

"Who was this Jakan? A weak spirit demon who preyed on weaker souls when he first came into this world and worked up to having the strength to do what he did? Or was he something else?"

"You love questions, don't you?" She spoke softly and there was a resignation in her voice.

He smiled. "And you seek answers."

There was a faint smile, then suddenly her eyes narrowed and the moment was gone. "Demons," she insisted.

Amirantha stood up and said, "It's easier if I show you." He motioned for her to accompany him.

She followed him into the keep and they passed the kitchen workers preparing a meal for those who hadn't eaten already. Brandos and his wife sat quietly in the corner, her head resting on his shoulder, holding hands. She had seen him go off to fight enough times that she knew there was nothing to say, apparently, so they luxuriated in the moment together in silence.

Amirantha led Sandreena up the stairs of the tower in which he had been housed, to the room set aside for his use. In the room they found Gulamendis avidly reading the volume. He looked up and smiled, the first openly friendly and genuinely excited expression either of them had seen on the elf since his first coming to the island.

"This is amazing!" he said. "Every time I reread it, I find new things about which to wonder."

Amirantha said, "If you don't mind, why don't you explain to Sandreena why this book is important?"

"First, it is genuine," said the elf. He slowly reached out and said, "Give me your hand," to Sandreena. He gently placed it on the book and in a second she snatched it back.

"Demon," she said. "I can feel it. It reeks."

Like a delighted child, Gulamendis asked, "Where to begin?"

Amirantha asked, "Did you make any sense of that battle you and your brother witnessed on Telesan?"

"I think so," said Gulamendis. "It would probably be better if I showed you."

He moved the book over and opened the back cover, lying it flat on the desk. He carefully unfolded the last page, until a map was revealed four times the size of a normal page. The map had been drawn in a vivid style, in garish colored inks, with many illustrations of demons of all stripes along the edges, with small narratives below each drawing telling something about that creature.

But Sandreena was instantly taken with the map itself, for it was a massive disk, divided into two circles, outer and inner, with the center circle being again divided into segments. "This outer circle is where the two of us have plied our craft," he said to Sandreena, while he pointed at Amirantha. "The beings we summon from here are what you most likely have faced before in your travels. The author of this work calls them the 'lesser infernals.'"

"Lesser?" Sandreena shook her head in disbelief. "I've confronted some very big and nasty demons in my time."

Gulamendis nodded slightly and said, "As have we all. No, lesser doesn't mean strength or magic power, I am certain. It's about organization, or rather lack of organization. It's a demon-eat-demon realm."

Sandreena put her hand near the map, just outside the border, and said, "What's here, beyond the edge?"

Gulamendis looked annoyed at the interruption, but it was Amirantha who spoke. "Consider this something of a metaphor. The Fifth Circle is no more a disk than it is a circle. It's a region, and I'm sure it has boundaries and what's beyond those boundaries . . . ? The void perhaps, or some other realm we do not know of, or perhaps it is the boundary with the Fourth Circle or the Sixth. In any event, it is this realm with which we are concerned, O seeker of answers." The last was said in a friendly manner, but Sandreena's dark look told the Warlock she wasn't in the mood for banter.

"May I continue?" asked the elf.

"Please," said Amirantha before Sandreena could ask another question.

"It's in this inner realm where all our answers lie." His finger stabbed around and he said, "It appears that chaos is something of the demonic nature, but at least in the inner circle, the circle of the greater demons, some semblance of order has emerged over the ages; these areas, what the author of this work calls 'cantons,' are each ruled by a demon lord, a self-anointed king, archduke, or some other like title."

"Maarg?" asked Sandreena, having heard from Pug of the Demon King's corpse being found on the Saaur world of Shila.

"He ruled the outer ring, as best I can tell," said Gulamendis. "It is an every-demon-for-himself sort of place, and he literally clawed and bullied his way to the top. As best we can tell from this, Amirantha and I feel that what we had discerned about demons before all this began was in the main true, demons have a loose organization of alliances and services. You either destroyed your rivals, absorbing their power, or you found service. Those who were weaker than you found a stronger demon to serve in exchange for protection, and the stronger demon had a retinue ready to aid him in conflicts with his rivals. A lot of rising and falling among the demons of the outer circle was the result of betrayal, ambush, and treachery. And it always raised the question in my mind of how anything remotely like a society could arise from this chaos. How could they evolve beyond animal states, to have a language and magic?

"But here," he said, indicating the inner circle, "is the answer. Each canton has its own society, apparently an army, and a ruler. Demons who somehow evolve enough to escape the outer circle but who don't contest for domination, they find their way to one of these cantons and . . ." He shrugged. "I'm not certain. Service? Slavery? Freedom?

"We struggle to apply mortal concepts to a race more alien than anything we've encountered, even trolls and goblins."

"Certainly true," said Amirantha. "The author of this work labeled these cantons with a variety of colorful names, 'Pandemonia,' 'Discordia,' 'Despair,' 'the Miasma,' and 'the Fallen.' We have no way to know what the demons themselves call these cantons, or even if the number of five is correct, or much about them."

"He writes a great deal on experiences here on Midkemia with demons, and the rest is inference as well as specifics about this place." Gulamendis sat back and crossed his arms over his chest. "Putting aside colorful embellishment, at the heart of this work stands this truth: there exists a realm that is threatening ours, at the heart of which stands a society or societies about which we know almost nothing. In fact, one about which we were ignorant until recently." With no vanity, he pointed to Amirantha and said, "And we are, most likely, as expert on the subject as any two beings you might find in this world today."

"Speaking of 'at the heart,' " said Sandreena, pointing to a dark spot in the middle of the map. "What is that?"

Gulamendis shrugged. "Another tiny realm perhaps? All I can say is it is marked with a single word, 'Void,' and about it nothing is written anywhere."

Laromendis arrived at the door and said, "Ah, there you are. Time to gather below. We are leaving."

Sandreena, Amirantha, and Gulamendis all looked out the window and saw the sun hanging low in the western sky. Without further discussion, they hurried down to the marshaling yard.

CHAPTER 16

Reconnaissance

Kaspar signaled.

They had ventured down the first trail, taking them to the rim of the valley, where they would begin the tedious descent down the switchback trails unless Pug decided he and Magnus needed to get everyone down in a hurry. All the magic-users had been cautioned to not use magic in any form, active or passive, unless they were attacked, as the defenders might have wards up to detect it. Looking at the long trail downward, and more trail beyond the distant rim, Amirantha turned to Gulamendis and said, "At least we should have a quick exit. I'd hate to have to run back up those trails."

The elf nodded. "Some of my people are hardy, able to do this for days. I am not one of them."

They had discussed this plan in detail, but arriving on the rim of the valley, where they could first see the construction, had caused them all to stop. "My gods," said Kaspar. "What is it?"

The construction apparently was finished. The four large arching towers now pointed to a center point above the vast open area in the center of the wall structure.

Pug said, "It looks something like the portal used by the Dasati when they invaded Kelewan, though they punched that through from the other side and didn't have all this construction around it. They used a magic shield that was very difficult to breach and expanded it as they sent more and more of their Deathknights through."

Sandreena said, "Where are all the laborers?" She pointed and said, "There were hundreds of them working, after sunset, and demon overseers patrolling the walls."

Pug said, "We need to get closer. I can see some movement in the distance, but it's too far to make out who it is."

Kaspar said, "Sandreena, lead us to that gully, please."

His band had worked their way down the switchback trails cautiously, Sandreena at his side, until they reached the gully she had used to circumvent the guard post at the bottom of the slope. In single file they followed her to the rim of the dry river basin, and after motioning for the others to wait, Kaspar and Sandreena crawled on their bellies up to the rim and looked over.

"It's quiet," whispered Kaspar.

"On the wall," said Sandreena.

Sentries could be seen walking the battlements, but between the basin and the wall was only empty ground. "It's going to be difficult to get close," said Kaspar.

"We should approach from the back," said Sandreena. "There's a dry river basin that flows close to the wall." She pointed off to their left.

Kaspar motioned for Pug to come join them and when he did, Kaspar said, "Are you going to be safe using magic?"

Pug said, "Magnus and I have been testing as gently as possible, and we don't sense anything unexpected." He looked at the massive construction ahead of them and said, "Something in there is very powerful, but it's dormant for the moment. There are a few wards to detect scrying, but they're basic, nothing we can't avoid." He looked at the five crouching figures down in the basin behind and said, "I think we stick to the original plan."

Kaspar nodded. "Wait ten minutes until we have worked our way around to the back of this fortress and then do what you think is best. If we hear any sounds of alarm from your group, we will have Magnus take us back up to the plateau above.

"If you hear any trouble on our part, do what you think best."

Pug and Magnus, along with Amirantha, provided a formidable magic force, and might make the difference between the others getting back alive or not; after a long argument, Kaspar had relented as Pug insisted that he should be the one to decide if he should come to Kaspar's aid or not. Kaspar was secretly relieved.

Sandreena followed Kaspar, Laromendis, Magnus, and Jim Dasher up the dry riverbed, while Pug rejoined Brandos, Amirantha, and Gulamendis. They slowly counted ten minutes, then Pug said, "Laromendis, be ready to make us look like a pile of dirt."

The elf smiled slightly and said, "That should be no problem, assuming no one is looking very hard at our pile of dirt and we don't have to be dirt for too long."

Brandos chuckled, then turned to listen. "Someone's coming," he whispered and they all scooted close to the face of the basin, looking upward.

A demon sentry walked close to the edge and glanced downward, blinking for a moment. He had a bovine head with massive red eyes and a prodigious pair of horns that swept up and out. He grunted once, blinked, then moved on.

When he was away, Pug turned and asked the elf,
"Dirt?"

"Dirt," answered Laromendis. "Next time, try to get
me a little more warning."

"Those cattle heads tend to be fairly stupid," said
Amirantha.

"It also helps they're nearsighted," said Brandos. "That
fact alone has saved my head more than once."

Pug shook his head. "A nearsighted sentry?"

Brandos whispered, "It makes them nervous. They
jump at any motion they detect. If we stay in the dark and
don't move, they'll probably miss us even without the spell
of seeming that brother elf just cast."

Pug said, "Let's go that way," indicating the direction
from which the sentry had walked. They crouched low and
moved up out of the basin, keeping low along the edge of
the depression.

They reached the road that led to the switchbacks up
the hill, and the sentry post Sandreena had described was
gone. Pug assumed they cleared everything from the perimeter once the gates and wall were finished, keeping the area
around the walls free of any possible concealment.

Into the darkness on the opposite side of the road they
crept, finding another depression behind which they could
crouch. Slowly they moved away from Kaspar's group.

Sandreena held up a balled fist, indicating those behind her
should stop. Kaspar gently put his hand on her shoulder,
letting her know he was coming up behind her so as not
to startle her. She signaled there were sentries ahead, indicating two of them. He slowly rose up to peer over the
edge of the dried riverbank and saw two demons walking
a patrol before a small gate. They had traversed the perimeter halfway around the structure and had yet to see a safe
approach. The fortification looked as if it were able to withstand attacks for a short time, but not able to withstand a

long siege. There was no central structure beyond the walls, so any storage and quarters were either in small buildings nestled inside the walls, or nonexistent.

Kaspar indicated they should move away and when they were safely distant from the gate, he whispered, "I don't know what this place is, but it's like nothing I've encountered. It's easily defensible with a hundred soldiers, damn near impregnable with twice that, but I'll be damned if I see much sense to it otherwise."

"My best guess," said Sandreena, "is they built this to defend for a short while in case someone tumbled to what they were doing and tried to stop it. I see no close-by water source, no decent supply route, and no quarters for any garrison. It's as if they are willing to walk away from this place once they've accomplished whatever it is they plan on doing here."

"My thoughts as well," said Kaspar. He turned and motioned for Magnus to come close. Whispering, he said, "Do you have any sense of what this place is for?"

Magnus's expression was grave. "There is some very dark magic occurring within those walls. It's . . . muted, waiting for something to be unleashed, but it's there."

Suddenly a fine silver netting appeared out of the darkness and landed upon the white-haired magician. Magnus stiffened, then his eyes rolled up into his head as if he had been struck from behind by a massive blow. Kaspar and Sandreena crouched low and drew weapons as figures apparently rose up out of the soil of the plateau before them. Sandreena turned toward Laromendis and Jim Dasher, only to see them gone, and as she raised her mace and Kaspar his sword, a pair of finely woven silver nets descended over them.

Sandreena felt a shock course through her body, and her mind became a tumbling cascade of thoughts and images. Part of her knew she was under attack, but years of training, both martial and magic, wilted under the effect of that net. Her defensive spells refused to coalesce in her thoughts; moves as basic as raising a shield or hefting her mace, ingrained in her body's memory as much as her mind, became spastic jerking attempts to control herself.

Kaspar was likewise overcome, jerking and twisting as he sought to command his body by force of will to meet the coming attack. But like Sandreena and Magnus, he quickly fell to the ground.

Looking up they could see three figures covered in suits of fine cloth from head to toe, with only the smallest slits for eyes. The cloth was the same color as the dirt that had hidden them and they must have been lying in ambush for quite some time, perhaps hours, waiting for the intruders to get close enough to render them powerless.

Another figure appeared a moment later, a grinning bearded man who looked down at the three prone bodies and said, "Bring them!"

As he turned away, Sandreena managed to whisper, "Belasco!" She didn't know if Magnus or Kaspar could hear her.

Pain coursed through her body when she tried to move, but if she remained motionless, the pain faded. Her thoughts were still chaotic but she witnessed enough and remembered enough to have a sense of time passing as she and her companions were lifted and carried toward a small rear gate in the wall.

Then she found her thoughts fleeing, then came darkness.

Jim crouched down behind the smallest of rocks, his cloak pulled over him, motionless. No doubt he was likely to be discovered in a moment, but he had an instinct for when to flee and when to remain still. Right now his "bump of trouble" was telling him to get as close to the ground as humanly possible. He could hear muffled voices and sensed some movement ten yards ahead.

He had felt more than seen the ambush, and his reaction had been to leap backward, away from the fight. It was not cowardice but caution that motivated him; he wanted to be sure no one was coming up from behind. Those three steps backward and ducking low as whoever threw the net at Magnus jumped down the side of the dry riverbank, saved him from detection. Something happened to Laromendis, but he couldn't be certain. One moment the elven magic-user had been there, the next he wasn't.

Jim had his dagger ready, but kept still. He waited until he could hear no sound, then risked peeking out from under his cloak.

The riverbed was empty.

He had heard the brief struggle and knew the instant Magnus went down without a sound they were over-matched. Whoever waited for them expected a powerful magician; he assumed the same magic trap prevented San-dreena from using her abilities, and the nets had quickly rendered both her and Kaspar unconscious.

Pug and Kaspar had been clear in their instructions to him; he was the last link to the outside world if all else failed, and given the level of power and talent in this recon-naissance, he considered himself a desperate choice.

He crouched low, willing to risk looking out from under his cloak, but not willing to risk moving just yet. Where was that elf?

Then he saw Laromendis move and suddenly the elf was standing before him. He turned and looked down at Jim and whispered, "They're gone."

Jim stood up and Laromendis reached out to touch his cloak. "That is impressive."

"I'm good," whispered the noble-turned-thief-turned-spy, "but I'm not that good. This didn't come cheaply. The artifi-cer who wove it for me called it his 'cloak of blending,' and I suspect it uses magic similar to your own." He looked around for any sign of lingering danger. "What just happened?"

"Your guess is as good as mine," whispered the elf. "They were lying in wait. They knew we had magic-users with us, and they were ready."

"They knew we were coming."

"Apparently. What troubles me is how the ambush was executed."

Jim's brow furrowed. "Explain."

"We were not moving especially quickly, in fact we were very cautious. For those three ambushers to have secreted themselves in that location, in anticipation of our arrival, meant they had to be lying in those shallow depressions, covered with dirt, for quite some time, perhaps an hour or more."

"How did they breathe?"

Laromendis nodded emphatically. "I'm thinking they didn't breathe."

Jim's face became a mask of concern. "Necromancy?"

"Pug mentioned to my brother and me that one of his concerns was trying to understand how death magic and demon magic were linked, and we understood that concern, though we have had no experience with any such connection." The elf paused, then looked at Jim. "There may be a more prosaic explanation, but if those were . . . reanimated dead?"

Jim was, for the first time in years, uncertain what to do next. "We need to send word to Pug, and we need to follow those captors."

Laromendis said, "I'll find Pug. I can stop and hide, better than you can, but I cannot track or skulk, and that cloak gives you more flexibility than my magic does." He asked, "What should I tell Pug?"

"Tell him what you saw, nothing more. Don't speculate unless he asks, and tell him that if I don't find you within one hour he's to assume I've been taken as well." Jim glanced over the verge and said, "Good luck," then he wrapped his cloak around him and almost vanished.

"Good luck," returned Laromendis, fascinated at Jim's subtle bit of magic. He could see Jim moving along the verge of the dried river, but only if he looked directly at him and concentrated. He knew that if he took his eyes off of the human, he'd vanish from sight. The cloak did not render him invisible, but rather let him blend in with the surrounding terrain.

Laromendis decided he'd ask more about that cloak if they ever got out of here. He glanced around to ensure he wasn't being watched, then started back the way he had come, hoping to overtake Pug before they ran into trouble.

Pug motioned for the others to halt. They'd been making very slow progress, frustrated by the need to loop far to the northwest and then return toward the wall in tangential approaches. There was simply no good cover until they reached a point farther to the west, and from there they could hardly see anything. Kneeling behind an overhang that sheltered them from any but the keenest observation, he whispered, "This is getting us nowhere."

Gulamendis whispered, "Amirantha and I sense demons, but there are not that many, and they were scattered."

"Where?" asked Pug.

"All over," answered Amirantha. "A heavy concentration of them near that big gate where we first crossed over the road, but after that . . ." He shrugged.

"How about here?" asked Brandos.

"Few," answered the elf.

Looking at Pug, Brandos said, "Perhaps a direct approach?"

"What do you propose?" asked the magician.

Glancing around at the deep night sky and shrouded landscape, Brandos said, "Unless they have night vision like friend elf here, or a cat's, I can get close and take a look. It won't be the first time I've crawled on my stomach to get a look at an enemy position."

Pug thought for a moment and said, "I'm loath to use magic that might be detected until I know what we face. Get as close as you can, then get back here, but secrecy is paramount."

"Understood."

Brandos went up over the edge and on to the berm, crawling at a surprisingly efficient rate. Amirantha said, " 'Enemy position'?" He chuckled softly. "He means seeing where the local sheriff or city watch was waiting for us."

"As long as it works," whispered Pug.

Time dragged slowly and then they could hear Brandos returning. He snaked down on his stomach to where they crouched waiting, rolled over, and sat up. "There's a small gate a hundred yards and a bit to the southwest. It looks like it's the one part of the wall that's not quite finished. There's a wooden barrier they have to move to bring anything like a wagon in or out, and there's only one guard. A demon," he said to Amirantha with a grin.

"What manner?" asked the Warlock.

"Big battle demon, ram's head, all decked out in black armor carrying a huge double-bladed axe."

"Ram's head?" said Amirantha, looking at Gulamendis. The elf said, "They tend to be tractable if you can subdue them."

"If you can subdue them," echoed Amirantha.

"What are you thinking?" asked Pug.

"If we can subdue that demon, even for just a few minutes," said Amirantha, "that gives us a point of ingress. If you have the means to get in unseen and look about—"

"I can do that," said Pug. "I can render myself unseen for a short period."

"That's good," said Gulamendis with a slight smile, "as we should only be able to subdue that demon for a short period."

"What do we do with him when he stops being subdued and starts shouting alarm?" asked Brandos.

"I expect it will be dead by then," said Amirantha pointedly.

Brandos rolled his eyes. "They tend to stop being cooperative as soon as you start killing them."

"Then do it quickly," he said to Brandos and Gulamendis.

"You hook him," said Brandos, "and we'll gut him and cook him." Gulamendis nodded. "I've got one banishment that's very quick, but it tends to be messy."

"I don't mind messy," said Pug. "If we need to leave in a hurry, we can."

"What about Magnus and his bunch?" asked Brandos.

"If they hear trouble, they know what to do," answered Pug.

"I hope so," said Brandos. "Because I certainly don't."

Pug said to Amirantha, "Take the lead."

Amirantha nodded, but instead of crawling forward as Brandos had, he stood, motioning for the others to follow, and started walking straight to the gate.

The sentry was looking the other way for a moment when Amirantha loomed up in the darkness, and when he turned his sheep-like head in the Warlock's direction, he uttered a curious sound, "Uh?"

Before he could make another, Amirantha had used a single word spell that stunned the creature, causing the huge axe he held to drop from limp fingers. Amirantha said to Pug, "You have perhaps ten minutes. Five is more like it."

Pug said, "I'll be back in five minutes." He took a quick glance at Amirantha who stood with hand outstretched, his magic controlling the demon. Brandos stood ready to strike a killing blow if needed, with Gulamendis ready to banish the creature.

Pug took a deep breath, then started walking toward the now unguarded entryway. As he moved around the makeshift wooden barrier, he unleashed a spell he had never used before. It was a difficult cantrip, causing him to be ignored. Not invisible, but rather when someone glanced at him, he didn't garner notice, as if he wasn't important enough to remember. It was a spell taught him by Laromendis the week before, and while the elf had judged Pug's mastery of it sufficient, Pug still had doubts.

He walked through the opening and paused a moment, glancing in all directions.

The four towers rose up overhead, arching toward an open center. This close Pug could sense there was power in them, faint, perhaps dormant was a better word, but there. A tiny flicker of light danced across the tip of each from time to time, but otherwise they were quiet.

Pug could not enjoy the luxury of investigating any one aspect of this place, no matter how much he wished he could. He moved toward the massive excavation in the center of the ring, glancing from side to side to see if he was being observed. A sentry on the wall looked directly at him for a moment, then turned away, looking out over the dark berm outside the wall. Apparently the spell was working or there were other humans in dark robes seen trekking around the facility after dark.

He reached the edge of the pit and glanced in. His stomach knotted. The pit was less than thirty feet deep, but he could see the piles of bodies. The stench that rose clearly indicated they had been dead for days. Elves, humans, dwarves, and even some demons lay sprawled in the mass.

Pug stepped back and felt the freshening breeze blow the stench away. Had the air been still he would have smelled the dead at the outer gate.

He hurried toward the only feature inside the ring that offered any invitation, a small building of some sort, with a single door and no windows. As he hurried to reach the door, a voice from nearby hissed, "Pug!"

It was only by the scantest margins Pug didn't incinerate Jim Dasher where he stood. "You have no idea," Pug whispered. "Where are the others?"

"In there," Jim pointed to the door. "There's a stair leading down to an underground chamber."

Pug said, "I have one minute before I must start back to where Amirantha and the others wait." He pointed toward the unguarded entrance.

"Magnus, Sandreena, and Kaspar were taken."

"What?"

Jim motioned for him to remain silent. "A trap. I think they knew we were coming." Before Pug could ask how, he continued. "I used my cloak and Laromendis his conjuring skills to stay hidden. He's heading around after you and if he hasn't overtaken his brother and the others by now, he will by the time you get back."

"Me?" said Pug. "My son is down there."

"And I'm better able to slip in and out than you. Your seeming is good. I had to look at you long and hard for almost a half minute before I realized I was looking at you, but I did recognize you, and if you're coming down stairs, even if those at the bottom think you're someone they should ignore, you'll be somewhere they can't go, so let me go and I'll meet you by the gates in five more minutes."

"If you're not back by then, I'll come after you," said Pug.

"What about the plan?" hissed Jim.

"Everyone is in place, and I'll send Brandos with instructions if I must. I've lost too much to not go after Magnus."

"Understood," said Jim. "Now, let me go down there and I'll find you."

Pug hesitated, hating to leave this in another's hands, but one complaint he had always had about his wife Miranda was her seeming inability to delegate important tasks to others. Feeling a rush of bitterness thinking of her, he nodded and turned away.

Jim Dasher knew it had been difficult for Pug to let him go. The recent loss of his wife and other son made him that much more protective of Magnus. Still, Jim knew from experience that this was exactly the situation where emotion would only get you killed.

There was a plan established, and it was the third option that only he, Pug, Kaspar, and Magnus knew of. Three companies of soldiers were assembled and ready to attack at a moment's notice.

Each was under the command of men who Pug trusted implicitly—his adopted grandsons, Tad, Zane, and Jommy. Jommy waited in a nice quiet estate on the island of Roldem, with three hundred Roldem Royal Marines under his command.

Zane was down in Kesh with a half Legion of Kesh's finest border Legionaries, "dog soldiers," nearly a thousand men.

Tad was waiting in Krondor with five hundred more of the Prince's own. Kaspar had another five hundred hand-picked shock troops from the army of the Maharaja of Muboya waiting half a planet away with the young magician Jason ready to bring them here.

Any or all of them could be here in minutes. The only critical thing was one person using a Tsurani orb to get free of here and back to Sorcerer's Island, where a simple order given would trigger a full-scale assault on this fortification.

As long as one person could get away.

Jim made his way slowly into the building, and down the circular stairs that began with a hole in the floor. He kept one hand lightly touching the wall on his left, while the other held the cloak firmly around him. The nature of this marvelous garment was reduced in proportion to his movement, but the steps were hardly wide enough to allow someone to pass, so he felt the need to reach the bottom as quickly as possible.

Five full circles and he knew he was approximately thirty feet below the surface, with the bottom still not in sight. Ten more and he saw light, and when he reached the bottom, he judged he was easily a hundred and fifty feet below the surface. It would be a wonderful climb back up, he thought, especially if he were being chased.

At the bottom, Jim discovered himself in a large room with ancient stone walls. Another of those damned ancient Keshian fortifications, he thought. This had all begun for him at that ancient site atop the plateau called the Tomb of the Hopeless, and now he found himself in one even more remote and dangerous.

Looking around for some sense of what to do, he noticed that only one of four tunnels leading away had a distant light at the end, so that's the direction he chose.

The tunnel was also ancient stone, dry and dusty, but the floor showed the tread of many feet. He still had no concept of what this place was and why the mad magician Belasco and his demon minions had chosen to occupy this place, but he suspected whatever the reason, it was something he was going to regret discovering more than he regretted not knowing.

Reaching the end of the tunnel, he hesitated, clutching his cloak around himself and looking into the room with surprise.

A massive altar, ancient and stained black with the blood of the slaughtered centuries past, now was stained with fresh blood. Before it knelt three figures, bound in chains and forced to kneel—Kaspar, Sandreena, and Magnus.

Well, at least they're still alive, thought Jim.

What had him stunned, to say the least, was that atop the altar lay the still form of Belasco, eyes closed. Dead, unconscious, or sleeping, he could not judge.

And standing on the other side of the altar was a slender man, whipcord strong in his appearance, stripped to the waist. His torso was covered in clan tattoos, and his teeth had all been filed to points. Jim had never seen one before, but he had to be a Shaskahan cannibal, practitioners of especially dark magic.

Only this time the magic didn't seem to be intended to destroy the body on the altar, but rather he appeared to be attempting to revive it. When the chanting stopped, the islander reached over and gave Belasco a gentle shake. "Master?" he whispered, loud enough that Jim could make out the word.

From out of the air came a voice. "Yes, my servant?"

"Are you with us again?" asked the islander. He appeared genuinely frightened by whatever was taking place.

"Not yet," came the answer.

"What must I do? We trapped those coming, as you said they would. We have them bound here in chains that make their magic not work." He looked at Sandreena and Magnus as he said the last, then at Kaspar. "We can spill blood if it will help."

Dryly, the voice in the air said, "Nothing can help."

Then another voice sounded, and it was as if the winds of hell had been given the power of speech. "Let me out of here!" commanded the other presence, and the body on the altar shook and the islander pulled back, obviously terrified.

Jim hung back in the shadows, now totally uncertain what to do next.

CHAPTER 17

SUMMONING

The pit exploded.

Pug and the others were thrown to the ground as a tower of green energy ripped up through the air from the pit to a point equally spaced between the four towers. There brilliant white energy lashed out like angry lightning, sizzling through the air with a hiss loud enough to make them want to cover their ears.

"Gods," said Brandos. "What was that!"

Pug felt the hair on his arms and neck stand up as an all too familiar and evil power began to coalesce. "Oh, gods, indeed," said Pug as a deep thrumming sound and a powerful vibration came from the ground beneath them and set their teeth on edge. "It's a summoning!"

"What?" asked Gulamendis. "I have never seen anything like this, and I've summoned my share of demons."

Laromendis said, "I have never seen its like, either." The Taredhel had found his brother, Amirantha, and Brandos while Pug had encountered Jim. Pug had just finished explaining what he was going to do when the mad energy erupted from the pit.

Pug turned to Brandos and said, "Here, take this." He handed him a Tsurani orb and said, "Push that button and you will find yourself in the keep on Sorcerer's Island. A magician named Pascal will be there, waiting against such an appearance. You tell him 'bring everything.' He'll know what to do."

"I'm not leaving," he said, looking at Amirantha. "He'll get himself killed if I'm not here to watch his back."

Amirantha took the sphere from Pug and pressed it into Brandos's hands. "I was keeping alive before you were born, boy." If anyone found the younger-looking Warlock calling the grey-haired fighter 'boy' odd, no one felt the need to remark on it. "Do as you're told and then get back here if you can; otherwise wait at the keep with your wife. Understand?"

Looking from face to face, Brandos realized that he was indeed the most expendable person there, so he grabbed the sphere and suddenly he was gone. "What now?" asked Gulamendis.

"Something beyond your ability to imagine may be coming through that portal soon." Pug saw that whatever guards were in the area, they were hurrying back inside the wall, a look of panic on their inhuman faces. "If you see anything heading for the small building against the far wall, kill it," he shouted, taking off at a run.

The two elves and Amirantha didn't hesitate and were off a half-step behind Pug, who sprinted past the wooden barrier and through the empty gate. Several demons of varying sizes were screaming at one another, looking for anything to vent their rage and terror against. Amirantha shouted, "Pug, to your right!"

Both the Warlock and Gulamendis began banishment rituals, but before they could get halfway through, Pug put out his hand, palm outward, and unleashed a withering beam of silver energy that tore the demon closing on him in half. The two portions of the demon fell to the ground, smoking, and erupted into flames, while the two Demon Masters and the Conjurer looked on in awe. "Remind me never to make *that* human angry," said Laromendis.

Gulamendis nodded, then shouted, "That got their attention."

A dozen demons had seen the display, and Pug had provided them with a convenient target for their fear and rage. They bellowed and shrieked as they charged him and the others. Pug made a sweeping gesture with his hand and a curtain of flames erupted on the ground in front of the demons. They were engulfed by flames and screamed and roared in outrage and pain and Gulamendis chose to stand next to the nearly frantic magician. "Those are demons. Fire will mostly annoy them."

"It has slowed them down for a couple of minutes," said Amirantha.

They reached the building and Pug made a quick decision. "Amirantha, go down the stairs and find Jim Dasher. Be careful." To Laromendis and Gulamendis he said, "We have to keep those creatures on the other side of the door."

The Warlock hurried down the circular stairs while Pug's right hand shot outward, palm forward, through the door. A ripping in the air, tainted an evil green glow by the light from the summoning device, showed a wall of force speeding outward, striking a dozen demons and knocking them backward. Several lay stunned and motionless, but the others seemed only to get madder.

Gulamendis took a talisman from his belt pouch and pointed it at one particularly nasty-looking demon, a thing of scales and crocodile teeth, bat wings, and blood-red armor. He spoke a quick phrase and suddenly the demon's yellow eyes blinked and it reached out with clawed hands to rip out the throat of the demon next to it, another scaly horror, but this one looking more like a lizard.

Laromendis closed his eyes and muttered, "Something big." A moment later the ground shook from the enraged bellow of a massive golden dragon as it sprang into being above the thirty or so demons ringing the hut.

Gulamendis said, "This will only buy us a few minutes, Pug. The bigger the illusion and the more violent, the faster Laro fatigues."

The dragon was a thing of beauty, looking exactly like the one the brothers had ridden with Tomas. It opened its maw and a scorching blast of searing hot fire rolled over the demons, scattering them. Pug felt the heat wash over him until he noticed that while some demons ran screaming, batting at nonexistent flames on their arms, their flesh blistering, there were no flames and there was no smoke or char on the ground. The moment he realized it, the heat stopped. He could still see the dragon, but it was now insubstantial and clearly an illusion.

Knowing the demons would soon come to understand their minds were playing tricks on them and they were the authors of their own suffering, he sent out another blast of flame, exploding in a tower of orange and yellow that did inflict real burns on the demons. "That will keep them confused a little longer," said Pug.

"Confusion will only work a while longer," said Gulamendis. "Whatever reserves they had outside the walls are now joining in."

Pug said, "They probably were given orders to return when the summoning started. I wonder what chance let these live while their companions lay at the bottom of that pit?"

"That battle we saw on Telesan was not an illusion,

Pug," said Gulamendis. "There's a demon war taking place, and it's our good fortune, all of us living here on this world, that the demons are now warring on one another—I've lived through losing two worlds to them. A third is one too many. Look out!"

Pug saw the fliers attacking the dragon illusion and Pug responded with a lance of purple light that caused one flier to burst into flames above the dragon. As the flaming corpse fell, it passed completely through the dragon and several other demons realized something was amiss.

"They're stupid," said Gulamendis, "but not that stupid. They'll turn on us in a minute."

Pug shot out another bolt of energy and said, "If we can hold out for another ten, fifteen minutes, the marines from Roldem should be the first here."

As more demons swarmed into view, Gulamendis said, "I think they're going to be overmatched unless we can help."

"We'll help," said Pug.

Gulamendis used his ward and reached out and took control of the largest demon he could clearly see and set it to attacking its neighbor. It didn't take much provocation for that conflict to spill over into a free-for-all as several other nearby demons were drawn in.

"Something is breaking down in their conditioning, Pug. These are battle demons and they're reverting to their old habits and starting to create makeshift alliances and start fighting for domination."

"Why?"

"I have no idea, but I think that whatever was controlling them is losing command of them."

As they watched, the demons began to turn on one another. Enough of those continued to rush the small building that Pug was forced to use all his skills to knock them back with another pulse of energy. "I can't keep doing this all day," he said, obviously fatigued. "There are so many of them."

"If they fully turn on themselves, we just need to bar this door." The Demon Master again selected a demon in the fray and had it turn on its neighbor. Then the illusion of the dragon vanished.

"That tears it," said Laromendis, coming out of his trance. "I've got little left to offer." He pulled out the wand he had harbored since they had fled the battle of Hub and pointed it at a particularly nasty beast charging the door. It went down in convulsions as energy consumed it.

Pug said, "I wish I knew what was going on below." He pushed aside thoughts of his son and the others and returned his attention to the battle before him.

Amirantha held up in the shadows, uncertain of what was occurring before him. He saw Jim Dasher hugging the wall by the door; the only hint the noble turned spy was there was the odd refraction of the light at the door's edge, which moved slightly, and if Amirantha stared at it for a moment, he could make out the vague shape of a man along the edge of the visual boundary between the door and the room beyond.

Then he took in what was occurring in the room beyond and his eyes widened. His brother, Belasco, was lying motionless across a sacrificial altar, and Sandreena, Kaspar, and Magnus were bound and kneeling before the altar. Amirantha assumed the bindings prevented the two magic casters from using their abilities, or this situation would have been resolved before either Jim and he had arrived.

A strange-looking man, thin with ragged hair and an impressive-looking set of pointed teeth appeared to be weeping piteously over Belasco, and seemed to be imploring Belasco to tell him what to do. Even more perplexing was a dialogue between two entities not visible. Amirantha stopped to ensure he wasn't losing his mind, because while his brother lay motionless on the altar, he could hear his voice, and then another voice, both demanding some sort of behavior by the witless man.

Amirantha came up behind Jim and as the cloaked figure tensed, he said, "It's me; what is happening?"

Jim gripped the Warlock by the arm and pulled him back into the tunnel and said, "I have no idea. That lunatic cannibal has been talking to your unconscious brother for five minutes, and I have no idea who the other voice belongs to."

Amirantha said, "I need to explain the subtleties of demonic possession to you, but now is not the time. Can you kill that man without giving him time to harm anyone else?"

"Easily, but why?"

"Because if he makes the wrong move, we're all going to die."

"That's a fine reason," said Jim, and Amirantha saw a dagger appear out of thin air, held by a hand and part of an arm, while the rest of Jim was still shielded by the cloak.

"Wait," said the Warlock.

"Why?" asked Jim. "Either we want him dead or not. Which is it? Our friends are stupefied and our enemy is overcome. As I see it, with two quick kills, this issue is resolved."

Amirantha whispered, "Ah, if it were that simple." He pointed to the confused islander. "Why is he so perplexed?"

"Because his master lies prostrate and he has no concept of what to do," said Jim. "I do not know a lot about magic, but I know enough to understand that sometimes a price is paid that was unanticipated. If that evil bastard on the altar made a mistake, why not advantage ourselves and end this?"

"No, to both. We can't end this, not yet, and moreover, that distraught minion is confused because *there are two beings within that one body!*"

"Two beings?" whispered Jim. "What does that mean?"

"It means my idiot brother summoned a demon recently who tried to take over his body. Now they're struggling for control."

"Is that why he's lying there motionless?"

"Apparently. Neither one has enough control to command the body and fight off the other entity."

"What should I do?"

"For the moment, regarding Belasco, nothing," said Amirantha. "As for the rest, can you kill that sharp-toothed fellow without bringing harm to our friend?"

"At any time."

"Do so now, if you don't mind, then cut the others loose. I most likely will need Magnus and Sandreena's help with whatever happens to Belasco, and if there's some lingering effects of their confinement, the sooner that's over, the better."

Jim faded into the shadow and for a moment Amirantha felt as if he were alone in the tunnel. Then there was a blur of motion on the left wall and the wailing Shaskahan islander's body went rigid and his eyes widened, then he slumped to the floor. Jim pulled back the hood of his cloak and stood over Belasco, and then motioned for Amirantha to enter. The Kingdom spy moved then to unfetter his companions.

Magnus and Sandreena were both tied with silver netting, while Kaspar was bound and gagged in a more conventional fashion. Kaspar gasped for breath when Jim pulled the gag from his mouth. "Gods! I thought I was going to suffocate they pushed that so far back." He cleared his throat and said, "Help me up. My knees are not what they once were and I have been kneeling too long in one position." Jim gave him a hand and said, "What did they do to Magnus and Sandreena?"

Both magic-users were mute, wide-eyed, staring into space. Kaspar said, "They went that way when those nets were cast on us. They quickly got me out of mine, but they kept those nets on them the entire time."

Jim nodded. "Slavers' nets. They use them in Durban if they're trying to snag a magic-user. The really fine and costly ones not only dampen magic but render the magician tractable.

"Help me get them out of those nets," said Jim.

Kaspar was stiff-legged for a minute and then set to on Sandreena's bindings, while Jim cut through the netting holding Magnus. When they were free, both went limp and Kaspar caught Sandreena and lowered her to the floor while Jim did the same for Magnus. Jim said, "Now we wait for them to recover."

"How long?" asked Kaspar.

Amirantha stood over the prone figure of his brother, whose eyes were trained on him. He said, "The effects should wear off shortly."

The lips on the altar's body didn't move, but a voice sounded in the air. "Is that you, little brother?"

Amirantha said, "It is, big brother."

"You don't find me at my best," came the hollow reply.

"I never did." Pulling out a dagger, he said, "Is there any compelling reason I shouldn't end this now?"

"Besides me wishing not to die any time soon, you mean?"

"Obviously; as you've shown little inclination in giving me that consideration, I hardly feel moved to grant it to you."

"Fairly stated," said the disembodied voice of Belasco.

Suddenly another voice, loud, raspy and harshly accented commanded, "Kill him and I will make you powerful beyond your dreams, Warlock!"

"That's the other reason," said Belasco's floating voice. "If you kill me, then Dahun here will get free. I'm the only thing keeping him from entering this world."

Amirantha glanced at Magnus and Sandreena, who were

still both stunned, though both were now blinking as if coming slowly out of a trance. Knowing that time was not in their favor above, Amirantha still knew that he needed a little more time here. "If Dahun is in you, what is that contraption on the surface about?"

"Ah, that would be telling," said Belasco with an evil chuckle.

"What madness have you undertaken now, brother of mine?" said Amirantha, prodding Belasco's shoulder with the point of his dagger.

"That hurt!" said Belasco with an almost petulant tone.

"Injure me at your peril!" shouted Dahun's voice. "A clean kill to set me free, I will accept, but torment will earn you repayment a thousandfold."

Kaspar said, "Not very reassuring, is he?"

"Neither of them is worth saving," said Amirantha, but his eyes flickered back and forth a moment between Kaspar and the others, and with a twitch of his head, he indicated he needed the General to play along. "Still, there are some things worth knowing that might prove interesting.

"Belasco, I can only assume you're controlling this monster inside of you for two reasons: your usual pure spite at serving anyone else's interest but your own, and because you have some idea that somehow you can manage your way out of this impasse?"

"You know me well, brother. But until I can conceive of a way of telling you anything is to my advantage, I think I shall keep my reasoning to myself."

"Well, you always did have an unwillingness to share."

"Blame Sidi. He was always beating me and taking my things."

"True, and both of you treated me the same until I started summoning help."

"That was an unfortunate day," said Belasco's voice.

"Warlock!" came the demon's voice. "Release me and

I shall make you a Prince of men, my first servant on this world."

Amirantha sighed and shrugged at Kaspar. "Sorry, Dahun, but experience tells me your promises are of little currency."

Belasco said, "Actually, he might keep that one. He doesn't plan on eating everything in sight. He plans on settling in and ruling things. That was our original arrangement, and he was as good as his word."

Amirantha closed his eyes as if he couldn't believe what he was hearing. He sighed slowly and then said, "Until you betrayed him," he said flatly.

"Of course."

Amirantha was silent for a moment, then said, "So, if I kill you, the demon within is freed, but if I let you live . . . well, sooner or later you're going to die if you can't eat or drink, unless you tell me of your plan."

"Not yet."

Amirantha saw Magnus and Sandreena begin to rouse and said, "Speaking of Sidi . . ."

"Yes," said Belasco.

"He's dead."

"Pity," said Belasco.

"Why? You hated him."

"Because I wanted to be the one to kill him. Mother may have been an evil witch, but she was Mother."

Amirantha glanced at Kaspar, who said, "Now that I've met all three of you, I can only imagine what she must have been like."

"Who's speaking?" asked Belasco. "I glimpsed him before, but he keeps moving where I can't see."

"Kaspar, formerly Duke of Olasko, and now General of the Army in Muboya."

"I'd bid you welcome, but I suspect you're not here to do me any good."

"Exactly. Unless there were exigent circumstances I can't begin to imagine," said Kaspar, "we came here to kill you."

"Ah, always murder in everyone's heart." That was followed by an evil chuckle.

"Now what?" asked Kaspar of Amirantha.

But it was Belasco who spoke. "We wait until I decide what's in my best interest."

CHAPTER 18

Attack

Pug unleashed another spell.

Demons in all forms and sizes were flung back, and Pug shouted, "Something is very wrong here."

Gulamendis shouted over the bellowing and shrieks, "What?"

"I'm not sure, but I sense something. . . ."

Laromendis was nearly exhausted to the point of being unable to stand. He had conjured every conceivable illusion he had learned in the years of fighting the demons, and had used up every one. The unexpected arrival of a myriad of threats, other demons, Taredhel sentinels, animals and monsters of every stripe, all had distracted or delayed the on-slaught of demons enough to give Pug the time to unleash his considerable power.

A voice from behind said, "Could you use some help?"

Pug turned and his face became alive with relief, as he beheld Magnus standing there. "Are you up to it?"

Nodding, he said, "They used a spell-binding net on Sandreena and myself, but the effects have worn off." Then his eyes narrowed and he said, "And I'm angry."

He moved to stand between Gulamendis and Pug and with his outstretched hand unlimbered a blast of crimson energy that moved like a thundering breaker on the beach. The demons to the last of them, irrespective of size and shape, were hurled backward. Those at the rear of the pack were cast down into the vast pit from which the green energy rose.

A shout from behind caused the remaining demons to turn and see what new threat was coming. Into the green glow cast by the tower of emerald energy ran armored humans, each dressed in the garb of Roldem's Royal Marines. Adept at battle on ship and land, they were the island kingdom's toughest combat soldiers. Leading the charge was a familiar face, though the usual boyish grin was missing. Jommy Killaroo, now Knight of the King's Court of Roldem and Captain of Special Services to the King, shouted orders as he raised his own sword and lashed out at a man-sized demon standing before him, rooted by surprise.

Pug let out a long breath. "Three hundred marines from Roldem will keep them busy until the rest get here, which should only be minutes away."

As if to punctuate his words, another shout from outside was followed by the arrival of Tad, one of Pug's adopted grandsons, leading a contingency of the Prince's Own, crack troops from Krondor. Their orders were simple: kill every demon in sight.

Pug said to Magnus, "Save your strength. We may need it soon."

Magnus nodded. "My tantrum was satisfying, but fatiguing."

"How're Sandreena and Kaspar?"

"Alive," said Magnus. "Belasco is incapacitated and in a struggle with some sort of demon presence"—he held up his hand before his father could ask a question—"I'm sure Amirantha can explain it later, but for the moment what you need to know is that if Belasco loses this struggle with an entity named Dahun, then the demon lord will appear in this realm."

Gulamendis said, "Dahun! He's one of the regional kings, and if he does get through intact, it'll take all of us to contain him." He shook his head in doubt. "I don't know if Amirantha and I together could banish him back to the Fifth Circle."

"We should have another half dozen magicians here within a few more minutes," said Pug.

"That should do it," said an exhausted Laromendis.

"Yes," agreed his brother. "If you damage him enough, wear him down, then Amirantha and I should be able to banish him back to where he came from."

"It's not like we're going to have any choice," said Pug. Looking at Magnus, he said, "We could use Amirantha and Sandreena up here."

"They're trying to puzzle out what Belasco is doing."

"I thought you said he was incapacitated."

"It's difficult to explain, Father, and I'm not sure I understand, but it appeared that Belasco is a host for the demon, and killing him will release Dahun into this realm. Belasco has kept him in check, but at the price of his own freedom."

Hearing this, Gulamendis said, "By the Ancestors, I need to get down there." He left the struggle as more arriving human soldiers were bringing a vicious fight to the demons.

"This should be over soon," said Pug, as a company of Keshian dog soldiers and another of Royal soldiers from Muboya hove into view.

Then a loud noise echoed from the pit accompanied by a company of flying demons, who seemed to erupt from within, and another host of monstrous creatures, who scrambled their way up over the edge of the pit and launched themselves into the fray.

"Perhaps not," said Magnus, as he sent a massive fireball into the midst of the fliers circling over the attacking human armies.

Gulamendis found Amirantha and Kaspar hovering over the prone form of Belasco, while a disembodied voice bellowed: "My minions will be here shortly, humans! This cursed magician who confines me will perish, then shall I be set free and your deaths will be agonizing and prolonged! Set me free now and I will reward you, but my patience is nearing its end!"

Jim Dasher stood ready with his dagger to end Belasco's life if there was any need. He glanced at Amirantha with a questioning look.

Amirantha shook his head in the negative, then looked at the elven Demon Master and asked, "Have you ever heard anything like that?"

"I've never heard a demon use the word 'patience,' nor have I heard of anyone confining his power once he's in possession of a mortal host."

Sandreena was fully recovered and said, "I've heard a lot of threats, but usually it was from a demon trying to rip out my throat, not from wanting to bargain."

"This is unique in my experience, as well," said the Warlock. "And my brother, true to everything I know about him, refuses to cooperate."

"You've given me no reason to cooperate, dear brother." Belasco's voice hung in the air.

"Give me a reason that will persuade you, Belasco."

"The conundrum is that for me to emerge victorious, I

must first rid myself of my demon possessor, and the only means I know of is to perish.

"Should I perish, however, Dahun reverts to his body, and soon that will be in this realm."

"Soon?" asked Gulamendis.

"Perhaps now," said Belasco with an evil laugh. "Had you killed me an hour ago, perhaps even minutes ago, he would have been cast back into the Fifth Circle of Hell, but now . . . ? It may be too late."

"I could kill you and find out," said Amirantha.

"But if you do that, and if he appears, then what, dear brother?"

"We may have enough strength to send him back?"

"Ah, *may*. What if you don't?"

"What is the truth?" demanded Amirantha.

Gulamendis said, "I may not be able to get the truth from your brother, but I can compel the demon within him to speak truth, at least for a while."

"You have a compelling enchantment that powerful?"

"I think so," said Gulamendis. He looked at the point of exhaustion, but closed his eyes. "I will try."

Long minutes dragged by with the distant sounds of battle reaching them from time to time. Kaspar asked, "Can I safely leave you here?"

Amirantha indicated the dagger in Jim's hand that was mere inches from his brother's throat. "I don't think your being here makes much difference."

"Good," said Kaspar as he turned to leave. "From the sound of things, they could use a general up there, or at least one more sword."

Jim looked at Kaspar, who said, "You stay here. Amirantha might hesitate, but I have no doubt you'll quickly cut Belasco's throat if needed." Jim nodded.

Amirantha was forced to smile. In the months since he had first come to know Kaspar, he had developed a genuine affection for him. Given Kaspar's reputation Amirantha found it surprising that a former enemy of the Conclave and friend to his dead brother, Sidi, would prove such affable company, but then he knew what Sidi had been capable of, and judged that much of Kaspar's villainy had been Sidi's doing. Jim was also someone the Warlock found likable, despite having a hard and cold side to him.

Gulamendis said, "It is done." To Dahun he said, "To truth are you bound. What reason have you for this possession?"

It was a question shared by all three of the demon experts in the room; possession was rarely employed by the more powerful demons of the Fifth Circle. It was against their nature; why trade a more powerful body for a weaker, more vulnerable one? Disguise was the only possible reason they could think of, but disguise was hardly necessary given the huge conflict above.

Silence was their answer.

After a long minute, Belasco chucked. "Your spell must have worked, elf."

"Why do you say that?" asked Jim.

"Gulamendis compelled him to tell the truth, but not to answer. His silence tells you he cannot lie to you, so he elects to say nothing."

Gulamendis looked from Amirantha to Jim to Sandreena, an openly beseeching expression on his face. They all shook their heads.

"What do we do now?" asked Sandreena.

"Come up with a bargain for my brother," Amirantha opined.

"What do you propose?" asked Belasco.

"Jim could cut your throat and we could deal with the demon when he gets in," said Sandreena, and her tone left little doubt she considered that a viable option.

Amirantha held up his hand and said, "Last resort." To

his brother he said, "We could banish the demon back to the Fifth Circle?"

"An exorcism?" said Belasco incredulously. "You must be joking."

"Sandreena is the Mother-Bishop of the Order of the Shield of the Weak," said the Warlock.

"I think I liked her better when she just wished to bash my head with her mace," said Belasco. "That would be quick and easy. An exorcism is as likely to get me killed, but a great deal more slowly and painfully."

Sandreena and the two Demon Masters exchanged knowing looks, and they conceded wordlessly that Belasco was right; the more powerful the demon when driven from the host, the more damage endured by the mortal. And no one in the record of any temple had successfully banished a demon king or prince.

Amirantha said, "Your choice, brother. A quick death and we deal with your demon, or we can try to save you, and then we'll most likely be forced to kill you."

"You know me well, brother." There was a long silence, and Belasco said, "Give me your word that should I emerge from this intact you'll grant me one day's grace to find a safe haven."

"After all you've done?" said Sandreena.

"That's the bargain," said Belasco.

"I vote for a quick death," said Sandreena.

"I think we should try the exorcism," said Gulamendis.

Jim shrugged. "I really don't know what's best."

"That leaves it to you, brother," said Belasco.

Amirantha said, "Give me a reason to grant you any mercy. You've been trying to kill me for a century."

"Well, that's a regret, really. I count it a bad habit. I just got so annoyed with you and Sidi . . . I didn't really think things through."

Amirantha closed his eyes a moment, then opened them

and said, "You may not be as mad as our brother was, but there's nothing about you that resembles sanity.

"Let me be clear; I'm leaning heavily toward ending this rapidly and clearly, which involves cutting your throat, unless you provide me with a persuasive reason why we should risk letting you live, and having to deal with a powerful demon anyway."

There was a long silence, then Belasco said, "I will tell you the truth."

Amirantha laughed. "That would be unusual."

"By the blood of the old woman of the moons, the nightmares of the child in the village, and the bones in the wicked man's hidden grave," said Belasco.

Amirantha fell silent. He looked at Sandreena and Gulamendis and softly said, "When we were children it was a pact we made; we imitated a curse our mother used . . ." He shook his head. "It was as close as any of us got to anything sacred. Even Sidi never broke a promise or lied after making that oath."

"It's the best I can do, brother."

Amirantha was silent. After a long moment, he said, "Very well. Begin."

Pug saw the demons before the doorway turn from attacking Pug's group and answer the attack from Jommy's marines. Kaspar arrived and said, "What's the situation?"

"Chaos!" shouted Magnus. "Our forces arrived, then a horde of demons appeared out of that pit!"

"It's a summoning pit, massive beyond anything I've heard of; even Amirantha and Gulamendis didn't recognize it for what it was: a Demon Gate."

"We have to shut it down!" said Kaspar.

"The problem," replied Pug, "is that it might take a while."

Kaspar looked out at the battle raging beyond the door while Magnus sent another blast of searing energy at a demon charging in their direction. "Keep discouraging them," said Kaspar, "while I get a better look." He tapped Laromendis on the shoulder and said, "You up to giving me a boost up to the roof?"

"Certainly," said the elf. They stepped sidewise out the door and Laromendis made a stirrup with his hands. Kaspar stepped up and the tall elf boosted him high enough to allow the General to clamber onto the tiles of the building.

Magnus stepped outside in time to destroy a flier who saw Kaspar as an easy target, and the General shouted, "Thanks!"

Kaspar saw that activity from the pit had ceased and shouted down, "I think that's all of them!"

He looked around the fight and cursed himself for not having had a better notion of how this struggle might unfold. He had made one poor assumption, that a quick strike by overwhelming forces would obliterate a disorganized band of cultists and a few demons.

What he hadn't expected was that the demons would be armed, organized, and getting reinforcements. Still, his forces were gaining the upper hand through sheer numbers. Which was a good thing, he considered, as it seemed to take three or four human soldiers to best the larger demons.

The stench from demon blood was making his eyes water and another flier came hurling out of the night sky and almost took his head. He felt the heat from its flaming body as Magnus dispatched it.

Kaspar sat on the eaves and then dropped to the ground with an audible grunt. "I'm too old and tired to be doing this," he said to no one in particular.

Pug and the others had come out of the small building as the ebb and flow of the struggle had taken the combatants to the other side of the large fortress. Kaspar said, "We've got the upper hand if something doesn't change unexpectedly." He nodded. "I've got to find my commanders and see if we can coordinate this a little better."

He hurried off and Pug turned to Laromendis. "Why don't you see what your brother and Amirantha are up to down there. Magnus and I will protect this building."

Laromendis said, "Of course," and ran back into the building.

"There's a new war under way," said Belasco. "It's been under way for centuries. The five demon kings have been battling for supremacy since time began, this endless Demon War. But this new war is something different."

Amirantha said, "How is it different?"

The sound of laughter filled the room, both Belasco's and the demon's. The demon's was hate-filled and bitter, while Belasco's was genuine amusement. "I don't really know," said the motionless magic-user. "Lying is as much a part of the demon nature as it is mine, dear brother.

"When I first began to dabble with summoning it was for the usual reason; I wanted to better you. I tried to kill Sidi once by creating a litch, did you know?"

"No," said Amirantha.

"It wasn't well conceived, really. Too much emphasis on irony and not enough on learning the craft. Sidi quickly disposed of the monster and I spent the better part of a year living in a very cold cave up in the Northlands, surrounded by ice bears, snow leopards, dark elves, and not a lot to eat." He sighed, more an emotional footnote than any real exhalation of breath. "You'd think I might have learned, but I really didn't.

"With you I decided to not just conjure up a random demon and turn him loose on you, as I knew you'd easily better it, but I thought I could subvert one of your spells so that you would summon in something you didn't expect. I thought that was very clever."

"It almost worked," said Amirantha.

"Almost?"

"I had help. Had I been alone, I would have perished."

"Well, that's some sort of consolation." He paused, then said, "To learn enough to do that I began studying demon lore, much of it familiar to you I assume. But I did find a few odds and ends, a scroll here and a book there that made it clear that there was far more to the demon realm than you suspected. I wasn't doing this for scholarship, really. I was looking for a very clever way to kill my brothers."

Gulamendis looked at Belasco and then at Amirantha and just shook his head. Sandreena kept her eyes fixed on Amirantha's face.

Amirantha said, "The Demon War?"

"Something is driving the demons. Something has come into their realm and is struggling with them for supremacy in their own realm," said Belasco. "Millions of demons have been destroyed in the struggle and three of the kings have united to oppose the invaders."

"Who?" asked Amirantha.

"I don't know," replied Belasco. "I only hear vague references to 'them,' or 'the invaders.' One time I heard 'from the darkness.' Other than that, they are a force that has destroyed the order, such as it was, of the Fifth Circle.

"Of the two kings who did not ally, one took a wait-and-see position, my friend here, Dahun."

That brought a sound of snarling but no coherent speech.

"The other was Maarg. Some fool on a world in this realm opened a Demon Gate, into Maarg's realm, and he unleashed the outer horde, the demons from the edges, into this world. There were great battles I was told, but in the end, the demons found themselves on a world with no way off."

"Shila," said Sandreena. "Pug has spoken of that world and the demon battles with the Saaur."

"But it was Dahun who saw the potential in this realm. The demons have their own magic-users and before Maarg devastated the entire world of Shila, Dahun sent spies and agents into that world, pillaging the libraries and studies of their priests and magicians. They returned with everything they could carry and for the better part of a half century they studied.

"Dahun first recognized the need to solidify his own position so he annexed Maarg's realm, trapping Maarg on the mortal world knowing the demon king would eventually starve to death after he devoured everything.

"He then allied with the three remaining demon kings and sent forces to battle the invaders—but the forces he sent were those he inherited from Maarg's realm, keeping his own loyal army close by.

"He then set about to leave the Fifth Circle."

"And come here?" asked Gulamendis, as his brother walked into the room.

"The battle goes well," said Laromendis, as Gulamendis held up his hand to indicate silence, while nodding that this was good news.

"Yes," said Belasco. "This realm is weak compared to the Fifth Circle. But Dahun is by far the most intelligent of the Demon Lords. He realized that changes would be needed to prepare the way for his entrance into the realm.

"You know as much about demons as any man can learn on his own, brother. You know that without control, a demon will continue to feed until he devours everything he can find. Dahun created that control.

"He created a hierarchy that was more than was known before in the demon realm, not only one of power and alliances, but loyalty as well. He orchestrated betrayal and infiltrated spies into the domains of the other rulers, and he began a series of conflicts between his neighboring rulers.

"He created the illusion that Maarg had suddenly returned, feigning his own defeat by Maarg and allowing the other rulers to believe what Dahun wanted them to believe. Then he escalated the Demon War to a new level, contriving to set allies against one another, against the mortal races he encountered in this realm, and against any who might pose a threat.

"In short he readied himself to enter this level of reality and assume supremacy over all he encountered."

"But we somehow managed to frustrate that plan," said Amirantha.

"More than you care to know," said Belasco. "At first I thought this merely another opportunity for some grim fun, a little nasty play that might net me some personal gain, but when I discovered what Dahun's plans were, in truth, it was too late."

"You were in his trap," said Gulamendis.

"Another voice," said Belasco. "Yes, demons are by their nature creatures that cannot be reasoned with, negotiated with, or pleaded with; they can only be forced to reach an accommodation and the only thing you can be certain of, they will betray you eventually, given an opportunity.

"Amirantha, you would not believe what your so-called minions think of you. Before you take personal offense, realize they feel that way about all humans. We are cattle to them. We are food. We provide things they desire, nothing more. To get what they desire, they will serve if they must, but it is always about what they desire."

"And Dahun desires to live on this world?"

"He desires to rule it. He sent every rim demon he could herd through his gates to vanquish the elves on a dozen worlds. He came here because—"

"No!" came Dahun's voice. "You may not speak of that!"

There was silence.

Amirantha said, "Belasco?"

More silence.

Gulamendis looked at Sandreena and then Amirantha and said, "What do we do now?"

"I have no idea," said the Warlock.

CHAPTER 19

Demon Unleashed

Pug cast a spell.

A wave of pulsating energy rose above the heads of those struggling on the ground and swept the sky clear of the few remaining winged demons. Somewhere in the midst of the fray Kaspar was bringing order and the diverse units were beginning to coordinate their efforts. Demons were still crawling up out of the pit but the rate had slowed to a trickle and Pug sensed they were on the verge of defeating this invading host.

A dozen magicians had accompanied the soldiers and they used their arts to contain the more fractious creatures, or to neutralize the magic-using demons. Pug turned to Magnus and said, "It's almost over I think."

Before Magnus could reply, a loud thrumming filled the air as a huge pulse of green light shot up each of the four towers to explode in a near blinding display at the top of the columns.

The effects were almost instantaneous, as the ground heaved beneath everyone's feet, knocking most of the combatants to the ground. Pug quickly regained his footing and pointed to the towers, which were now pulsing as ripples of green energy ran up to the top, where they fed into a growing, bright white ball of energy.

"Oh, gods, I know what that is."

Magnus said, "It's a summoning device of some sort, you said."

"But it's what ties the necromancy and demon lore together!" said Pug. "It's why those death rituals that Jim told us of, and why there were bodies down in that pit when they needed the workers no longer, and it's why Dahun doesn't care how many demons we kill." He pointed to the pulsing energy running up the towers, increasing in frequency and tempo. "When the gate is fully open, he'll come through."

"But he's here already," said Magnus. "He's possessed the body of Belasco!"

Pug said, "It's a ruse! He's buying time." He gripped Magnus by the arm and said, "Get back down there. Tell Amirantha and Gulamendis what is occurring." He looked at the massive struggle and said, "I've got to come up with a way to stop the killing!"

The human forces were coalescing around Kaspar who was orchestrating a containment attack, pressing in on all sides around the remaining demons. The tactic forced demons to confine other demons, so only those on the outside could engage the human soldiers.

Then another wave of demons exploded out of the pit. "Oh, damn!" said Pug.

. . .

Magnus hurried into the chamber. "They're using death magic to activate the Demon Gate!"

Amirantha looked at Gulamendis and said, "Now, I wonder who contrived that idea?"

Dahun's contempt cut through the air. "Your brother thought to use me, human! He was bending power to his own ends. He envisioned a demon army here, serving him on this world, as he conquered and ruled. The fool!"

Amirantha's brow furrowed. "I've never known him to be that ambitious."

Gulamendis said, "People change."

Laromendis said, "Whatever the motivation, am I correct in assuming this melding of death magic and demon summoning is creating unexpected problems?"

Magnus said, "Each life taken up there fuels the device, and it appears as if it has begun to open the Demon Gate. Lesser demons are coming through in waves."

"Can you shut that creature up?" asked Sandreena.

Gulamendis closed his eyes and said, "No. But I think I have a trick . . ." He chanted something and abruptly the sound of Dahun's "voice" in their minds retreated to a distance.

"What was that?" asked Magnus.

Amirantha smiled. "A very nice trick that I'm going to get him to teach me if we live through the rest of this day." Looking at the still face of his brother, Amirantha shouted, "Belasco! Can you hear me?"

A distant whisper answered, "Yes."

They all had to strain to hear him over the still-ranting demon, but that was a very soft voice.

Amirantha said, "Was it you who created the death magic portal?"

"Yes," said Belasco. "I almost killed Sidi once in Kesh, forcing him to abandon his lair. I found several interesting tomes and books."

"You always wanted to better us at our craft," said Amirantha.

"Because I *am* better!"

"Well, you're about to get everyone here and probably half the world murdered to prove you're not as clever as you thought," snapped Sandreena. She was obviously tired and not feeling this was going well.

Jim narrowed his gaze and gave her a silent warning to keep still.

The magician's ethereal voice took on a moment of urgency. "I can feel the tug! The gate is opening! Our bargain? If I tell you how to defeat this monster, do I get my day's head start?"

Jim started to shake his head no, but Amirantha's eyes warned him this was coming to a head. Finally Jim nodded once in the affirmative.

"One day," said Amirantha. "You get nothing else, not food, water, horse, or weapon."

A sound of distant laughter drowned out the railing demon. "Done! Here is what you must do. Within the next ten minutes, you must render me unconscious."

Sandreena hefted her mace where the prone figure's eyes could see it held in menacing fashion. "That's no problem."

Belasco laughed at the threat. "I like her!" In faint tones that seemed to be growing more distant, he said, "No, brother, you know what to do."

Amirantha nodded and looked at Gulamendis. "His body isn't the issue; it's his mind. You need to keep aware of what Dahun is doing, while I stun Belasco's consciousness."

"Excellent," said the recumbent magic-user. "As soon as you do, I will lose my hold on him between the realms and he will come through the gate."

"This is your plan?" said Sandreena. "I thought we were trying to keep him out of this realm!"

"You must utterly destroy the gate while he is still

within. You will have less than a minute once he begins to manifest, but he will be completely vulnerable during this translation. That is when you must strike.

"Then revive me and I will be on my way, dear brother."

Amirantha said to Magnus, "You need to alert your father. It's going to be very nasty up there in a couple of minutes."

Magnus closed his eyes. "I'm not the best at this, but I'll try to save the time needed for me to run up there."

Father, Pug heard in his mind.

"Magnus?" he whispered.

Yes. Listen closely as I don't know how long I can maintain this link. In less than ten minutes Dahun will manifest within the Demon Gate. He will be vulnerable for a minute, perhaps two. If you destroy the gate at once, you destroy him before his full power is manifest.

Pug let out a long breath. "I have it."

Pug saw Kaspar a short distance away, but he was blocked by a half dozen demons. A particularly brutish one, with a head something like a rhinoceros and two large curving horns coming out of his shoulders sweeping upward, lowered his head, hefted a massive sword, and charged. Pug shouted, "Get back!" to those soldiers nearby and sent a pulse of force at the creature.

Pug was trying his best to stun or disable the demons without killing them, but it was not going well. Several of the monsters were so hearty that nothing short of a killing blow seemed to slow them down, let alone stop them.

Pug reached Kaspar and said, "We need to withdraw."

"Why?" said the General, his sword actually smoking from the black demon blood on it. He had a nasty gash on his right cheek, but ignored it. "We've taken command of the field, have them surrounded, and are forcing them into a knot. We can cut them down from the edges and should have them all dead within a half hour!"

"Because in about ten minutes, each death here will cause that thing"—he pointed to the green column—"to bring a Demon King in and he, I feel safe to say, will have to be put down by magic that will level this entire structure. Nothing within a quarter mile of this place is likely to survive."

"Withdraw!" shouted Kaspar, not waiting to hear any more. He had known Pug long enough never to doubt him in matters pertaining to magic. Zane, one of his key captains and a foster grandson of Pug, hurried over and looked as if he was about to question the order. Like Kaspar, he saw the human forces as having the upper hand.

"Get them south of here! We don't want to be trapped on those bloody switchbacks! I want everyone at least a quarter mile away in the next six minutes!"

Zane knew better than to question an order like that, and began shouting the command, ordering it relayed to the other commands. The order was quickly passed and the soldiers confronting the demons launched a fierce assault for thirty seconds while those behind turned and began a hasty retreat.

Kaspar said, "This is where I'd normally use archers, but as I didn't bring any . . ."

Pug said, "I understand." He raised his hand and launched a red ball of light straight up. It was a signal every magician at that struggle had been prepared to see, though not if they saw the struggle as going well. Still, it was an order to cover an orderly retreat.

Those magicians who could fly or hover took to the air, laying down withering blankets of flame and shocking energy like lightning. Others climbed to the walls and used wands and staves to rain all types of destruction on the demons. Pug cursed the need to retreat. They were verging on repulsing the Demon Legion and if he could spend any time investigating this gate he could render it inoperative without destroying the entire structure.

Still, what one wishes and what is are often two very

different things, the magician thought. Of Magnus he asked, *Are you safe down there?*

I'm coming up. This chamber is deep enough the others should be safe, but you may need help with Dahun.

Pug knew better than to argue. His son was most likely right. For a brief moment he pushed aside a rising fear, for he knew he was fated to see Magnus dead alongside his mother and brother, and he wondered if this was the moment. He prayed not as he rose into the air and began blasting demons back into the pit.

Kaspar's soldiers were as well trained and disciplined a group as Pug had ever seen, despite most of them not having trained together. They withdrew in rapid order, leaving it to the magicians to hold the demons at bay. The advantage to the human forces was enough that even with the soldiers withdrawing, the demons could not pursue due to the punishing magic directed at them from all sides.

Magnus appeared in the air next to his father and said, "You've gotten good at rising into the air, Father!"

It had been something Miranda, Pug's wife, had been able to do with ease, but Pug had trouble managing. It was a point of pride with Pug that he labored to master those skills at which he was not gifted and he smiled as he said, "I can't let you get better than me in everything, now, can I?"

Magnus tried to chuckle at the quip, but knew his father was nearly frantic with worry. "It will be fine, Father," he said, trying to reassure Pug.

Both magicians unleashed as much destructive energy as possible, creating a curtain of death between the demons and the retreating humans. "Now it gets dangerous," said Pug, as the last of the human soldiers turned and ran.

Only the magic wall of flame and crackling energy confined the demons, and Pug said to Magnus, "Tell Amirantha to do whatever it is he's going to do."

Magnus sent word to the Warlock.

Amirantha's eyes widened as he heard Magnus's voice in his mind. *Father says in two minutes the area will be clear.*

Amirantha said to the others, "Two minutes."

Belasco's voice said, "Good. I am getting very tired holding this beast in check." There was a sense of a dark chuckle, a humor rooted in pain and anger. "I guess we can both say this time I overreached myself, brother."

Amirantha looked around the room and saw Jim ready to cut Belasco's throat, Sandreena ready to bash his head in with a mace, and the two elves ready to do whatever they needed to subdue him should the need arise. "Given there are five people here ready to see you dead in an instant, and you're stuck in some mental struggle with a Demon King, and thousands of lives are at risk because of your choices . . . yes, I can agree you overreached."

"Well, I'd tell you I was sorry, but we both know that would be a lie," he said with what seemed to be an echo of evil glee. "You may be right, you know."

"About what?" asked the Warlock.

"About me being insane. I'm not sure, because I've always felt this way. I know Sidi was mad, but that was easy to see. You, probably not, or you hide it well. But I realize now that a lot of what I've done . . . Don't get me wrong on this, dear brother. I still don't care, but I realize that one must be a little crazy to try what I've tried.

"I saw myself as just too smart." There came a hollow laugh. Then suddenly the tone changed. "It's starting! You must do it now!"

Amirantha nodded, and Gulamendis said, "I will delay the demon within for a few minutes."

Sandreena said, "I can pacify your brother, Amirantha."

"Begin," said Amirantha.

"Farewell, brother," came Belasco's voice. Amirantha's eyes widened slightly, for in his lifetime, his brother had never offered him the slightest wish for good fortune. As if understanding this, Belasco added, "For if you do not fare well, I most certainly perish."

They began their spells.

Demons withered under the blistering attack of the magicians surrounding them. Pug could sense more than see that some of the magicians on the walls were failing, exhausted from the tremendous demand on their willpower and endurance to channel so much magic in so short a time. Only Magnus seemed unfazed by the demands placed on him.

A massive wave of energy swept up the four towers and suddenly a figure began to appear, suspended in the air, slightly translucent in appearance.

Twenty feet tall, Dahun's massive torso was heavily muscled, descending into huge legs and a scaled black lizard's tail below his spine. His black legs and tail blended to red at his stomach and turned crimson at his chest. His face was contorted in pain, as if this transition was causing agony. He bellowed and it was a distant, hollow sound. His eyes were solid black orbs, opened wide, looking, seeking something as he came into this world. His head moved side to side, the hair braided with human skulls swinging over his shoulders. His brow was adorned with a massive golden circlet, set with a dark stone pulsing with purple light. The fingers of his left hand ended in black talons and flexed slowly, restlessly, as if in anticipation of rending apart his enemies. In his right hand he held a flaming sword. His hips were girded with a metal-studded kilt, and two large leather bands crossed his chest with a massive golden emblem.

Pug said "Now!" to Magnus, and the two of them unleashed every destructive magic they possessed.

Two waves of sizzling light shot from their hands to strike the figure full in the chest. Dahun trembled and started to fall backward, his hands outstretched, as if in supplication, and a single word escaped his lips, "No!"

As he fell out of the confines of the four towers, energy like purple lightning erupted from his body, striking the pillars rising above him. The Demon King screamed in outrage and pain, his arms flailing as he tried to reach for the nearest pillar and keep from falling out of the pit boundaries.

"Destroy the towers!" Pug said to Magnus.

Pug kept the assault focused on the demon while his son sought to topple the towers. Pug's strikes of searing energy caused smoking welts on the demon's body while keeping him falling off balance, until he struck the ground between two towers. A sound like a groan and a piteous cry came from Dahun as he touched the soil.

Magnus used the power of his mind to reach out and find a keystone in the foundation of the tower closest to where his father and he floated, while noticing that most of the other magicians nearby were fleeing. One or two of the stronger were still on the wall, directing their magic at the demon in aid of Pug.

Magnus used the power of his mind to grind the keystone to dust in moments, then he sent a massive wave of energy at the sudden void in the masonry. The entire tower shuddered and began to collapse, stones coming apart as the construction moved side to side. As it fell, massive discharges of green magic swirled upward, like mad dust devils spilling away into the night sky.

Dahun shrieked in agony as the now unbalanced forces in the pit began to discharge massive explosions like lightning and balls of fire. Pug could feel waves of heat rising up and instinctively raised a protective shield around himself and Magnus.

With the shield in place, they could only watch.

Dahun lay writhing on the soil, his mouth gasping much like a landed fish. His body contorted in spasm and twitched wildly, while around him flames roared up from out of the pit.

His legs and tail still hung over the pit and they began to smoke and blister and he screamed in pain but was unable to move. Magnus sent to his father, *It's over.*

Pug replied, "Not quite yet."

A second tower began to tremble and Pug used his magic to send a warning to the remaining magicians. "Get out!"

They fled, two flying, and one just leaping from the low wall to the outside of the fortress and running south as fast as he could.

The third and fourth towers also began to come apart and tumble inward, and another tower of flames erupted from the pit. Now all of Dahun's lower body was consumed, and his eyes rolled up in his head and were vacant.

Then suddenly a huge sucking sound was followed by a trembling from below and Dahun was jerked from where he lay and vanished back into the pit in an instant. All the masonry, towers, loose stones, and dead bodies nearby were sucked into the pit as if a massive vacuum had inhaled everything around the pit. Anything loose within the confines of the walls vanished into the pit, including dropped weapons and armor.

Then it was still.

"Now is it over?" asked Magnus.

"I think—"

The explosion was massive.

A shock wave that was visible to Pug and Magnus rolled out of the pit, carrying dirt, parts of dead bodies, and debris before it. It blasted out with enough force that the small building and the outer walls of the fortress were swept before it like a child's hands knocking away toy blocks.

Only Pug's shield kept his son and himself safe, but the ferocity of the blast caught him off guard.

The speed of the shock wave had the area before them

cleared in seconds, and when they looked down, there was no sign of the pit, or any construction. The blast area was also devoid of any plant life and as smooth as a patch of marble floor, but otherwise unmarked.

"What happened?" asked Magnus.

"The rift closed," said Pug. "We unbalanced the magic and it . . . rebalanced itself."

"It looks as if there's nothing down there."

"Well, we have some people down there, if they survived." Lowering himself and his son down, Pug said, "We'd better start digging them out."

"I hope Kaspar got his men far enough away to survive that blast," said Magnus.

"I suspect he did," said Pug. "I'm not so certain about poor Timothy. He was running when last I saw him."

Magnus said, "He's fast."

"Let's hope he's fast enough."

They reached the ground and Pug said, "Now, where was that building?"

"Somewhere over here," said Magnus, as he closed his eyes and started probing magically for the entrance.

Amirantha was the first to regain consciousness. It was pitch-dark in the room. The massive explosion above had momentarily sucked all the air out of this chamber, rendering all within unconscious and extinguishing the lights.

His lungs burned and he felt his head pounding, as he reached around in the dark and felt the base of the altar. He used it to steady himself and got to his feet. Obviously the air had quickly returned to the room, but the decompression really had caused some damage.

He reached into his belt pouch and took out a crystal, incanting a single word. The crystal began to glow, casting enough light in the room so he could see the others. Sandreena was stirring, with a groan, and he knelt next to her. Shaking her shoulder gently, he said, "You're alive."

She shook her head and focused her eyes on him and said, "What?"

"In case you were wondering; you're alive."

She grunted, then said, "I was wondering."

He helped her to her feet as Jim and the two elves began to review. Looking at the prone figure of Belasco, Amirantha said, "Did he survive?"

As if prodded by the question, Belasco groaned and moved slightly.

A thump from above and a burst of dust coming down the corridor was followed by Magnus's voice in their minds. *Is everyone all right?*

Amirantha shouted, "We're alive, if barely."

A moment later the two magicians entered the chamber and Pug said, "It's over."

"The demon's gone?" asked Jim, blinking as if trying to clear his vision.

"Everything's gone," said Magnus. "The pit is filled, the ground is flattened, and the stones are scattered across miles of desolation. It's as if this place never existed."

"Good," said Jim. "That means no explanations to the Keshian government."

Belasco stirred and groaned as he sat up. In a gravelly voice he asked, "It's over?"

"Yes," said Amirantha. "And your day's grace to find a safe haven begins this moment."

Moving to gingerly get down from the altar stone, the magician stood on uncertain legs for a moment, then he said, "I'll go."

He began walking in a halting fashion, stopped, took a deep breath, then repeated, "I'll go."

He was almost to the door when Amirantha said, "Wait."

Turning, Belasco said, "What?"

"One more time, your word."

"You have it," he said with a contemptuous snarl.

"Again, say it again."

"What?"

"The oath."

Belasco was silent for a long minute, then said, "Very well. By the old woman's blood—"

Amirantha shouted, "Kill him!"

Pug, Magnus, the elves, and even Sandreena hesitated, looking at the Warlock, as Pug said, "What?"

Jim Dasher didn't hesitate. The dagger that had not left his hand since coming into this chamber now flew straight across the room, taking Belasco in the throat. The magician's eyes grew round, and he reached up as if he would staunch the blood flow with his fingers.

Crimson flowed from his mouth as he tried to speak, then out of his nose, then his strength gave way and he fell to his knees. With blood pouring down his face, neck, and chest, he fell over on his right side.

"Why?" Pug asked.

"Because that wasn't my brother," said Amirantha.

"What?" asked Sandreena.

"Belasco would never have gotten the oath wrong. It begins, 'By the blood of the old woman of the moons,' not 'By the old woman's blood—'" Pointing a finger at the prone body on the floor, he said, "That was no longer my brother. That was Dahun!"

"The demon?" said Gulamendis.

"Yes," said Amirantha. "When we were being so clever, he was being much more clever. Everything we did was being manipulated. He convinced us there was a struggle—because he permitted it. Belasco remembered the oath, but when it came time to act, Dahun cast him out, into his body emerging from the demon realm. It was a foregone conclusion you two"—he pointed to Pug and Magnus—"would destroy Dahun's body; Belasco had no ability to use the demon's magic. He was an easy target."

Magnus said, "It required a lot of magic to destroy that construction, but before that, there was no real fight."

Pug said, "But why? Why go to all this trouble to come here, to possess your brother?"

"I can only speculate," said the Warlock.

Jim said, "Well, we're going to be back on Sorcerer's Island soon, so let's leave it to then."

Pug said, "Agreed. Now, let us leave this gods-forsaken place and go home."

No one in the room objected.

AFTERMATH

Pug motioned for everyone to sit.

The mood in the room was slightly festive but subdued. Despite their victory over the demons, they had lost lives.

Pug said, "With Belasco dead, I hope this means our days of conflict with your family are over, Amirantha."

The Warlock smiled and put his hands outward in a sign of supplication. "Assuredly. That both my brothers served some dark agency who caused so much harm is beyond my ability to amend, but I plan on doing what I can to help, Pug."

"It's welcome. It's clear we have very little understanding of the demon realm."

The two elven brothers were speaking softly, and Gulamendis said, "My brother is going to return to

E'bar, Pug, to see if we are able to help our people," then dryly he added, "or if we're even welcomed back."

"I'd like to remain here, a while, and study with Amirantha."

"Of course," said Pug. "You are both welcome here at any time." He looked at Laromendis and added, "Your task may prove difficult, if I understand what is occurring with your Lord Regent and his Meet. Still, if we must, we shall endeavor to extend our hand and offer friendship."

Laromendis smiled. "Remember, we are a long-lived people, Pug. Give Tomas a few more years to come to terms with the Lord Regent, then we'll introduce you."

Jim laughed and drank his wine. Wiping his mouth with a dirty sleeve, he was once again dressed as the ragged head of a Krondor street gang, Jim Dasher, also known as Quick Jim, Jimmyhand, or, to a select few, the Upright Man. He had said earlier the Kingdom could do without his services for a few more days, but he doubted the Mockers, the thieves of Krondor, could. "I must be off in a few minutes, but I have a question, and this seems the perfect time to voice it, while you're all here."

Pug nodded, looking around the room. Only Kaspar was missing, having returned to his responsibilities in Muboya with those soldiers who had come up for the fight. Brandos was sitting next to Sandreena, and had complained for most of the day about having missed the fight, much to Amirantha's amusement.

They had all returned a few hours before sunrise and had bathed and rested and were now enjoying a late breakfast or a very late supper from the night before, depending on one's perspective.

Jim asked, "What was really going on down there, Pug? I know what I saw, both times I visited, but what did I really see?"

Pug looked around the room and said, "One way or

another you're all members of the Conclave, even if you don't consider yourselves as such; you've all shown a steadfastness in defending this world beyond any duty you owe to any crown or faith"—he looked at Sandreena as he said the last. "You deserve to know what I know.

"For over a century I have been confronted by a dark agency. I have had suspicions over that time as to who the agency is, but twice now I've had to rethink my assumptions." To Amirantha he said, "That your brothers were servants of that agency is, I think, a coincidence."

Amirantha nodded. Putting down his wine, he said, "It must be. They would never knowingly work with each other; they were as anxious to kill each other as they were to kill me. Sidi was driven quite mad, and Belasco was . . . less mad, but certainly not sane."

"Which tells me this evil agency you speak of, Father," said Magnus, "draws to it those inclined toward dark madness."

"You can't cheat an honest man," said Jim Dasher.

"What?" asked Gulamendis.

"It's an old saying among confidence tricksters. To inspire confidence in a mark—a victim—you need two things: the mark must be greedy and must think he has an edge over you." He sipped his wine, then continued. "Your two brothers were conned, Amirantha. Whoever they worked for gulled them into thinking they were getting something more than they were giving up in service, that somehow they had the advantage."

Amirantha nodded. "Anything that appealed to Sidi's need to gather power to himself, or to Belasco's vanity, yes, that would work."

Pug said, "However this agency recruits its servants, it has many, and they come at us when they think they are strong enough to win."

"So you think they'll come again?" asked Sandreena.

"Almost certainly," said Pug. Then he smiled. "We will

be ready. We have resources, as you have seen. Those in high places who are in the Conclave, or who are allied."

"Creegan?" asked Sandreena.

"He is in the Conclave. I recruited him when he was a young Knight-Adamant. Now he's Grand Master of the Order. We have closer ties with your temple than any other, though we have a good relationship with some others."

Sandreena said, "I assumed as much." She took a drink from a mug of tea, then said, "I'm not entirely sure about this Mother-Bishop role, though."

"Oh, that," said Pug. He smiled as he said, "It was temporary. I think Creegan failed to mention that to you."

Sandreena was caught between outrage and relief. "Yes, he did. Who and why?"

"Who is Brother Willoby, who is a loyal member of the Conclave, and an adept administrator. You are too good at what you do to coop you up in an office all day. As to why, Creegan had no idea how much you might require from the temple before we were done. Knight-Sergeant would get you a bit, but Mother-Bishop would get you anything you could ask for."

Sandreena considered for a moment, then laughed. "Sneaky bastards, all of you."

"We need to be," said Pug. Returning to Jim's question, he said, "Exactly what it was we witnessed, I don't know. He looked from Gulamendis to Amirantha and said, "Have you given it consideration?"

Gulamendis said, "We have. This was so unlike what we know about demons, we have to stop all our assumptions and build a theory based on what we saw."

Amirantha said, "We know there's a civil war in the Fifth Circle. This Demon War has raged there for centuries, as far as we can judge; it spilled over into our world for the first time, but that doesn't mean it won't happen again."

Gulamendis said, "I doubt that's the last we've seen of the demons, but perhaps we won't have to confront them as we did on the Taredhel worlds.

"They seem to have sent most of those demons from the outer circle, and while it probably didn't seem like it to those of you, my brother and I can tell you what we saw down in Kesh was nothing compared to the onslaughts we endured on those worlds."

"So then, why was the Demon King Dahun trying to sneak into this world?" asked Jim. "Or rather, why all the big magic, murder, and mayhem? Either take over Belasco when no one is looking or just come in like a demon and start ripping things apart?"

"That's the heart of the mystery," said Gulamendis.

"I have a theory," said Amirantha.

"Let's hear it," said Jim, sitting back in his chair. His beard was starting to grow and Sandreena had no doubt by the time he was seen on the streets of Krondor the next day, he would be his disreputable-looking self. She might someday forgive him for the role he played in the most painful part of her past, but she'd never forget his hand in it.

Amirantha said, "Dahun was fleeing. He came here to hide."

Pug and Magnus exchanged glances, and Gulamendis said, "That would explain a great deal."

"Hiding from what?" asked Brandos. "I've faced enough demons in my day to know they're hardly a shy lot."

"That I don't know," admitted Amirantha.

"Perhaps those other Demon Kings?" suggested Laromendis.

"Perhaps," said Pug, "but I doubt it. There's something behind all of this, a deeper, darker cause of all the troubles that have visited this world since before any of us were born." He let out a long sigh. "It will eventually make itself known to us, but until it does, we can only pride ourselves on this victory, wonder how long we have to enjoy the newly won peace, and prepare for the next attack."

"You're certain there will be one?" asked Sandreena.

"As certain as I am of anything," said Pug.